THE BONE ANGEL TRILOGY

NAMELESS: THE DARKNESS COMES

I

NAMELESS: The Darkness Comes
Mercedes M. Yardley
Ragnarok Publications | www.ragnarokpub.com
Text copyright © 2014 Mercedes M. Yardley.
All rights reserved.

Published by Ragnarok Publications
Tim Marquitz, Editor-In-Chief | J.M. Martin, Creative Director
206 College Park Drive, Ste. 1
Crestview Hills, KY 41017

ISBN-10 0-9913605-1-6
ISBN-13 978-0-9913605-1-2
Worldwide Rights
Created in the United States of America

Cover art by George C. Cotronis
Book design by J.M. Martin

NAMELESS

MERCEDES M. YARDLEY

RAGNAROK PUBLICATIONS

CRESTVIEW HILLS, KENTUCKY

DEDICATION

For Janyece, who has dealt with me the longest. In exchange for everything, I give you Mouth.

Prologue

The demonic love the taste of little girls.

Luna Masterson went to her first sleepover when she was six, armed with a Superman sleeping bag and a pink pillow, pigtails and sour candies. Before she left, her dad pulled her onto his lap.

"Sweetheart," he said, and looked worried. Even though she should have been too young to tell, Luna could see the anxiety running under the linesW of his face. "You're sleeping somewhere other than home tonight. And I know you see things in the dark…"

"You don't want me to talk to the Tiptoe Shadow tonight."

His face broke a little. A man's face isn't designed to carry so much emotion at one time.

"Sweetie, I never want you to talk to the Tiptoe Shadow. He's a bad thing and he lies. But especially not tonight, because I won't be there with you. Do you understand?"

She understood. Her mother didn't see the shadows, and neither did her brother, Seth. But for some reason, her Daddy could, and it made her feel better. Even a child knows about the word *crazy*.

"All right, Daddy."

He kissed her hair. "I love you, Luna. Don't let him use you. Now go hop in the car."

The night was everything she had dreamed of. They had cake and ice cream, watched a movie, made up silly dances, and fell into bed exhausted. Penelope, the birthday girl, was the first to fall asleep. Luna was the last.

Her eyes were starting to close when she heard it. The surreptitious sound of something slyly skittering her way. She squeezed her eyes shut.

"Oh girl Luna," called a voice. It was high and squeaky like the brakes of a car. "Luuuuuuuuuuna. Let's, *mmm*, play."

She didn't move, tried to act like she was asleep. Something leaned over her face and chuckled.

"Girl is awake. I know girl. I smell girl. Girl smells like fear and dying and oh, oh, oh."

Long, tapered fingers ran down her face. She knew them well.

"And more girls, *mmm*. Lots of choices." He pranced away from her, and she cracked open an eye. The demon was tall, hunched as he picked over the girls sleeping on the floor. He was made of nothing but shadow cast onto the wall. Impossibly tall, impossibly thin, he minced around on his tiny tiptoes instead of walking fully on his feet.

"Girl smells like happy. Yuck," he said, and moved on to a brunette. "Girl smells like, *mmm*, anger. I taste it, yes." He ran his thick tongue over the girl's face and into her hair. Luna shivered. The demon tottered to Penelope and inhaled deeply.

"Girl smells like hurting. Smells like her father. Smells relieved to have, *mmm*, friends here to sate the father, maybe he chooses one of *you*, maybe he leaves her alone tonight, maybe he doesn't come. But he will, oh yes! He will come, and he will look, and he will see her, and you, and all your, *mmm*, friends, so pretty, so sweet, so *little* and *helpless* and *small*—"

"Stop it!" Luna shouted, and the shadow whipped its head in her direction. Although it had no face, she could feel the burn of its eyes, sense its grin. "Leave her alone. Leave us all alone!"

"Luna, who are you screaming at?" Penelope said. She sat up, rubbed her eyes. The Tiptoe Shadow yelped in glee and nuzzled her hair. She didn't see it. "Don't be so loud. You'll wake up my parents, and we'll get in trouble."

"Here comes father!" squealed the demon. It danced around on tiny, broken feet.

"Girls," Penelope's father said warningly, standing in the doorway. Luna looked at him with new revulsion.

"Don't touch me. Don't touch her." She stood in front of Penelope, spreading her thin arms wide to keep him away. She bared her teeth at him and the groggy girls gasped in horror.

"Luna, what's gotten into you?" Penelope's father asked. He reached for her and she screamed, hitting and kicking and biting.

"I know what you do. The Tiptoe Shadow told me you're a bad man. I want my daddy!"

Luna was never invited to another party at Penelope's house, or anybody else's. When Luna the Lunatic's mother died, her father tried to teach her how to handle the demonic on his own.

"I don't think they'll hurt you," he told his daughter one day. She was sixteen and had just run a demon down with the family car. "At least, not usually. You're too much fun for them."

"Thanks, Dad. That's extremely disheartening."

He put his arm around her. "Cheer up, Sweetie. We can beat this, you and I."

And they did, for a while, until her world was destroyed and she was left alone.

The darkness comes when she's all alone.

Chapter One

Dude, that guy has a demon," I said to my brother. We were sitting
side by side on the front porch, but he wasn't looking at me. I
nudged him in the ribs and pointed at the guy, discreetly.

"What's it doing?" Seth asked, still flipping through his *Runner's
World*. He never even looked up. I'm not surprised in the least. I squint
at the guy across the street.

"Well, the guy's carrying groceries into his house, and it looks like the
demon's trying to open the door. And you're not listening."

"I'm listening." *Flip, flip, flip.* He wasn't even looking at the pages,
flipping them so fast. Trying to keep his cool, as usual. Sometimes his
calmness was maddening. I wanted him to get excited sometimes, to stand
and shout until the veins popped out of his neck like Dad's did. But he'll
never be Dad. He'd die first.

"There's a *demon*, Seth. Hanging around the guy next door. And you're
completely unfazed by this?"

"Completely."

"Of course," I muttered and took a bite out of an apple. The green
kind, my favorite. And suddenly it didn't matter anymore, if he believed
me or not, because that wouldn't change anything, would it?

"I'll be late. Don't wait up," I said, and my voice sounded harsher than

I intend. It sounded mean. I wanted to turn back and apologize, but I made myself keep walking.

I think about my brother. I think about him a lot lately, especially since his wife ran out on him six months ago. After the first five, I moved in to help him take care of his baby girl, Lydia. She's a little over a year old and still doesn't sleep through the night. Nightmares. I think they're hereditary. But then, with a mom like Sparkles, I'd have nightmares, too.

Yes. Seth actually married a woman who called herself Sparkles. Maybe he deserved everything he got.

"Where are you going?" a soft voice asked me. I didn't turn to see the speaker.

"You don't belong here," I said, not breaking my stride. "Go home."

"Where is home?" The voice floated along at my side. I could see the wispy darkness out of the corner of my eye.

"I meant your home. You are not invited to mine."

"I want to come to yours."

"Uninvited, demon."

"I want to see where you live."

I was getting irritated. I wanted to turn and face the demon so I could yell at it properly, but I kept walking, kept my eyes straight ahead.

"I'm on to your tricks, demon. You'll get no sport from me."

There was a snorting laughter, and the earlier foggy vagueness was gone from its voice. "Oh, I'll get plenty from you, *Luna*." It faded away.

The first time a demon called me by name, I about had a heart attack. *How does it know me? How does it know?* I had thought. But I was young then, only a little girl in school, and I was not wise to such things. They know me because I know them. Really, it isn't very mystical at all.

Ah, but knowing a demon's name? That gives you power. Good luck finding it out, though. Half the time the demons themselves can't remember what they were originally called.

I walked all of the way down to the harbor. The air had that heavy scent of fish and soft rotting things that somehow managed to be fresh and almost pleasant. I love the sea. I leaned over the railing and stared into the dark water.

Something even darker stared back.

I sighed, shoved my hands in my pockets and turned my back to the railing. Sometimes this *gift* of mine really sucks.

My phone rang, and I fished around in my puffy down vest until I found it. It was my brother.

"What's up?" I said.

There was a pause, and then a shadowy voice warbled out, "I am a demon."

"What, using my brother's phone?" I asked.

"Yes."

"Don't be a moron. Demons can't use electronics. What's going on, Seth?"

My brother took a big breath and let it out slowly. It was purifying just listening to it. I found myself breathing out with him.

"I don't want you to be mad at me, Luna," he said. I could hear splashing and happy noises in the background. He must be giving Lydia her bath. This made me smile.

"I'm not mad at you. I'm just, you know, frustrated. I'm not lying."

"I never thought you were," he said, and I heard little girl giggling and more splashing. And something different, a kind of low humming. This was a lot closer.

Great, I thought.

I turned my back to the humming and stalwartly refused to look into the water. There's always a lot of activity that goes on near the sea. A lot of things there.

"You don't think I'm lying, you just think I'm crazy, right? And this is supposed to make me feel better?"

Seth didn't say anything, and I bet he was mentally counting to ten. I try his patience, I know this. At the same time, he's my brother, the only family I have left, and I almost feel like he owes it to me to believe.

"Dad used to hear voices," he said slowly, and I snorted and hung up the phone.

"You," I said, pointing to a demon three steps away from me. His eyes were already upon mine. "And you, and you." I pointed at two others, one of which was trying to reach the phone in my hand.

"It's not going to work. You think I'd help you touch something from my world? You, too," I said, peeking over the railing into the water. "You guys aren't real. You're all products of my ultra-deranged mind. What do you think of that?"

They started laughing.

"Thought so," I said and turned toward work.

Chapter Two

I'm sort of a jack of all trades, I guess. I do a little bit of everything, and all of it is mediocre. Except sticking people with needles. Being stabby seems to be the only thing I really excel at. So when I blazed into town full of glory and good intentions, I snagged a phlebotomy job, no problem. Something about siphoning healthy-looking blood soothes me. I'm sure a psychologist would have a field day with that one.

I was busy prepping my station for a routine blood draw when a shadow fell across me.

"Hey, hotshot, I'm not ready for you yet. Wait for me to call you, okay?" I said, not looking up.

The shadow didn't move. I bit the inside of my cheek in frustration, and raised my eyes.

There was nothing there. That I could see, anyway.

Well, *this* was new. There was always a person or a demon, but an invisible presence? Something unseen casting a shadow? I don't know much about physics and its laws, but I'm thinking they'd have a hard time accepting this.

"So…" I said, waiting for the thing to take the lead. It didn't. And frankly, I didn't have time for this.

"Okay, nice chatting with ya. Obviously it's time for you to scram.

Working, you see."

I grabbed the tubes I needed and rechecked my order. Satisfied, I stood up and went to the window at the front of the office. The presence followed me.

"Reed Taylor," I called out, and waited until a relatively handsome guy with tragically bland hair stood up. I nodded toward the back room and he followed me. So did the presence.

"What's up?" I asked this "Reed Taylor". He smiled benignly. I suppressed a sigh. Let's do a quick stick and get this over with. Then afterwards maybe I could go play in traffic.

"Would you roll up your sleeve, please?" I asked him. He blanched a bit, and then slowly pulled his sleeve up. I could see the old track marks on his arm.

"I haven't used in years," he told me quietly. I flicked my eyes to his, but he was carefully looking away.

"You don't have to explain yourself to me," I said, and started prodding at his arm. There was a lot of scar tissue to work around.

"I know that. I just…" He laughed. "I don't want you to think badly of me, that's all. Which is funny, considering you're a complete stranger. So it shouldn't be important, should it? I mean, I could be murdering people right and left, and it shouldn't matter to you." He paused. "That was so inappropriate." His head dropped.

I laughed. I couldn't help it. I hit his vein and filled the tubes, one after another. The presence moved closer. Its shadow fell across my hands.

"Back off, I can't see," I said without thinking. Reed's head flipped up, and I froze.

"Who are you talking to?" He asked. His eyes were shining with an intensity that made my spine stiffen.

"Nobody." He didn't look like he bought it. He probably thought he was getting his life's blood siphoned off by a complete psycho. "Uh...you?"

He shook his head. "No, you weren't talking to me."

I pulled off the last vial and pressed a cotton ball over the needle. I pulled it out more hastily than usual and Reed hissed.

"Sorry about that. Here, hold this," I said, and Reed pressed down on the cotton ball. His eyes were still trying to catch mine, but I made a big show of gathering all of my paperwork together.

"So you know the drill, Reed Taylor. Drink lots of water; don't use this arm to lift anything heavy. If there's any strange bruising or a painful lump that arises..."

"Hey," he said, and I finally looked at him. His eyes were vibrant and green. Not bland at all. Kind of almost...beautiful.

"W-what?"

Reed spoke slowly and gently, like he was talking to a scared child. "This is very important. We both know you weren't speaking to me. "

Suddenly I wanted to tell him. I don't know why. Something about guarding myself every minute of the day, being careful not to look at things nobody else saw, to speak to things nobody else heard. It was wearying. But I can't just say to a stranger, "Hey, you know what? I see demons. They're everywhere. Everybody else thinks I've just gone bonkers." But he didn't ask about demons, did he? He only wanted to know what I saw right now. And I didn't see a darn thing.

"I didn't see anything," I said honestly, and something changed behind his eyes. He looked disappointed and angry at the same time. He turned his face away from me.

"Whatever. It doesn't matter. Nice meeting you..." he squinted at the name sewn onto my borrowed lab coat, "Bartholomew." Good heavens, he can't be that stupid. He frowned slightly, looked at me one more time, and then abruptly stood up and walked away. The presence drifted off behind him. I had the impression it was trying to tell Reed Taylor something, but he wasn't having it.

Something about his walking off made me sad, and being sad made me angry. Anger was easier to deal with, anyhow. Forget him and his mysterious presence. But even while I turned my back to him, I felt my shoulders tense up. A cognizant something I couldn't see? That was new. And *new* in my world usually got me nothing but trouble.

Chapter Three

Seth slammed the milk down on the table. The Raisin Bran followed suit. "So tell me about the demons." He sounded frustrated.

I smiled to myself and scattered some Cheerios on Lydia's high chair tray. She chirped and dove for them with pudgy hands shaped like stars.

"It's such a lovely day, big brother. Why do you want to botch it up with talk of the dark side?"

"The dark side?" He flopped down in his chair and rubbed his hand over his unshaven face. Not a bad looking guy, all in all, but he was looking particularly harsh this morning. Worn out. Maybe he had more dreams about the Elusive Miss Sparkles. Like I said, I think the nightmares were hereditary.

I sat down next to him, stole the milk for my own cereal. "Seriously, Seth. You haven't believed me in years. Why the sudden interest now?"

He leaned back in his chair, covered his eyes with his hands. "Gar! Just tell me already. I might never ask again."

I sighed and pushed my bowl away. I was never into Raisin Bran anyway. Too soggy. And it tried too hard to be good for you. Pretentious.

"Well. What do you want to know?" I crossed my hands neatly on the table and tried to look helpful. Secretarial, even.

"Is there one in the house?"

My friendly smile stuck to my teeth. "Right now?" I asked.

Seth looked at me. "Yeah, right now. Is there a demon hanging around here now?"

I shook my head. "Inside, no. They can't come in. Not usually, anyway. But outside...that's different." I pointed to the demon that had its featureless faced pressed to the kitchen window. "There's one there."

Seth looked. The demon looked. I studied my fingernails, which were a bit ragged.

"I don't see anything," Seth complained.

"Don't worry. Neither does the demon. I made sure of it."

"I don't have a clue what you're talking about."

I scattered more Cheerios for Lydia. "Well, it's hard for demons to come into your home, right? They can't just waltz in. They have to be..."

"Invited?" Seth interrupted. "Like vampires?"

"Don't be stupid," I said. "Vampires aren't real."

He squeezed his eyes shut, and I knew he was mentally counting to ten. That happened a lot. "Keep talking, Luna. I'm trying to be serious and supportive for once."

He was, and it was killing him. "Thanks, Seth. I appreciate it. Really. So, anyway, I guess they have to be invited, in a way. Demons can't just wander into random homes so much. I mean, they can, but it's really rare. And if they do, they tend to be the really dumb ones who don't know any better."

"Dumb demons?"

"I know, right?" I said, and Seth grinned. "Demons are like everybody else, at least from my experience. You have your smart ones and your dumb ones, and ones that are worse than the others. You know. Just like us. So it's bad news to wander into somebody's house if you have no reason to be there. They tend to get in trouble."

Seth washed Lydia's hands with a washcloth. She squirmed when he reached her round face. "Get in trouble by who? Is there some kind of demon police? What do they call them, the Demon Patrol?"

I almost laughed. "I'm not really sure. They get in trouble by somebody, because I've seen it. They look all panicked and explain themselves to somebody, but I have no idea who. I don't see or feel anything. It's like they're talking to somebody who isn't there."

Seth raised an eyebrow at me. "That's what you look like a lot of the time, for your information."

I blushed. I knew this. I worked really hard on not having conversations unless I was alone, but I slipped up. A lot.

Seth noticed my face and tried to smooth things over. "No, you're okay, Luna. It's really not a big deal. I just tell people you're practicing lines for a play, or something. It's nothing to worry about."

Well, great. My dorky brother has to cover for me. Now that's just embarrassing.

Now Seth looked embarrassed, too. "Okay. So usually demons can't come inside. And they can't look inside, either, right?"

I nodded. Then I thought, and shook my head. Then I kind of bobbed my head in a half nod, half shake.

"Explain," he commanded.

I took a deep breath and looked up, thinking. I didn't know the best way to approach this.

"Well, usually they can see inside, and it isn't so much of a big deal. But…" I paused. Seth glared at me.

"Spit it out."

I did. It just seemed easier. "Okay, so there was a demon in the house and I saw it and it was a mean one and I didn't want it to come back so after it was gone I did a sort of special thing and now none of them can see in the house anymore." I spit it out in one breath, then looked at him warily.

He was staring at me like I'd gone completely off my rocker. Which it sounded like I had, I'm sure, but I couldn't stop talking. I babble when I'm nervous sometimes. It really sucks.

"And maybe I shouldn't have made it so they can't see in because they're really curious, and now they're here all of the time, but since she left—"

"She?"

"—it just seemed like the safest thing to do to keep her out. Forever, you know. Because *she* was bad news."

I snapped my mouth shut. Seth's eyes were completely goggled. Lydia looked at him and laughed.

"Is Daddy doing a silly face?" I asked her. She laughed again.

Seth blinked. "So not only do you see demons, but we had a Princess Demon in our house. A particular nasty one and you performed some sort of a *magic spell* so they can't be Peeping Toms? Is that what you're telling me?"

I frowned. "Now that sounds absolutely ridiculous." I reached out for Lydia, but he swept her out of her high chair and away from me.

"It does. Utterly ridiculous. I'm sorry I asked." He walked carefully up the stairs, adamantly refusing to stomp.

Right then I was pretty sorry he had asked, as well.

I was still stewing when the phone rang. "Talk to me," I said, picking it up.

There was a silence, and then a haughty voice. "Who is this?" I recognized it immediately.

"Ah, Sparkles. My sweet Princess Demon. We were just talking about you."

Silence again, and then she spat out, "Luna. What are you doing at my house?"

Oh, this was going to be good.

"Your house? I'm sorry. I thought when you moved out and abandoned your husband and child you forfeited your claim to this house."

Sparkles laughed. It was hard and cold. It made me want to shut my eyes and turn my face away. It felt like her laugh could shred bits of skin off my face. I had to admit it, the woman scared me. And that was even before she picked up her little demonic friend.

"Ah, sweet girl," she cooed. There was nothing comforting about it. I curled my toes to keep the chills away. "I am afraid you misunderstood. I never abandoned anyone. I just needed some time to think, and…clear my head. Surely you can see that."

My face felt like rock. "I'm not the one you need to be explaining your actions to, am I?" Immediately I wished I hadn't said that.

"You're right," Sparkles fairly purred. "Is Seth around? I would so love to chat with him."

"He's not here."

Her voice cooled even more, if that was possible. "Are you lying to me, girl?"

"Maybe. Why don't you stand out on the front porch and take a peek inside? Tell me whether I'm lying or not."

Sparkles hissed, and I nearly slammed the phone down in fear.

"So it was you," she said, and her voice had teeth. I couldn't breathe. I sat down and put my head between my legs, still holding the phone up to my ear. *This is crazy*, I thought. *She doesn't have any power over me.*

I took a deep breath and made myself smile. I wanted her to think I was as calm as possible.

"Well, that's that," I said. "Thanks for calling." I pushed the button on the phone and touched my fingers to my forehead. I was sweating.

"Who was that?" Seth asked, walking into the room. He was dressed for work, and pressed a happy Lydia into my hands.

"Nobody. Telemarketer," I said quickly. Lydia looked at me and her lips turned down.

"Really? You look awfully upset for somebody who just got off the phone with a telemarketer." Seth put his hand on his hip, studied me up and down. I rubbed my forehead again, and forced a smile.

"You know how it is with them these days. Nothing but scare tactics."

"Right-o," he said, and turned to go. He paused.

"I won't, uh, hit anything with the door when I open it, will I?" he asked me. He shifted uncomfortably from foot to foot.

"Nah, they can't touch our stuff. Not unless they have a pretty firm foothold on somebody, or if I help them materialize. You're good."

"Okay. Bye, then," he said, and threw the door open with extra exuberance. It passed right through the demon, who grabbed half-heartedly for the knob. It shut itself with a click, and the demon stood on its toes to peer in through the window set into the top of the door.

Chapter Four

The encounter with Sparkles rocked me more than I cared to admit. How could somebody so vile have a child as sweet as Lydia? She's definitely cute, I can tell you that much. And smart. And astute. I can tell she has my genes in there somewhere.

And, like me, after a few minutes swabbing at the counters with a washcloth and the like, she was bored.

"Right, let's go shopping," I told her, and then I sprayed her down with sunscreen. Hey, even out here in the Northwest, you can't be too careful. Demons and sunburn and cancer, oh my. Not my little girl.

I ran a dark red lip stain around my mouth, pulled tall boots up over my jeans and threw on my sunglasses. Suddenly I was a femme fatale, a woman of mystique. And all under ten minutes.

Lydia had pulled out her pigtails, so we did them over again, and that took nearly another ten minutes right there. She has a knack for yanking beautiful doodads out of her hair. For this, I blame her father.

"Ready, Princess Pretty Fingers?" I asked her.

She pursed her lips and twisted her chubby wrist in a wave. "Mama," she said.

"No, Luna. *Luna*."

"Mama."

"Have it your way, kid," I said. I buckled her into her car seat and lugged her out to the car. It was heavy, and I had to use both hands.

I like taking Lydia to the grocery store, quite honestly. I like showing her off. People always peer and coo at her, and Lydia takes it as her due. And I like it because she can usually put a smile on the face of the most dour crone and codger. Lydia has charm.

It's me that gets us into trouble.

"What a beautiful baby," the woman next to us exclaimed. Lydia flirted from her seat in the wonky-wheeled cart.

"Thanks, she's my brother's," I said, and the woman narrowed her eyes and scurried away from me, still glancing back over her shoulder from time to time.

Anyway, I was standing there comparing prices on ground beef, when I felt a presence. I turned around, and again, there was nobody there.

I firmly ignored it. If it wasn't going to be polite enough to show itself, then I wasn't going to give it the time of day.

"What do you think, Lydia? It's never too early to learn about economics and the state of the nation's food supply."

Lydia apparently didn't care about the state of our food supply, because she was smiling and peeking out from under her lashes. At who, you ask? Well, me too, because I couldn't see the darn thing.

"Lydia, ignore it, darling."

Lydia ignored somebody, all right, but it wasn't the mysterious presence. It was Luna Mama.

"Lydia, I'm being serious. Talk to me about hamburger, okay? Don't pay any attention to that thing."

Lydia waved at the empty space. "Hi, hi, hi, hi, hi," she said.

I tossed the hamburger back into the case and whirled around to address the presence.

"I know you can hear me," I hissed. I was absolutely furious. "I want you to know it is completely unacceptable to hang around a baby girl, do you understand me? I simply won't have it, you freaking perv. Back off!"

"Did that beef do something to offend you?"

I spun around, and faced the green-eyed, bland haired man from the clinic earlier. He was trying valiantly not to smile, and if I hadn't been half blind with protective rage, I would have given him props for it.

"You," I accused. "It hangs around *you.* Anyway, it started it." I grabbed the cart to push it away.

Lydia pointed at the presence. "Pretty," she said. "Pretty." Then she started to cry.

I looked at the presence, but of course there wasn't anything there. Bland-haired Reed Taylor was eyeing Lydia quietly, but that wasn't causing her tears.

"What about her?" I heard him ask, but he wasn't talking to me and my attention was elsewhere.

"Oh good heavens," I said under my breath. Reed Taylor tore his gaze away from Lydia, and looked at me curiously. I didn't have time for him.

"Duck," I said, and the strain in my voice startled even me.

Reed Taylor hesitated only a second, and then hit the supermarket floor like a pro. I'll have to give him props for that later, too.

Behind him, darkness was gathering. Right there in the refrigerator section, the very jaws of Hell were opening up. This wouldn't be good.

It had happened before, so I knew what to expect. Nastiness. Complete and utter nastiness. The first time it had happened, the darkness had been so consuming that I was overwhelmed. Out of that darkness had climbed an even blacker shadow who hated me. *Hated me.* I had never been on the receiving end of so much hate.

The idea of it happening now, right in the middle of the Turk's Goodie

Grocery, was enough to make me puke. The idea of it happening in the presence of my sweet and pure Lydia was enough to make me tamp down the sickness and stand up and fight.

"What's going on?" Reed Taylor asked from the floor. I didn't have time to answer him.

The darkness had gathered fully, and I couldn't see the rest of the grocery store anymore. A cold wind blew past me, and I felt my hair ruffle.

"Holy crap," I heard from the floor, but I ignored him again.

A featureless form was zipping out of the darkness. It came at me in short diagonal bursts. I felt my breath become too heavy for my chest, felt the strength pulled from my body as the shadow tried to feed on my essence in order to take shape. I felt pieces of myself unspool from my soul like intestines. This was trouble. A demon is one thing, but a demon that's fully formed and can manipulate things in the real world? It's the proverbial double-edged sword. On one hand, if it has enough substance, I can usually beat the crap out of it. On the other, well, it can do the same thing to me, and anybody else that's around. I couldn't chance it with baby girl. I pictured my essence as a rope and tried to mentally pull it back into my body, a tug-o-war between myself and the demon. I wasn't winning easily.

The thing slowed down a little bit, but still continued toward us. My teeth began to chatter.

"Get back. Get back. Get back, *get back!*" I shouted and continued my invisible tug-o-war. The wind grew colder and blew harder, and my hair and clothes whipped around me like I was standing in a hurricane. The shadow wasn't slowing down any more, not at all.

It's stronger than I am, I thought, and despair overcame me.

There was a sound from the floor, some type of order, and suddenly the unseen presence rushed out from behind me and tackled the thing coming out of the darkness. The shadow seemed enraged and panicked, and I saw it grappling against air. Its struggle pulled me out of my trance.

I growled, willing my body to absorb all of the power the demon had leeched from it. I felt it weaken.

"Get back," I commanded, my voice strong and low. The thing turned its head in my direction, and the invisible presence used this distraction to literally stuff it back into the darkness. It howled angrily, and the darkness wafted in all around it, and was suddenly gone.

"My hero," I said to the presence, and then I blacked out cold.

Chapter Five

Somebody was saying something indecipherable, and it was much too loud. I groaned and tried to put a hand to my head, but the effort made my stomach heave.

"Cleanup in frozen foods," the muffled voice shouted again. It sounded slightly hysterical.

"Cleanup. That would be you," said a different voice. A calmer voice.

I managed to force open one eye. It was teary from the effort.

"Bartholomew? Are you back with me?" Bland-haired Reed Taylor was kneeling over me, peering at me with his fantastic eyes.

I groaned, and shut my eyes again. Suddenly I shot up into a sitting position. It made my head spin. "Lydia!"

Reed Taylor put his arms around me. "Calm down. She's okay, just sitting right there in the cart. Can you see her?"

Lydia peered down from her seat and smiled at me. "Mama," she exclaimed.

Reed Taylor's arms loosened around me. He stood up and started to pull me off the floor.

"She's my niece," I said a bit too quickly.

"What's going on around here?" A red-faced, beefy man came waddling furiously up the aisle. He eyed Reed Taylor heaving me off of the floor. It was obvious this paranoid Chef Boyardee suspected shenanigans. Golly.

"Bartholomew here has a little sugar problem. If she doesn't eat, her blood sugar goes all wacky and she passes out. Isn't that true, dear?"

I rolled my eyes. "Please, honey. How many times do I have to ask you to drop the formality and call me Bart? I was named after my father," I confided to the man. He looked appalled.

"That's a terrible name for a woman," he sputtered.

"I see your point..." I leaned in to read his nametag, "Shannon." *Shannon?* "But Mother was a sentimental old thing."

Shannon Boyardee continued glaring at us. "But the yelling and screaming. You can't tell me that's low blood sugar."

Reed Taylor hung his head. "Nah, that would be me. I just can't resist when Bart here gets all swoony. It's every romantic fantasy I've ever had, come to life. I can't seem to help myself." He looked properly shamed. I snorted in laughter and tried to cover it up with a cough.

"Well, thanks so much for your concern, *Shannon*, but I really ought to be going now. Obviously I need something to eat, and then everything will be just fine." If the extra hostile demons manage to keep from flinging their soul-destroying selves at me, that is. A girl can always hope.

I pushed the empty cart out of the store with as much dignity as I could muster, which wasn't much, because that stupid wheel kept sticking and I had to throw my whole body weight against it in order to make it move. Every eye on the store was upon me.

"See ya, guys," Reed Taylor said, waving at everybody. "I'll try to keep my hands off her until we get home, but I can't make any promises."

"Blood sugar?" I growled at him as we walked to my car. Well, he walked. I was trying to do an angry stalk-like thing, but the cart was ruining it for me. Finally I snatched Lydia out of it, and did a much more satisfying stalk that way. Go, me.

"Well, what else was I going to say? 'Bartholomew here had a psychotic breakdown? Help, run away, save yourselves and your children?' You should be thanking me."

I turned to face him. "My name is not Bartholomew. Nobody names their daughters Bartholomew. I'm Luna."

"I'm slightly relieved to hear that. I think."

"Get bent." I turned away. He jogged after me.

"Hey, why are you so angry at me, anyway?"

I stopped, and Reed Taylor nearly ran into me. He had a point.

I decided then and there that I would try my very best not to be horrible to him. After all, it wasn't his fault I saw the things I did. Besides, he hung around with a strange invisible presence that had the power to mess with the demonic. I needed to know what it was. I needed to know why Reed Taylor could see him.

I smiled sweetly at him.

"Thank you for your help, Reed Taylor."

He stopped short, eyed me a little bit. "That sounds highly unnatural coming from you."

My smile quickly dropped into a scowl. "I was trying to be nice," I nearly shouted. And winced. My head was killing me.

Reed Taylor shook his head. "Wait," he said, looking frustrated. "This is going all wrong. Let's start over, shall we?"

He stopped and held out his hand. I resituated Lydia so I could take it.

"Hi," he said, and smiled winningly. "My name is Reed Taylor. It's nice to meet you…?"

"Luna. Luna Masterson." I shook his hand demurely.

"Well, that's quite a moniker."

My handshake became quite firm. Crushing, even. "I thought things were going to go well this time?"

Reed Taylor smiled at me. "Maybe you and I are bound to create sparks, Luna."

I snorted. I couldn't help it. That was so corny.

Apparently Reed Taylor agreed. "I just…I'm just not batting a thousand. I swear I'm not so much of a loser."

"I don't believe you."

"Want to go to dinner?"

"I don't date losers."

"That's pretty harsh. Eight?"

I grabbed my lipstick from my back pocket and scrawled my phone number on his arm.

"If you're more than five minutes late, I'll kill you."

We glared at each other, and then we both grinned. He bounded away, and I was humming as I strapped Lydia into her seat. He seemed like a nice guy, and heaven knows I could do with a nice guy every now and then. But more than that, I needed to get a bead on that mysterious presence. What was it? Could it help me?

I was going to find out. And I needed Reed Taylor in order to do it.

Chapter Six

So I have a date tonight," I told Seth over the phone. He was eating at his desk, as usual. Noisily. In my ear. Brothers never change.

"You? A date? With who?" He slurped loudly from his drink. Obviously his body was crying out desperately for hydration.

"Well, his name is Reed Taylor, and he has awful blah-colored hair. And he was a user way back, so he says. He has this invisible thing that hangs around with him all of the time. It kind of gets in my way, but it has its uses. Like today when the demon attacked me in the middle of the hamburger section—"

"What's wrong with his hair?" Seth asked. "I mean, what is it exactly that you don't like?"

And that's Seth for you. He has this amazing mind, right? Quick, eager. His brain has tentacles and is always waving them around, ready to grab something interesting and suck it all in to its brain-mouth, or whatever. But the things Seth finds interesting, well. They just baffle me. I mean, I am *boggled*.

"His hair, it's like...I don't know. Nondescript. Nothing stands up and shouts. If his hair was a man, he'd always dress in beige. And eat mayo on white with the crusts cut off. All of the time. And say things like, 'That is very interesting,' even when it's not. You know that type of person?"

"Does Reed Taylor's beige-man hair wear a tie?"

"Yes, he does. It's a washed out gray, and very wide."

"Are you done?"

"And I think his beige-man hair guy's name is Nathanial."

"Not Nate?"

"Nope. Nathanial. And he'll politely, but firmly, correct you if you call him anything else. 'Hey, man,' 'No, my name is Nathanial' type of thing. Cripes, I don't know if I can go out with him."

"Because of his beige-man hair guy named Nathanial?"

"Maybe. And because I think I might like him."

"Nathanial?"

"No, Reed Taylor, you dork. Keep up with the conversation. Sheesh. I can't believe you sometimes."

Seth swallowed more mouthfuls of something crunchy. "Sorry. Guess I'd better stick to what I do, eh?"

I shook my head, although of course he couldn't see me. Unless he was mysteriously psychic, and perhaps that wouldn't surprise me at all, not with my family.

"Stop that, Seth. There's nothing wrong with being a legal assistant."

"Yeah, not if that's what you'd like to do. But if your goal was to be a lawyer…"

This was an old argument. "So go back to law school. Sparkles is gone, Seth. She doesn't need you to wait on her hand and foot anymore. I'm running the place now, and I say to get thy degree."

He almost laughed, which was good. I shifted gears.

"Anyway, you're good to have Lydia tonight, right? So I can go out with the hair man?"

"I am always available to facilitate your dating endeavors, my horribly, tragically single sister. May you have better luck than I did."

"Here's to that," I said, and clinked an imaginary glass.

I hung up. Lydia was napping, exhausted by entertaining so many callers at the grocery store. I went to front door and peered out of the window. A demon peered morosely back.

I stepped outside, and the demon reached out for the doorknob. It slipped right through his wispy hands.

"Were you here yesterday, too?" I asked it. It looked at me blankly.

"Yesterday?"

Ah, one of those. Totally disoriented, almost totally benign. I felt sorry for them, actually. I sat down on the step.

"Come sit with me, demon."

He did. He wrapped vaguely transparent arms around black robes like fog.

"So why are you so interested in the window there? What are you looking for?"

The demon peered at me, like he had never seen a human before. "Window?"

This might not be worth the effort. I tightened my muscles to stand up, but watched the demon turn his head, this way and that. He seemed so lost. It made me feel bad for abandoning him. I tried again.

"What are you looking for, demon?"

He was silent for a while, and I watched the light breeze disturb his flowing blackness. Like watching ink in water. It was strangely beautiful in a disquieting way.

Then he spoke. His voice was breathy and weak. "I'm hungry," he said.

Well. That had me shooting to my feet. I had my hand on the door and was ready to dart inside when he spoke again.

"For..." he fluttered his hands, unable to find the words. "For..."

"Food? Delicious people?" I offered, still poised to run.

He shook his head, distressed. "No. For...not this." He looked down at his body, his misty arms hanging loosely. He grabbed his robes and swayed slowly from side to side. "For not this," he said again, and then it was almost sing-songy. "For not this, for not this. I'm hungry for not this."

It was eerie. And heartbreaking. I stood there, horrified and saddened. There was nothing I could do for this guy. *What is the use*, I thought bitterly, *of seeing these things everywhere if there's nothing I can do?* It was too much to take.

"There's nothing in there that can help you," I told the demon. He acted like he didn't hear me, still swaying back and forth, speaking mostly to himself. I opened the door and stepped inside when suddenly the demon spoke again.

"That," he said, pointing. "I want that."

"What?" I asked him, craning my neck to see.

"That," he said again, firmly.

I looked at where his translucent finger pointed. I stared hard. The demon made a moaning, almost happy sound.

There was absolutely nothing there.

"I don't see anything," I told the demon. He looked at me, his gaze suddenly sharp and intense. My hand froze on the door handle.

"Ah, Luna," he said knowingly, and I swallowed hard. His eyes were penetrating. "Then you really can't see anything at all, can you?"

And he smiled.

Chapter Seven

Iwas still freaked out by the demon's change in personality when Reed Taylor came to pick me up. On a motorcycle, nonetheless. He roared to a stop in front of my house and pulled off his helmet. I couldn't feel the invisible presence anywhere, and that might not be such a bad thing.

"It's me," he said helpfully.

Thank you, Captain Obvious.

I eyed the bike. I was standing there in a filmy, light blue skirt and top. Ethereal looking, even. He was so killing my mystical vibe.

"Do I, uh, need to come in and…meet your brother or something?"

I'd filled Reed Taylor in on the phone earlier. "Come pick me up, and oh yeah, I live with my brother. And be sure to kick the demons in the face when you come. In the face."

Okay, so maybe I made that last part up.

I blew my hair out of my eyes. "Nah, he's my brother, not my warden. Besides, if you really want to say hi, you can wave from here. Most likely he's peering at us discreetly through the kitchen blinds."

Reed Taylor tucked his helmet under his arm and waved a bit wildly toward the kitchen. I saw the tell-tale movement of the blinds as my brother slunk away from them. Typical.

"So," I said, chewing on my index fingernail. I can't help it, it's a bad habit. There are always worse things I can be doing. "What's the plan, Stan?"

"The plan is that you get on this bike and hold on tightly to ole' Reed, because we are going to tear all around this town. Ready, baby?"

It is to my credit that I didn't laugh. Sure, I had to bite my lip, and I made a strangled sound that sounded like I was choking, but I kept the laughter at bay.

"If I had known," I said, "I would have worn jeans." Not only for modesty's sake, but also because Reed Taylor looked like he had just rolled out of bed ten minutes ago. After sleeping for about twenty years. And a shave would have been nice. Oh well.

"You look fine. Now will you please get on the bike? You don't need to be afraid. Motorcycles can be quite safe if you're a good driver, and I am a very good driver."

He revved the engine in what he hoped was an intimidating manner.

"You think I'm scared of your bike?" I asked sweetly.

"There's no reason to be," he said, still revving.

"But there's only one helmet."

"You can use mine," he said graciously. "I'll go without. It's important the lady always be protected."

Good heavens. I smiled flirtatiously at Reed. "I forgot something in the garage. Do you mind waiting just a second?" I batted my eyes. Gosh, I'm good.

"Sure," Reed Taylor said. He brushed his terrible hair back with his hand.

When I walked out of the garage, he gawked at me.

"Let's go," I said, pulling my own motorcycle helmet over my head.

"Where did you get that?" he asked. His wide green eyes were gorgeous.

"Dude, I never ride without a helmet. Are you crazy?" I swung my leg easily over the bike, wrapped my arms around his stomach. "I've been riding since I was a kid. Know what else?"

"What?"

"My bike's a lot bigger than yours."

Reed Taylor yanked his helmet onto his head and took off. The force of it made me tighten my arms around him even more. I couldn't stop laughing.

Except there is a downside to a full-face motorcycle helmet, and that is every sound you make is amplified like crazy. After my laughter finally quieted down into almost hiccupy sobs, and then snorting smirks, I had a monster of a headache. It sounded like the very demons of Hell had been cackling maniacally in my ears. But nope, it was just me.

"So where are we going?" I shouted at Reed Taylor. My amplified voice nearly made my eyes cross.

"No idea," he called back over his shoulder. "How about wherever the wind takes us?"

"Ah, so you're a free spirit," I yelled and promptly decided I was finished talking. My voice was driving me insane. Funny, I had dates tell me that before. Losers.

Reed Taylor was laughing, and I decided to lean against him and enjoy the ride. I hadn't been behind another rider in years. I used to ride with my father, but he had one of his episodes once and we'd crashed. He came out of it okay, but I broke my leg a pretty good one, and he sold the bike after that. He swore he'd never ride again, and he kept that promise for about five years. Then he'd bought a new one, and we'd gone tearing around again. It was in our blood.

And it was nice. I liked the feel of Reed Taylor, and I loved the feel of the bike. I closed my eyes and there were no demons, no invisible presences, nothing I didn't want to see. It was heaven.

Until an hour later, and I was starving. I mean, seriously, howlingly starving. Reed Taylor's shoulders were starting to look delicious.

"When are we going to eat?" I asked him. He flicked his eyes to mine in his rearview mirror.

"Hey, Luna, I thought you were sleeping back there."

I nearly was. "Of course not. Do you think I'm crazy? Feed me!"

Reed looked around. "You know, I don't really know where we are. I just kind of drove up the coast for a bit."

Normally this is the type of behavior I would applaud, but I was dying. I could feel my skin burning high up on my cheeks, a sure sign I was going to go ballistic without food. And Reed Taylor seemed like such a nice guy. It would be a shame to see him go. Just then, a blue sign caught my eye.

"Pull over here," I shouted, and pointed. The motorcycle slowed down, and Reed sprayed gravel as he stopped short. I hopped off the bike.

"You know this place?" he asked me, yanking his helmet off. His hair was an absolute mess. I liked this guy better and better.

"Know the owner. You'll like it."

I tugged my helmet off and hung it on his handlebar. Then I set about to the business of fluffing my hair.

"All right, let's go," I said, and pulled Reed Taylor by the hand.

"I wouldn't go in there right now," a demon said to me. He was leaning casually on the doorjamb, his robes fluttering around him like black wings.

I ignored him and kicked open the wooden door.

"You'll regret it," he called after me. I muttered something not very nice under my breath.

"What's that?" Reed Taylor asked me.

"Nothing. Two," I said to the girl at the front, and dragged my date to an extremely tall table. I hopped up on my stool, and he climbed onto his.

"Diet Coke," I demanded before the waiter asked, and then I tented my fingers together patiently while Reed Taylor ordered lemonade. Hmmm. Refreshing.

"I don't drink anymore," he explained while the waiter ran off to get our drinks. He looked almost embarrassed to tell me, but he was doing it anyway. I liked that.

"I told you, you don't have to explain yourself to me," I said, but I was pleased. He could tell.

He looked around. "What kind of hole in the wall is this?" The paint on the walls was blue at one point, but most of it had chipped off and faded by now. There was an old fishing net tossed haphazardly over our table like a tablecloth. Reed Taylor tried to extract his fork from it, but it wasn't working. It was tangled in there pretty well.

"This is the best fish and chips place you'll find, Reed Taylor. And it's dirt cheap. Even more importantly, it's quick," I said just as the waiter rushed up. He set down our drinks and whipped out his pad and paper. He ducked into himself, like he was trying to hide from me. For good reason.

"Hey, Owen, where's your hat?" I asked him. He scowled and pulled a paper diving helmet out of his apron. After carefully putting it on, he scrawled down our order, did a little nautical dance because we had ordered the special (why else would I order the special?) and zipped away.

"You liked giving that guy a hard time," Reed Taylor accused.

"I dated his brother for a bit," I explained, but my attention wasn't on Reed Taylor. It was on the demon following our waiter around. The way it was moving, it wasn't right.

"So did you like his brother?" Asked like he didn't even care. And maybe he didn't.

"Not especially." My body was very still.

"What's wrong?"

I didn't answer. The demon had gone from a drifting, ramshackle gait to a hurried, quick one. He had matched it directly up to Owen's.

"Luna?"

"This isn't right," I mumbled under my breath. Reed Taylor turned around to see. Frustrated, he turned back.

"There isn't anything there."

The demon inched closer to the waiter. He was only half a foot away. Realization slowly dawned.

"No!" I said, jumping off of my stool so quickly that it fell over. The few customers in the place started.

"Luna, what's going on?"

I heard Reed Taylor yelling after me, but I didn't stop. I leapt over my chair and ran as fast as I could toward the waiter. I felt a quick draining of energy, and the demon was reaching a suddenly much more tangible hand toward the boy's shoulder.

"Owen!" I screamed, and the waiter turned to stare at me in shock. "Owen, look out!"

I crashed into Owen a second before the demon did. The force of my body knocked him flat to the floor, and his trays went flying. The demon's hand landed hard between my shoulder blades, and I arched my back from the freezing pain.

It was agony.

I felt the will of the demon as it tried to burrow deep inside of my skin and my soul. Its fingers were tapered at the ends, sharp, and they pushed through my skin like pins, trying desperately to drive down to the very core.

"Uninvited," I gasped out. "Uninvited."

The demon panted, its face right beside my ear. "You took him from me," it hissed, and pushed harder into my body. I could feel tendrils of it, waxy and cold, sliding across the protective top layer of my soul. It wanted in. It wanted in so desperately that I could taste it. It made me taste it. I twisted up onto my tiptoes, my body spasming.

"Let me in, Luna. Your soul for his. Fair trade."

Reed Taylor watched me, his mouth open. The other customers in the restaurant looked confused, as if they couldn't decide whether to applaud the floor show or call an ambulance. Or, more likely, the men in white coats. I felt a brief burn of shame until movement caught my eye.

Owen scooted away on the ground, his face terrified. He was much younger when I had seen him last. An awkward little high school punk who didn't fit in anywhere, didn't have anybody but his brother. I felt my eyes narrow.

"You will not touch him," I spat and twisted around to face the demon. Its red eyes sparked, but I knew it was wearing out, too.

"You fight, Luna." Its smugness ticked me off.

"Better believe I fight," I said, and then I let it explode out of me.

That's the way to put it. All of the rage, all of my loathing for the darkness I'm bombarded with, all of my despair shot out through my skin. I could feel it. More importantly, the demon felt it. It was being forced to solidify against its will. It withdrew its fingers a fraction of a centimeter from between my shoulder blades, and howled.

"Keep screaming," I yelled, and let the power continue to flow.

"Stop," it gasped out. Its eyes were burning bright red. I had to act fast.

I slammed my forehead into its face. Something crunched, teeth or nose, I didn't have time to think about it. The demon's cry was shrill and agonized. It made my blood burn.

I yanked myself away, ripping its fingers from the blazing pain in my back. The scream that came out of my own throat was almost as harsh.

"Luna?" Reed called my name tentatively.

"Stay back!" I barked at him. "You don't want to become a target."

"A target for what?" he asked, but I hissed as the broken demon snapped toward Reed Taylor like a leather belt in the hands of an abusive lover.

"Don't touch him!" I growled and elbowed the demon in the jaw. It tried to dematerialize, but I pushed more of my anger and energy into it, holding it fast in its solidity. "No, you don't. No hiding." I elbowed it again, aiming toward its smashed face. It threw its hands up, and I elbowed it in the stomach instead.

"Just let me have the boy," it moaned.

"Never."

The demon spit something up, something dark and phlegmy and disgustingly alive. It mewled and crawled across the floor with wet, stubby legs. I was killing it, I knew.

"Please," it begged. "Please don't."

"I'm strong enough to defeat you," I snarled.

The demon bent itself in half backwards and shrieked. It was a horrible sound. The mewling thing tried to scramble away but I stepped on it, impaling it on my high heel. Its cry echoed the demon's.

"You are destroyed," I cried, and pushed my clawed hands through the demon's body. My hands felt like cold fire. The demon looked at me with utter contempt.

"I know you, Luna Masterson," it said. Its voice was surprisingly calm. "They want you, and I shall deliver you." The pain between my shoulder blades ramped up, nearly drove me mad. I felt my teeth clench in terror.

"I *Mark* you," it said, and vanished.

I took a deep breath, and realized I was panting right there in the middle of the fish and chips place. Every eye was on me. Owen was still on the floor, nearly incoherent with panic.

"Tell your brother hi," I said to him, my hand on my ribs. I felt like I had just run a marathon.

"W-will do," he promised. He dropped his head to the floor and closed his eyes.

I turned around, and Reed was staring at me. I tried to smooth my hair down with my hand.

"Uh, so that was…um," I started, but suddenly the ground rumbled under my feet. I felt the feeling of dread begin to prick at my skin.

"Oh no," I whispered, and ran to Reed. His pupils were slightly dilated.

"What's going on?" he asked me.

Well, drat. This wasn't how I meant to do this, but there just wasn't time. I cupped Reed face in my hands and looked him directly in the eyes.

"Listen to me, Reed Taylor, and listen well. I see demons. They're everywhere, and now we're in trouble. We have to get out of here. Do you understand?"

"Demons?" he asked dreamily. The ground shook violently, and blackness began to gather in the corner of the restaurant. A glass of water tipped over and shattered on the floor.

My heart nearly failed me.

"Reed Taylor!" I barked. He jerked like I had hit him. This ticked me off. "Give me your keys! Now!"

He fished the keys from of his pocket, and I ripped them from his hand. "Your bike! Go!" We ran outside, and I hopped on the motorcycle, then threw his helmet back to him. I could hear a sick snarling coming from inside the door. I started the bike, yanked my helmet over my head.

"Hold on!" I shouted and was nearly crushed by his arms. Well, good. He'll have to hold on tight with the driving I have planned.

I screeched off, bike roaring. Darkness swirled around us on the left and the right. I knew if I looked up, I would see no stars.

"Where are we going?" Reed shouted. I checked his eyes in the rearview mirror. They were completely wild.

"Home," I answered and coaxed more speed out of his bike.

I only hoped we made it there.

Chapter Eight

Reed Taylor's bike purred like a kitten, but I needed it to roar like a tiger. I was pushing it as fast as I dared, but I knew it wasn't fast enough. You can't outrun these things, but it didn't mean I wasn't going to try.

Even now, darkness twined around the trees and buildings like the searching tendrils of a plant, but these were tendrils of despair. They were loss personified. The closer they got to me, the more I felt like throwing my arms in the air and giving up. Except I'm not one to bow down. They ought to know that by now.

"Hang on," I shrieked. The bike squealed and we hung a sharp left. We zoomed down a smaller side street. The darkness pooled around us, momentarily confused.

I chuckled.

"You're enjoying this!" Reed Taylor sounded panicked.

"Stick with me, kid," I said and pushed the bike to full speed again.

Demons were coming out of the woodwork. Literally. I saw them spill out of houses and vomit themselves up from the ground. I had never seen so many at one time. They scrabbled and crawled and flew.

"This looks bad, Reed Taylor," I said, and suddenly my muscles contracted.

"Luna! What's wrong?"

I couldn't speak. The pain radiated out from between my shoulder blades and ran down my limbs. All of my energy was spent on keeping us upright. The bike slowed, and I struggled to push it up again.

"I. Will. Not. Lose," I hissed and felt my eyes narrow. The motorcycle let out a roar as I accelerated.

"Do we have to drive so fast?" Reed Taylor asked me.

"They run fast," I called back.

As if to prove it, I saw a dark shape out of the corner of my eye. I turned to look, and my heart nearly stopped. A demon was running alongside the bike, its face turned sharply toward me. He had visible legs, not the foggy, featureless robe of darkness that most of them had. This one was nearly tangible, even without my help. Seeing it loping eerily alongside us, its eyes on mine, nearly made me lose my mind with terror.

Dear heavens, please let this trick work again. I slammed on my brakes. Just for a second, enough for the demon to shoot past us, but it rocked the bike and made Reed Taylor go haywire. As it should. His bike was a beauty, and it would be a shame to drop it out here in the middle of the road.

Oh yeah, and to die while doing so.

"What are you doing?" Reed Taylor screamed. He was holding me so tight I could hardly breathe. I stuck my foot on the ground and made an abrupt right turn. The demon was doubling back.

"Saving your life," I called out, then gasped. The pain was excruciating.

"You're hurting. Where?"

"My back. Shoulder blades." I could barely bite out the words.

Reed pulled up my shirt and muttered something I couldn't hear in the screaming wind.

"What?" I demanded. I could feel the demons behind me, but neither they nor the darkness were in my line of vision.

"It looks like frostbite, or something. You have holes. Like skewers or claws, maybe. I've never seen… What did this?"

"Demon," I said, and the running demon appeared at my side as if summoned. I shrieked.

"What?"

It was close, only a few inches away. Its eyes seared into mine, and I had to force myself to keep my attention on the road. The demon reached for me. My muscles contracted.

"On your left! Kick it!"

Reed Taylor didn't need to be told twice. He kicked spastically, connecting with the demon once or twice.

"Holy crap, I felt something!" His voice was full of wonder.

"It's the demon. Keep kicking!"

He did. The demon was getting clobbered by a size 13 steel-toed boot, and by the sound of it, it wasn't enjoying it at all.

"A little higher. More to the right."

Reed Taylor kicked a mighty kick, and the demon grabbed at its face and fell to the ground. I cheered, but that was cut short when the demon's *Tracing* on my back seared into my soul. It was excruciating.

"Hey, you're losing control of the bike. Pull yourself together!"

I tried, but the pain was too much. I coughed and something warm and wet bubbled out of my throat and ran over my lips. The air grew heavy, and I felt my eyes start to roll up.

"Pull over. *Pull over.*"

I did exactly as Reed Taylor said. He took one look at me and pushed me forcefully to the back of the bike.

"My turn. You need to go to a hospital."

"No. Home."

"Dude, you totally look like…"

"Take me *home*, Reed Taylor!" I commanded, and he shook his head bitterly. I wrapped my arms around him and leaned my cheek against his back.

"So, uh, are they still after us?" he asked. I met his beautiful eyes briefly in the rearview mirror before I looked away.

"No. I mean, yes, but not like they were before. You hurt the main one when you slammed it in the head. It was almost fully formed, and they're pretty vulnerable when they're like that. Strong, too, though." I was really tired.

"I didn't think you could feel a demon."

"Usually you can't."

"Sounds like a long story. Up for telling me later?"

"Mmm," I said. It was the best I could do.

"Hold on, Luna. I'll get you home. I think I can help with that wound, too. "

I didn't answer. A while later, he said something else.

"Hmm?"

"I said, no wonder you always wear a helmet when you ride. You're a freakin' maniac."

He sounded pleased. I nearly smiled.

Chapter Nine

Reed Taylor parked the bike haphazardly in our driveway, grabbed me off it, and ran me up the steps and into the house. In his haste, he slammed my head against the doorframe. So much for grace. Thank goodness I was still wearing the helmet.

"Well, it's good to see you're—what happened?" Seth demanded. He set Lydia on the floor and raced over to us.

"Luna! Can you hear me?" Seth demanded, and yanked the helmet off of my head. He ran his fingers over the dried blood on my lips. The look he shot Reed Taylor even chilled me. "What have you done to her?"

"I didn't do a thing, man, it was this... I don't even know how to explain it. It was wild." Reed Taylor laid me down on the couch and knelt down beside me.

"Luna?" he asked quietly. I could feel my eyes rolling in my head, but somehow I couldn't make them stop.

"Hurts," I managed, and Seth shot to my side.

"What hurts? Where?"

Reed rolled me onto my side and pulled my shirt up to show the demon's Mark between my shoulder blades.

"See how it's white around the edges? It looks like claw marks. And put your hand here. It's cold."

Lydia babbled and gibbered and crawled over to the couch. She pulled herself up to look at me.

"Don't touch, baby," Seth said, and scooped her against his chest. She struggled, wanting to see her Mama Luna.

"What did you bring her here for? She needs a doctor," Seth said grimly and crossed the room to the telephone.

"No," I said from the couch.

"She didn't want a doctor, she wanted to come home," Reed Taylor said. He ran his fingers lightly over the bloodless wounds. His fingers felt scalding hot.

"Luna, you're nuts," Seth said to me. "Seriously, that's a really nasty wound. What did you do?"

I opened my mouth to answer, but heard myself groan instead.

"She said…a demon did it," Reed Taylor said, and Seth stiffened. Reed Taylor was watching him closely. "She just went kind of ballistic in the restaurant, said a demon almost possessed some boy she knew. Owen something-or-other."

Seth glanced up at Reed Taylor. "She drag you to that fish and chips place? The one with the nets on the table? That has to be so unsanitary."

Reed Taylor's lips turned up a bit, but Seth had already grabbed his car keys. Lydia snatched at them. "Seriously, she's sick and she's weak. And there are two of us, and we're bigger. We can totally stuff her into the back of the Pinto—"

"You own a *Pinto*?" Reed Taylor scoffed.

"—and get her to the hospital with little mishap. What do you think?"

I shook my head, barely. "Not safe," I whispered. Here I was protected, at least a little. Sending me out into the Big Outside World with the demon's Mark was akin to sending me out to sea in a tiny little ship. And setting it on fire.

Reed had my back. "Of course it isn't safe! Don't you know Pintos have the reputation of being 'the barbecue that seats four'?"

My breath rasped out of my body in such a way that both of them turned to look at me.

"Shut. Up," I managed.

Reed Taylor closed his eyes and took a deep breath. When he opened them, they blazed brilliantly.

"I can do it. I can heal her."

Seth blinked in confusion. "What, you're a doctor now?"

Reed Taylor's smile was beautiful. "Nah, I'm not a doctor. In fact, it isn't even me. But it's what she needs, and it'll be better than any doctor can do. Especially on something as ghastly as that. I know how it sounds, but I'm pretty sure it will work."

Seth was struggling with himself. I could feel it.

"Hi, hi, hi, hi, hi," Lydia chirped suddenly, waving. The invisible presence was back.

"Get lost," I told it, annoyed. I didn't have the patience just now.

"I…I'm not sure what's going on," Seth said. He breathed in the smell of Lydia's brown hair. He always did that when he was nervous.

"It'll be okay," Reed Taylor told him, and then he kissed my ear. "You're going to be good, my crazy girl. It'll just take a minute."

His eyes flicked up, bored into my brother.

"You," he said, "are really, really going to hate this."

Chapter Ten

Before Seth even had time to respond, Reed Taylor was murmuring softly. He was so quiet that I couldn't make out the words, but his tone sounded like he was politely asking for something. It was lovely.

I felt the presence step closer. I started to shake my head.

"I don't want it near me, Reed Taylor."

He quietly shushed me. "You're going to be all right. Let him do what needs to be done."

"Who?" Seth asked, his head rocketing from Reed Taylor to me and back. "There isn't anybody here!"

"Yes. There is." Reed Taylor said it with such easy conviction that Seth simply shut his mouth and held Lydia firmly.

I gasped as the presence ran its hand down my back. It felt comfortably warm, not blazing hot like Reed Taylor's hands had been. It hovered around the demonic Tracing.

"I know," Reed Taylor said aloud. "Please, just do your best."

"Do I even want to know what's going on?" Seth was practically whining.

Reed Taylor ignored him. "Luna? This is…*really* going to hurt."

He wasn't kidding. Before the words were even fully out of his mouth, I had flipped on my back in agony, trying to keep the presence away. I didn't want it to touch me, didn't want anything to touch me. My heels and top of my head were still connected to the couch, but the rest of me had arched off. The sounds of my own screams were making me even more hysterical.

"Luna! Reed, tell me what is going on! Tell me now!"

I didn't hear Reed Taylor's answer. My nerves were on fire. Somebody was scraping a knife blade against my bones. I could feel it under my skin.

Lydia started to shriek, and Seth cast a last look over his shoulder before he fled with her outside.

Reed Taylor scooped me up into his arms and held me on the couch. "I'm sorry, I'm so sorry," he said, and rocked me like a baby. I squirmed and writhed and fought him with all of the strength I could. I felt my nails scratch against something, and I focused on that, on the feel of something firm underneath my hands, on anything but the fire consuming my body.

I felt something push at my soul, trying to find a soft spot where it could get in.

"No," I gasped, and struggled harder. "Stop, no! Uninvited! Uninvited!"

"Are you done with her yet?" Reed Taylor was trying hard to sound calm, but I could sense the fury was barely being reined in. I was practically climbing his body in terror. His muscles bunched with the effort of holding me down.

"Well, hurry it up!" he shrieked, and his shrieking made me shriek even more. Honestly, I didn't think it was possible. The holes in my back were being filled with chemicals. They burned, they burned, they burned.

And then it stopped.

"Finally," Reed Taylor muttered. I flopped into his lap, exhausted. I was panting like I had just run all the way here from the docks. Reed Taylor smoothed my sweaty hair from my face. He had a row of bloody scratches on his cheek.

"How are you, my lovely maniac?"

I was dying. I was dead. My body had just been burned away to nothing. I truly doubted if I wanted to live, if living ever meant going through something like that again.

I looked into his concerned, green eyes.

"I sort of hate you a little right now."

Reed Taylor laughed.

Yeah, so I was okay. Better than okay, now that I was stuffing turkey sandwich into my face as fast as I could. My brother? Makes a killer sandwich. It's worth coming back from death's doorstep for.

"So tell me. Who is that?" I asked between snarfs. Seriously. I felt like I hadn't eaten in days. It had been at least four hours. And trust me, that's more than long enough in my book.

"Who?" Reed Taylor asked innocently, but I wasn't buying it, not anymore.

I pointed at the presence, which was hovering near my fridge. Whether looking at Lydia's finger painting art or wishing we had crème Brule, I don't know.

"That."

Reed Taylor's eyebrows lifted. "I thought you couldn't see anything."

I gulped down some milk. "I can't. It's just a big…I don't know. There's something there, I can feel it. I can see its shadow. And I know it listens to me, yes it does," I reprimanded, shaking my finger at it, "but it never says anything. It just sits there and…glares."

"Glares?"

"Glowers. Stares. Stalks. I don't know what it does, but it's very rude." I looked up at Seth. "Do we have any more cookies?"

His lips were pursed together. He pulled some cookies out of the vegetable bin and tossed them onto my plate with a thump. Now I knew his cookie hiding place.

"Cookie?" I asked Lydia, holding a piece out to her. She smiled and put it in her mouth.

Reed Taylor clapped Seth hard on the back. Seth staggered.

"Sure you're ready to hear this, Seth?" he asked.

Seth rolled his eyes to the ceiling, as if for divine help. Then he sat down at the table beside me. Good for him, showing that he was on my side. Go, Team Luna.

"Shoot," he said.

Reed Taylor looked grim. He took a deep breath and the seriousness in his green eyes nearly stopped my heart.

"This is my angel," he said, nodding at the presence. The presence shimmered somehow.

Seth and I both pushed our chairs back at the same time.

"Whatever," Seth said, stalking out with Lydia.

"An angel?" Was he mocking me? I'd never seen an angel. Never. I didn't necessarily even believe in them. With angels came a whole bunch of other things that I didn't want to think about. But I couldn't deny that the presence was *something*.

Reed Taylor's face stayed carefully neutral. "An angel. I would never, ever lie to you, Luna. I promise you." It was taking all of his control to stay so calm, I could see it. But I was rattled.

"I told you about the demons in order to save you. I wish I didn't see them, you have no idea. *No* idea. But if you're making up angels—"

"Luna."

I didn't want this. I wanted to know what the presence was, but this wasn't something I could accept. Angels? Beings of goodness and light? Reed Taylor was playing me. That was easier to accept than the idea that maybe there were angels and they appeared to random junkies, but they didn't appear to me. How many times had I asked, no, *begged* for something beautiful in my life to take the horror away?

"It isn't something I earned," he said, like he could read my thoughts. This was uncomfortable for him. He didn't seem like a guy who was used to sharing.

"I didn't earn this either," I told him, and looked away. The things I had seen, they were just…wearying.

He swallowed hard, rubbed his fingers absently over his scarred arms. "I didn't know how to deal with it when I was a kid. You know. Seeing things nobody else saw. Everybody thought I was…"

I glanced at his scars and was surprised to feel my anger being replaced with understanding. I reached out and took his fingers, held them loosely. He met my gaze and slowly slid his hand fully into mine. Nothing more needed to be said.

Chapter Eleven

I was viciously pulling weeds in the garden when a demon came sauntering by.

"Remember me?" it called out cheerfully.

"Whatever," I said. "You all look the same."

It edged closer. "I told you not to go into that restaurant. Should've listened, huh?"

I narrowed my eyes and gave a particularly stubborn weed a good, hard yank.

"Luna. We need to talk. I'm not going to go away until we do."

I turned and threw the weed at it. It sailed right on through. "Oh, all right. What do we so desperately need to talk about, demon? I'm busy here."

The demon *tsked* sarcastically, and I felt my muscles tense.

"Poor baby," it said, and flopped down on the grass. "Listen. You're going to be in a boatload of trouble soon. I'm talking serious, serious trouble. Dig?"

I attacked another weed. "You're threatening me, now? Typical."

The demon sighed and leaned back, staring at the sky. "That's the thing about you people. You always expect the worst. Why can't I be doing you a favor? Why can't I be your friend?"

My muffled snort didn't seem to faze it. It kept on talking,

"You don't know what it's like to constantly be the buzzkill. I mean, come on. A demon walks into a party and…it's like a bad joke, right? I'm not like that. I'm not like everybody else. It's not my fault."

That did it. I turned to face it, my eyes burrowing into its orbs of blackness. "It's not your fault? What are you, demon? Think you're an angel that lost his way? I don't think so. Demons are demons because they chose to be so. Either you made the choice recently, or you made it long ago. Doesn't matter to me. I don't deal with evil if I don't have to."

The demon surged to its feet, wispy robes blowing in a wind created by rage.

"You don't know anything about me!" it hissed. "You think you're so savvy, but do you know what I see? A scared little girl. I terrify you. We terrify you. And you're right to be afraid. We—"

I interrupted. "Are you going to start in on that 'We are legion' thing now? Please. I see you guys every day of my life. You don't help anybody. Why would you suddenly warn me of trouble, unless you wanted to see me crumble under the anticipation of it?"

"You need to trust me."

"Want me to trust you? Then tell me your name. Give me that power. How's that for trust, huh?"

It was silent.

"I thought so." I stood up.

"Luna, halt!" it shouted after me. Its voice had deepened and darkened to the commanding voice of death, but I didn't turn around.

"Save it," I said and pulled my gardening gloves off of my hands. I opened the kitchen door and stepped inside.

"Luna!" screamed the demon. Its voice had changed again, high and desperate. The Marks between my shoulder blades began to tingle. "Luna!"

The kitchen door slammed. I could still hear the demon shrieking my name, so I went upstairs and turned on the radio. I lay on my bed and stared at the ceiling for a while, but when that refused to calm me, I picked up the phone to call Reed Taylor.

"'Sup?" he said. Just the sound of his voice made me smile.

"Hi," I said. "How are things with you and your invisible presence?"

He laughed. "Good. We've been working out in the yard."

"So was I. You mean to tell me that you're a tidy guy?"

"Almost fanatically tidy. If you ever see weeds at my place, call for help, because something's wrong."

The demon squalled outside.

"Hey," Reed Taylor said. "Demon Patrol is kind of bored and wants to go to the store or something." There was a beat. "You want to go to the store or something?"

A shadow fell across the room. I turned to see the demon glaring through the window, still calling my name. He couldn't see me, but it didn't make it any less disconcerting. He was two stories above the ground, and that was just creepy.

"Reed Taylor, you have no idea. Meet me at the corner in fifteen."

I reapplied my lipstick, ran out to the garage, and hopped on my bike. I was strapping on my helmet when the demon appeared in front of me.

"You're a frustrating person," it informed me.

"What? I can't hear you. I have this big helmet on."

"You can so hear me. I'm not stupid, you know."

"Sorry," I said, and gave an exaggerated shrug. "Helmet on, demon's voices tuned out."

It opened its mouth to say something else, but I flipped the bike on, turned the key and revved the accelerator. I backed out of the garage without another word.

It was a pleasant little drive, and I hummed a little as I playfully swerved down the winding streets. Demon or no demon, I was off to see Reed Taylor and his little angel, and that just made my day.

He was parked at an old drugstore situated on a corner. Nice place with an old fashioned soda fountain and ice cream parlor. They also had just what I needed.

I hopped off my bike and Reed Taylor hopped off his. He turned his gorgeous eyes on me.

"So. Whaddya wanna do?"

I smacked my lips. "First we're getting a soda. Then I'm going to fix your hair."

He frowned. "My hair? What's wrong with my hair?"

"Oh, Reed Taylor, don't ask."

We shared a root beer float, much to the delight of the old people who hung around the counter. Charming, we. Then we headed to the back wall in the pharmacy.

"I don't belong in here," Reed Taylor said. He eyed the boxes and bottles suspiciously.

"Trust me, my friend. You'll be stunning by the time we're done. What do you think about me. Black with, what, purple tips?"

"Blue tips. And how do you know how to do this stuff?"

I handed the stuff to the cashier and winked at Reed Taylor. "Told you I was a jack of all trades."

He laughed. "What, you graduated beauty school?"

"Nope. Dropped out during the last semester. They wouldn't let me wear my combat boots on the floor, and those heels were killing me."

Suddenly I gasped and my legs nearly gave out. The Tracing between my shoulder blades was on icy fire.

"Luna! What's wrong? What can I do to help?"

Reed put his arms around me and tried to steady me. I bit my lower lip. "My back," I said.

He ran his fingers over the Mark. "It's cold. I can feel it even through your shirt. What does that mean?"

I glanced out of the window and growled. "It means the demons have shown up. They're on our bikes."

I stomped past Reed Taylor and blew through the front door. A demon was clambering around my bike, trying to wrap his filmy hands around the handlebars.

"Hey!" I shouted, and stormed over there. I put my hands on my hips. "What do you think you're doing?"

The demon didn't answer. A second demon wandered over and peered into my rearview mirror.

"Off the bike! Off! You can't use it anyway, and you know it. Go!"

The demon tried to rest his feet on the pedals. I was getting more and more steamed.

"Get off now, demon, or I'll sic Reed Taylor's Demon Patrol on you, so help me." I was so angry that my voice sounded perfectly calm. Reed Taylor stood quietly at my side, ready to pick up the pieces if I blew.

The demon looked at me lazily. The bright spots of his eyes were drifting in his head. "I want it. I want to ride."

I snorted. "Yeah, well, I want it, too, and I didn't choose the life of a demon, did I? I'm pulling rank."

The demon didn't budge, but the pain intensified on the Mark. I tried not to gasp. The second demon ran its hands over my controls.

"Watch it, bud," Reed Taylor said to the demons he couldn't see. "She's really ticked."

"You don't want to get me started," I began, but the demon's head swiftly turned away from me. I followed its gaze.

There was the mouthy demon from this morning.

Great.

Mouthy demon breezed right past me. He said something to the other demons in a language that I didn't understand. The demon on the motorcycle squeaked a question.

"What's going on?" Reed Taylor asked me.

I shook my head. "I don't know. I don't speak Demonese."

Mouthy demon nodded. He pointed away from the bike.

The smaller demon shook his head and said something that sounded like a protest. Mouthy demon roared in rage, and quite frankly I was taken aback. My fists were clenched at my sides. Mouthy demon scared me, I have to admit. The force and depth of his anger commanded a respect that I gave. Grudgingly, to be sure, but I gave it.

Apparently he frightened the other two demons as well, because they zoomed quickly and obediently over the hillside.

I turned back to mouthy demon. "You've got some chops, I've gotta say."

He cast me a withering glance. "You're not going to thank me or anything?"

I hated to admit it, but he had a point. "Thank you, Mouthy Demon, for chasing them off of my bike."

He preened. "Ain't no thing. But you owe me. We'll talk later."

"Hey, I never said—"

Mouth's eyes floated over to Reed Taylor, and he immediately bristled.

"What is he doing here?" Mouth hissed. He advanced toward Reed Taylor, and I automatically stepped between them.

"What's going on?" Reed Taylor asked. He put his hand protectively on my shoulder. "What do you need me to do?"

"He's here because he's with me, Mouth. Got a problem with that?"

The demon glared at Reed Taylor standing behind me. "Are you kidding me? For real? Out of everybody on earth, you actually hooked up with this guy?" His dark eyes locked on mine. "What, are you attracted to trouble?"

"What's wrong with him?"

"What's wrong with who?" Reed Taylor demanded. He was getting impatient, stamping his steel-toed boots on the ground angrily. "You're not talking about me, are you? Can demons even talk?"

Mouth rolled his eyes. I caught the shine of them from inside his hood. "Can demons even talk. That's rich. Hey, you!" he shouted, flowing past me and standing nose to nose with Reed Taylor. "Hey, you! Trouble! Yeah, you, big guy. Wake up and see what's right in front of your face sometime, yeah? Then maybe you could be some help that way."

The invisible presence beside Reed Taylor shimmered menacingly. Mouth took a few steps back.

"Yeah, yeah, I'm backing off," he told the presence. "You know what I'm talking about, though, don't you? If you have any sense, you'll keep him away from her. She's too important."

It was my turn to be confused. "Wait, what? Who are you talking about now? Me? You and Demon Patrol are having a conversation?"

Mouth threw his hands in the air. "Humans are so frickin' dense sometimes. Sheesh, Luna. You and this idiot," he jerked a thumb at Reed Taylor, "need to get some awareness, you know what I'm saying? You're all tooling around on your bikes, ga-ga eyed and thinking life is pretty darn sweet. Well, it isn't going to be for much longer, and that's what I've been trying to tell you. You're in serious, serious trouble, and you're only making it worse by hanging around with this clown. Him. Sparkles. What is it with your family and bad news?"

"I'm not going to ditch him." Reed Taylor watched me intently as I answered, his beautiful green eyes flashing. "I'm sorta into this guy right now, and no demon is going to talk me out of it. You guys are all liars, anyway."

Mouth's eyes narrowed. "Watch it, Luna. I'm going out on a limb to try and help you here."

I yawned. "Whatever."

Reed Taylor turned toward the invisible presence. He nodded. He turned back to face the demon, his eyes scanning the air for something he wasn't able to see. "My friend here says you aren't lying, demon. He says something big is up. Why are you trying to help us?"

The demon snorted. "Oh, I'm not doing a thing to help *you*. You can burn, for all I care. In fact, I hope you do." He sharply turned his back to us.

"Good riddance," I muttered.

"Oh, Luna," Mouth called over his shoulder. "Don't say I didn't warn you."

Chapter Twelve

It was a week later and I was still hot under the collar. I fairly sizzled with anger. Even stabbing innocent passers-by at work did little to appease me. I ranted. I grumbled.

"That demon is a pain," I said. "They're all pains, but that one's just extra irritating." I shook the bottle of hair dye viciously while I talked. "He just pops up, starts talking like he's my best friend come back from the dead, or something. You know, he really—"

"Don't you need to be calm for this?" Reed Taylor asked me. His voice was tight.

"What, Reed Taylor, are you scared?" I brandished the bottle of dye at him like a weapon. "Of this? This right here?"

"Watch it! That stuff can blind me. I read the package." He shuddered and wrapped his arms across his skinny bare chest. I told him to lose the shirt so the dye didn't ruin it, but secretly I was enjoying this way too much. Fan service.

"Yeah, you read it like a million times. Relax. Think I'd steer you wrong?"

"You say that an awful lot," he pointed out.

I caught his eye and winked. "Hey. You. Honestly. Do you really think I'd let anything happen to you?"

He grinned, and I grinned back.

"Okay, pretty girl. Make me a star."

It wasn't hard. A bottle of vibrantly red hair dye, a few white streaks here and there, and a haircut later, Reed Taylor was exactly my kind of man.

"I love it," I said, and sat on his lap. "You're perfect."

"You're not so bad yourself," he said, and ran his hand down my newly black hair. "Seriously, these blue tips rock! Who would have thought a little hair stuff could make such a big difference?"

Me, but I wasn't going to remind him how blah his hair had been before. There was nothing blah about him as a person, and now he looked as striking as his personality was. He looked like fire personified.

"Any other girl so much as gives you a second glance, and I'm killing her," I said sweetly. Reed Taylor laughed. "No, I mean it," I insisted. "I'll track her, beat her down with a shovel, and throw her body to the gators."

"Where are you going to find gators out here?"

"I'm resourceful. I'll come up with something."

But even while I was smiling at him, I was thinking about Mouth and his warning. As much as I wanted to ignore him, he *was* pretty persistent in trying to warn me about Reed Taylor. Maybe it was worth looking into.

Maybe later. My phone rang, and suddenly I had other things to think about.

"Hey, big brother. What's—"

I didn't get the chance to finish. "You know who just called? Sparkles. You know what she wants? Lydia." Seth's voice was absolutely wild. He had abandoned all attempts at calm. I leapt off of Reed Taylor's lap.

"Where are you? Where's Lydia? Is she trying to do this legally or by force or by—"

Again, Seth interrupted me. "I don't know. Legally, I guess. By force.

I have no idea. I just… I mean, she walks out. She just walks *out,* and suddenly she cares about her daughter? She never cared about Lydia! The second she was born, Sparkles ran out and found herself *that* guy, and—"

This was approaching meltdown.

"Seth. Seth, listen to me. We'll figure something out, okay? Sparkles is one nasty beast. She's a terrible mother. Nobody will ever give Lydia to her."

Seth sighed. "Luna, that isn't the way things work. Kids usually end up with their mothers unless their mothers are horribly abusive monsters."

"But she—"

"She never abused Lydia. She just didn't care. And face it, with our family history, and your proclivity to…well. It doesn't…I'll talk to you later, okay?"

He hung up before I could say anything. I stood staring at my phone.

Reed Taylor came up from behind me and put his hand on my shoulder.

"What's going on?" he asked.

I shook my head but didn't turn around to face him. "Seth's wife wants custody of Lydia. It sounds like Seth has already given up."

He stood quietly and waited.

Finally I broke down.

"Reed Taylor, I'm part of the problem. Everybody thinks I'm crazy. Like Dad was crazy. I thought moving in to help Seth was the thing to do, but maybe I'm more of a liability than I thought. And Sparkles, well, she isn't normal, you know. I mean, a normal bad mother. She walked out on my brother with some guy, which was terrible enough, but somehow she got involved in the whole demon thing."

"Involved how?"

I turned and looked into his fantastic eyes. He wasn't judging me. He wasn't laughing at me. For the first time in my life, somebody believed me wholeheartedly. It was terrifying. It was also wonderful. He made me want to tell the truth.

"It's like there is a protective layer on the soul. Your soul. That soul belongs to you, right? But you can keep doing things to damage that layer, until finally it's thin enough a demon can just hop on in, take a ride around with you. Sometimes you know they're there, and sometimes you don't. Sometimes the person actually digs it. That was Sparkles. She got herself a demon, and they made quite the team."

Reed Taylor looked wry. "That sounds like my last ex-girlfriend."

"It sounds like everybody's last girlfriend. Sparkles and her demon, they liked to hurt. If she wants Lydia, it's not because of motherly love, that's for sure. There's something else going on."

"So what are you going to do?"

I sighed. Curse it all.

"You're a good time, Reed Taylor, but Seth and I need to scheme. It sounds like I need to gear up for demonic battle."

Chapter Thirteen

I walked in the front door and knew something was wrong. The house didn't feel right.

"Seth? Lydia? I'm home," I called out and dropped my backpack on the floor. Nobody answered.

"I'm leaving my jacket on the couch like a slob. I'm wearing my boots in the house, and I didn't even wipe them. You should come yell at me."

Silence.

The sticky weight of the atmosphere nearly took my breath away. The Mark between my shoulder blades tingled and burned, making me slightly nauseous. I tiptoed to the kitchen and peeked through the door. Nothing. I reached in and slid a heavy duty kitchen knife out of the block, just in case.

"Seth? Are you here?"

I walked through the downstairs, checking closets and under tables as I went. The knife shone dully and I swallowed hard. I hoped I didn't have to use it. I took a deep breath and nearly decided not to go upstairs, telling myself I was obviously alone in the house, but the sickly, oily ambiance made me grind my teeth and continue on.

"Stupid demonic presence," I muttered to myself as I climbed. I pressed my back against the wall and held the knife tightly in front of me.

I thought of Seth, I thought of Lydia. I thought of this whole mess, and the idea of Sparkles ending up with sweet Baby Girl. Wasn't gonna happen.

Seth wasn't in his room. He wasn't in Lydia's. Not in mine. With every door I opened, I felt my hope turn to something ugly and full of despair. Where could they be? Why did the house feel like this? It felt like back in the old Sparkles days, but worse. Much, much worse.

There was only one door left. I turned to the bathroom and felt like my legs were going to give out. It was so quiet. So unnatural. I could barely get my legs to move. Had I ever been this frightened before? My hand fluttered up to my heart, which was pounding almost painfully. I gripped the knife tighter and forced my legs to walk. One step. Two steps. Maybe I was under a lot of emotional duress. Maybe Seth and Lydia were at the park. Maybe I was just going crazy. Please, let me be going crazy. I'd been expecting that for years. I was prepared to handle it.

I turned the door handle, and even before I pushed the door open, I knew. I knew.

Seth was fully clothed in the filled bathtub. His head was flopped to the side, half of his face submerged.

"Oh, Seth!"

I dropped the knife and ran to him. I fell to my knees and lifted his head out of the water.

"Seth! Seth, can you hear me? Wake up!"

He didn't move. I felt for a heartbeat, but my hands were shaking so hard that I wasn't sure if I felt a pulse or not. If he still had one, it was terribly weak. I pushed his hair out of his eyes and tried to take his pulse again. My knee bumped into something on the floor. It was a bottle of prescription medicine. A bottle of Lortab that I kept around for when my old injuries flared up. It had been nearly full. Now it was mostly empty.

"Why would you do this? What about Lydia? Where's Lydia?"

I tried to pull Seth out of the tub, but he was too heavy. Panicked, I yanked the stopper out of the bottom of the tub, bouncing from foot to foot while the water drained. I needed to call the ambulance, but I couldn't just leave him unconscious with the tub full of water. My head was spinning. My stomach roiled. I stopped, covered my face with my hands, and took a deep breath. Then I was back in action.

The water drained to the point where I felt I could race for the phone without Seth drowning during my absence. I ran downstairs, grabbed the phone out of its cradle, and dialed 911 as I took the stairs two at a time.

"911, what is your emergency?"

"My brother is dying and my one year-old niece is missing!" I gave them the address and dropped the phone. I pushed Seth's hair out of his eyes, and whispered that I loved him. I told him I needed him, that he couldn't leave me alone, that I wasn't strong enough to lose Mom, Dad, and now him, too.

"And Lydia! Where's Lydia?"

He didn't move. I couldn't feel any breath. His skin was white and his lips were blue.

I sat down on the floor next to my only brother, put my head on my knees, and sobbed.

Chapter Fourteen

Somebody was banging on the door.

"Paramedics! We're coming in."

I leapt to my feet. Somewhere along the line I'd picked up the knife again. Somehow it made me feel a little bit better.

"Up here! Up here, up here," I screamed, and ran for the stairs. The paramedics were already on their way up.

"Where is he, Miss?"

"The bathroom. That door. I don't know if he—"

"We have it from here."

They pushed past me in the small hallway.

"He's alive," one of them yelled. I wrapped my arms around myself and started to cry. The other paramedic turned back to me.

"Miss? Do you have somebody to call? Somebody to give you a ride to the hospital?" He eyed me. "We have a current policy that we can't take anybody with us, and you're in no condition to drive."

"I, uh, yes…" Somewhere in the back of my brain, I realized I was only getting in their way. I pulled myself together. "Yes, I have somebody to call. Excuse me."

The paramedic nodded and turned back to his work. I stepped into Lydia's room and dialed Reed's Taylor's number.

"Yeah, this is Reed."

"It's me."

"Luna! Listen, I was just about to call you. I think we should—"

"Seth just tried to kill himself."

A beat. "You're kidding me."

"I'm not. The paramedics are here. He was in the bathtub, and he had taken a whole bottle of pills. He always was prissy like that, hated to get dirty. Dad was always after him about it."

"You're rambling, baby. Where's Lydia?"

I started to cry again. I had never cried so much in my life.

"I don't know. She isn't here. I looked, before I saw…the house has this strange feel, and I couldn't find them anywhere. I had a knife and—"

"Hold on. I'll be right there, Luna. Don't go anywhere, do you understand me?"

He hung up, and I cradled the phone to my chest just to be closer to him. The paramedics had Seth on a stretcher and were maneuvering him down the stairs.

The blond paramedic looked very weary. "We're taking him to St. Marks. See what we can do."

I nodded. I didn't know what else to do. I followed as they loaded Seth into the ambulance, turned on their sirens, and roared away.

Chapter Fifteen

I had my helmet in hand by the time Reed Taylor squealed into the driveway. I climbed onto the bike behind him, wrapped my arms around his waist, and rested my head against his back.

"St. Marks," I said.

"Hold on, baby," he answered and took off. I closed my eyes. I tried not to think about Seth. Instead, I tried to figure out where Lydia could be.

Seth wouldn't do anything to hurt her, so obviously she wouldn't be in the house when he tried to…do what he did. Is she at the babysitter's? Except I *am* the babysitter. Who could she be staying with?

It didn't make sense, not any of it. My brother would never do this.

Except that he did.

Did something happen to Lydia, and that's why Seth didn't think he could go on?

My eyes snapped open, and I flinched.

"What's going on?" Reed Taylor yelled back to me.

"Just thinking," I yelled back. He nodded and kept up his breakneck speed.

No, if something had happened to Lydia, Seth would have called me. No matter how bad it was, we would have figured something out. It has to be something else.

I remembered the atmosphere in the house, the dark depression and loathing that hung in the air. I felt like I'd be combing despair out of my hair tonight. The ambiance felt greasy and that could only be one thing:

The demonic.

We reached the hospital. Reed Taylor pulled up to the doors, and I hopped off.

He reached out and took my helmet. "I'll park the bike and meet you inside."

I nodded and ran through the doors. The signs pointed toward the empty registration desk and I slapped my hand on the table until somebody peeked out from behind a partition.

"My brother. Seth Masterson. Attempted suicide, pills and drowning. The ambulance just brought him in."

The girl looked at me with wide cow eyes. I wanted to poke them out with my thumbs.

"I'm sorry," she began.

I slapped the desk again. "Tell me where he is. Can I go in? Do I have to wait outside?"

She shook her head. "I don't know. The woman who works at the desk just ran to the bathroom. She'll be back in just a minute, so if you can wait until then…"

I leaned over the desk, and I'm sure that every demonic visage I have ever seen had nothing on my expression then. I could feel the hatred and anger in it.

"Listen, lady. Tell me where my brother is, or I will run all around this hospital and find him myself. I will call upon the powers of Hell to help me. And believe me, you don't want to know what that will be like."

I felt a hand on my shoulder.

"Hello, ma'am. My name is Reed, and this is Luna. She's a little upset right now. Will you let Seth Masterson's doctors know we're available in the waiting room, please? Thank you so much."

He steered me over to a seat and sat me down. "Coke?" he asked.

"I'm not thirsty. I can't sit here in a waiting room. I need to see Seth. I need his help to figure out where Lydia is. The demons..."

Reed Taylor walked to the vending machine and got two sodas. He set one in my hand and opened the other one.

"Luna," he said after a swallow. "I'm sorry about Seth, but they're not going to let you in there while they pump his stomach. You know I'm right."

He *was* right. I scowled and sucked down my soda.

"Ms. Masterson?"

I turned to face a short policeman with a jolly face.

"Yes? Oh, good. You're here to look for Lydia. Look, I have a picture of her here in my wallet."

"Lydia is with her mother, ma'am. She's safe."

I felt my whole body jerk.

"She's with Sparkles? And you call that safe? Where are they? I need to get her back."

The officer held out a warning hand. "Sit down, Ms. Masterson. You're getting excited. There is no reason to—"

I didn't sit down. Instead, I put my fists on my hips. Reed Taylor whistled and took a step back from us.

"Listen here, *officer*. Sparkles is a terrible woman who walked out on her family with some pretty young thang. She has no love in her cold, black soul. She only wants Lydia because she doesn't want Seth to ever be happy."

"Now, miss—"

"What? You think I'm lying?" I felt like my eyes were sparking, I was so angry. A demon slid along the floor on its many legs like a centipede. It flowed over the policeman's shoes, but I ignored it. "She's a nasty woman. She's a demonic presence. I don't know how she even got into the house because she is so utterly wicked that she shouldn't have been allowed in."

"Now I understand you don't like her, but you don't have to be so harsh. It's unbecoming." The officer looked perturbed at my rudeness.

I snorted. "Unbecoming? She is the most evil person I have ever met, and believe me, I have seen a lot of yuuuuuck in my time."

"Now, miss—"

I was ready to really lay into him when the doctor poked his head out of the door. "Family for Seth Masterson?"

My head whipped to the doctor, back to the officer, and to the doctor again.

"Talk to the doc. I got the cop," Reed Taylor told me. He winked at me with his fantastic green eye.

I nodded, flashed the officer a "You're so lucky I have to leave right now" look, and strode over to the doctor.

"So what's going on? How is my brother?"

The doctor smiled. It looked fake, but he had a hard day, too, so I was prepared to let it go. "He's alive. We pumped his stomach. He had some water in his lungs, but not very much. He's a lucky man."

"Can I see him?"

He nodded. "Just for a minute. He's pretty groggy."

I followed him through the door into the triage unit. A little boy was getting his head bandaged. Weak cries came from behind a curtain. I could see something leggy winding around the hospital bed. That thing from earlier.

"Here he is. Like I said, you only have a few moments."

Seth looked like death. His color was bad and his eyes were tiny slits.

His body looked small and horrifyingly frail in the hospital bed. I checked his heart rate and blood pressure on the machines. Weak, but better than I expected. I pulled out the single chair and straddled it.

"Hi, big brother. How are you?"

I saw the shine of his eyes flick in my direction.

"Luna."

"Yeah, it's me. Good to see you. You scared me to death, you know."

"Sorry."

"Yeah, I bet you are. Do you know Sparkles has Lydia? What were you thinking? Did you go crazy?"

He flinched at the word 'crazy,' and it only served to anger me.

"That's right. I said The Forbidden Word. *Crazy.* You hear that? Killing yourself, Seth? You, of all people. What about your daughter? What about me? You said you'd never forgive Dad—"

A nurse swung the curtain open with an irritated scowl. I hadn't realized that my voice had gotten quite so loud. Or hysterical.

"Now that is quite enough, young lady. This man needs to rest, not be badgered. Out. Scoot."

"But—"

"*Now.*"

I was pretty mad. I hate being told what to do, and Attila the Hun here was getting on my last nerve. I jumped to my feet and opened my mouth to tell her exactly what I thought. Then I took another glance at Seth, and he looked awful. The anger quickly drained out of me, and I was left with gratitude and worry.

"I'm sorry," I said to Seth. Then to the nurse, "I'm sorry. Give me just a second, will you?"

The nurse *hmphed* and looked away to give me some semblance of privacy. I noticed she didn't budge, though.

I leaned over the bed and smoothed Seth's hair with my hand.

"I love you, Seth. You and Lydia are the only family I have. I never want to go through life without you." I patted his cheek. "Now get better or I'll have to amputate your toes for you. With a hunting knife. And no anesthesia."

The nurse looked alarmed. Seth's lips twitched in a brief smile, and then he was asleep again.

"He likes it," I assured the nurse. "If I didn't threaten him daily with bodily harm, nothing would get done around the house. That's just how it is."

I blew past her into the waiting room. Reed Taylor was sprawled across the chair, staring at nothing. He stood up as soon as he caught sight of me. There was no sign of the policeman.

"How is he?" he asked.

I tapped my foot rapidly. Suddenly I was full of nervous energy. "He's all right. He's alive. The nurse is a real tyrant, I tell you. Wouldn't let me talk. I didn't get a chance to ask him anything."

Reed Taylor's smile almost made me forget everything. For just a second, anyway. "Yeah, I heard you. You were pretty upset, and your voice really carries, love." His smile faded. "Listen, about Lydia—"

"Right. Let's go get her." I started for the door but Reed Taylor stopped me.

"It isn't that simple. I was just talking with the policeman there, and he was saying that…well, it doesn't look likely you'll be able to get her back right now."

I narrowed my eyes at him. Shooting the messenger, sure, but curse it all, somebody was going to be shot around here! "Why not?"

Reed Taylor sighed. "There's no easy way to say it, Luna. Lydia's father just tried to commit suicide. There's history of mental illness in the family.

You're also suspected of being mentally unstable. So here comes Luna's mom, who basically looks pretty clean right now, riding in on a white horse to save her little girl."

"What?" I shouted. Every head in the hospital snapped my way, and Reed Taylor put his arm around me.

"Luna. Calm down. I know how you feel about Sparkles. But let's face it. You don't really have a leg to stand on right now." He looked grim. I wanted to run my hands through his hair of fire to assure myself he was really there, or maybe just belt him in the stomach, but I was too wooden to move. "Besides, there's more than that. Notice who's missing?"

"The angel. I told you things were going down."

I spun toward the voice. Mouthy demon was standing behind me. He looked angry and possibly even a little defeated, but it flashed across his dark face so quickly I couldn't be sure.

"Mouth," I said. I nearly wanted to hug him, which only proved how out of sorts I was. "I'm so glad you're here."

He snorted. "You are?"

"I am. Reed Taylor and I need to talk to you."

Mouth turned away. "You know I want nothing to do with this guy. Talk to me when you're alone." He started to flow away, but I grabbed for his arm. A faint resistance, but that was it. My fingers went right through. Mouth stopped, though, and looked at his arm. He looked at me.

"Mouth, Lydia is gone. I…" I was no good at this. I didn't even know what words to say. "I could use his help. And yours. Just get over it and let's go figure some stuff out, all right?"

Mouth muttered some very angry, crass words a lady never chooses to repeat but I've never had a problem with, and then he sighed.

"Okay. All right. Not here; you're causing a scene. Your house." His eyes flicked to Reed Taylor. "I'm telling you it's best if he doesn't come, but you're not going to listen to me anyway."

He dissipated into darkness.

I turned to Reed Taylor. "Man, he really does not like you. Have you had a run-in with him before? Killed his mama?"

Reed Taylor laughed. "Not that I know of." He took my hand. I closed my eyes for just a second, taking the chance to collect myself. His hand was warm, callused, and very reassuring.

My father's hands used to feel the same way. I slid my fingers out of his grip and stepped away.

"We're meeting him at my place," I said. I couldn't look him in his beautiful eyes, couldn't take a chance of what he might see. "He's willing to talk to us. Maybe he knows what's up with Seth and Sparkles and the absence of your Demon Patrol."

Chapter Sixteen

The ride home took forever, and the worst part was it gave me time to think. Obsess, really. If Lydia was with Sparkles, then that means she's hanging out with her mom's demon. Who know what was going on, wherever they were? Seth was in no condition to go after his daughter. I think Reed Taylor would be willing, but what good would he be without his own personal Demon Patrol? He can't even see the things. And Mouth seemed like he might know what's going down, but he is, after all, a demon himself. We all know demons are liars.

Mouth was waiting for us when we pulled in. He looked irritated.

"All right, let's go."

He stalked up the porch stairs.

"Hey," I called out, "you're not going to be able to—"

Mouth glided through the front door. I froze. I couldn't make myself breathe right.

"What's wrong?" Reed Taylor asked me. He cursed. "I can't see anything."

I licked my lips. "He just…he just went through the door. He's in the house." I turned to face Reed Taylor, hoping his gorgeous greens would calm me down. They didn't. "He isn't supposed to be in the house. I did that protection thing. It should work against any demon that isn't fully

83

possessing a human…"

Mouth's head popped back through the door. "Coming?"

I took a shuddering step forward, and Reed Taylor wrapped his arm around my waist.

"You shouldn't be able to get inside there," I accused Mouth.

He shrugged. "I had no problem. So are you staying outside all night or what? Your neighbors are already watching you mill around."

Ugh, the neighbors. First the ambulance and now I'm freaking out on the sidewalk. I growled in my throat and started marching forward. The things I do to keep up appearances.

"We have a *lot* to talk about," I threatened.

"Can't wait," Mouth replied demurely. The Mark between my shoulders tingled.

I worked the key in the lock and threw the door open with exuberance. Quite a bit of exuberance. Too much exuberance.

"Ouch!" yelped Reed Taylor.

"Oops! Sorry."

He rubbed his shoulder and stepped through the door. He stopped. "Whoa," he said.

Whoa was right. The ambiance. The heaviness. But more than that, the house was packed. Demons crowding around the staircase, demons on the furniture. A tiny demon that looked like a fruit bat stuck its head out of the garbage disposal.

I had never seen so many demons in one place before. I felt dizzy and looked for a place to sit down, but there were demons of all shapes and sizes propped on every surface.

"I think I'm going to be sick," I said, and slid down the wall to the floor. I wrapped my arms around my knees, trying to keep myself as small as possible. I didn't want a demon to touch me if I could avoid it.

"Your house," Reed Taylor said. He moved his head around like a blind man who was straining to see. "It feels terrible. So dark. What happened here?"

"It's become Demonic Utopia, you screw-up." Mouth looked Reed Taylor up and then he looked him down. "Seriously, Luna, what do you see in this guy? He's got nothing."

"Shut up, Mouth." I struggled to my feet. "There are demons everywhere," I told Reed Taylor. "I mean hundreds. One just…one just walked right through you. Did you feel it?"

"No, I didn't."

Thank goodness. I took another step into the room. I hated to see them in our space, trying to touch our things. Something slinky slid down the banister.

They're upstairs, in our rooms, looking at our pictures, at our clothes, touching as much as they could touch. I wondered if I'd find a tiny demon in Lydia's crib. The thought of it nearly made me throw up.

"You okay?" Reed Taylor asked me.

I shook my head. "This is so uncool. I mean, seriously. You should just see the place. Actually, it's probably better you can't."

Reed Taylor's muscles were tense. "I don't have to see them. I can feel the air. It feels dangerous." He looked at me. "Besides, there isn't a single angel here. Not one. I wonder why that is?"

"Because they're not welcome here, doofus!" Mouth stabbed his finger into Reed Taylor's chest.

"Knock it off, Mouth. But what do you mean, they're not…ugh."

My eyes practically crossed, I was feeling so sick. I doubled over and wrapped my arms around myself.

Reed Taylor was instantly at my side. "What's wrong? You look awful. Is it the house?"

"It's the—" I started to gasp out, but I couldn't finish. I dropped to my knees. I screwed my eyes closed, but I could still feel the demons' gazes upon me. The area between my shoulder blades screamed for their attention, I could feel it.

"It's the Mark," Mouth finished for me. Which was very helpful, except Reed Taylor couldn't hear him at all. Still, it was a rather conciliatory gesture, offering an explanation to the man he despised so much and without good reason, and I'd have to thank him for it later.

If I didn't die right here on the living room floor.

Mouthy demon closed his eyes and the want in his voice made me shiver. "Oh, man, that Mark. The Demon Tracing. You have no idea what…" His eyes snapped open. The other demons were inching closer.

"You need to get out of here, Luna," Mouth said. "Like, right now."

I couldn't move. It hurt to breathe. I was curled up on the ground and my muscles were starting to twitch.

"No," mouthy demon said, and stood between me and the other demons. He used the commanding voice and strange language I had heard from him before, his eyes flashing. I didn't need to speak Demon to know he was angry.

The demons stopped advancing for just a second, but the pull of the Tracing and my deliciously deliciousness was apparently too great. Mouth turned to Reed Taylor and swung at him in frustration.

"Get her out of here, you moron! Use your head. Be useful for once."

Of course Reed Taylor couldn't hear him, but if there was one thing that man knew how to do, it was to think on his feet. He swept me up, threw me over his shoulder, and took off out of the house.

Just being out of that oppressive environment made me feel better. I breathed in through my nose. The Mark still hurt, but it wasn't a blinding, screaming pain like it had been before.

"You can put me down, Reed Taylor," I said. My voice sounded weaker than I liked.

"When we get to the bike."

He trotted over to his motorcycle, and set me down gently. "How are you feeling?"

I rubbed my eyes. "Not so great, but better. The house…"

I didn't know what else to say. The house was a cesspool of demons. It felt like death. The house was no longer safe. I didn't have anywhere to go.

"What did your little demon friend have to say about it?" he asked me.

Mouth didn't come out of the house, but other demons were starting to drift over from across the street. It seemed like tonight was going to be a big demon block party.

"He didn't say anything. Wait, except that he started yelling at them in some strange language. He was telling them to back up, or something. I'm not sure." I reached back to rub the pain out of the Mark. It wasn't helping. Plus it's in a really awkward place. I sighed and grabbed my helmet and motorcycle.

"What was that all about, anyway?" I asked bitterly. "Why would he bring us here if he knew it was going to be so disastrous?"

Reed Taylor shrugged. "Maybe he didn't know. Maybe he thought you'd be more comfortable at home, I don't know."

Suddenly Mouth was standing at my side. "Or maybe I wanted to give ol' Luna here a wakeup call. Show her how things were really shaking down. "

I bared my teeth at him. "Oh, is that it? You couldn't have just told me, instead of driving me to my knees because of the horrible demony power of my mystical, magical Tracing?"

He bared his teeth right back. I almost took a step back but reminded myself it was only the pesky mouthy demon, and he didn't scare me. Good, because I had almost forgotten.

"Telling you does no good, *Luna,* because you never listen to me. *Luna.*" He wasn't kidding this time; he was really, genuinely angry. I really did take a step back, and nobody could fault me for it.

"I take it he's here again," Reed Taylor said wearily. He pulled his helmet over his head. "Fantastic."

Mouthy demon heaved a great sigh and visibly pulled himself together.

"Listen, you two. I tried to tell you, and I tried to tell you. That wasn't getting us anywhere, was it?" He gestured at Reed Taylor. "He can't hear me. You won't listen. What else am I supposed to do?"

"I'm sure you could have thought of something."

He wheeled on me quickly, and his eyes were blazing fire. That's not a figure of speech, either. It's a real true thing. Fire licked up out of the sockets of his eyes and danced around his forehead. I could actually feel the heat.

"You," he said, and his voice dripped with venom and, I want to say, disgust. "Stop with the jokes. Drop the wisecracks and sarcasm. You don't even grasp what I—" He glanced over his shoulder. "They're coming. They can't forget the scent of your Mark." He glared at me, and I kid you not, I was actually afraid. "Go somewhere. Anywhere. Get away from here. And if you're smart, you'll get away from him." He spit at Reed Taylor, and disappeared.

"What did the punk have to say?" Reed Taylor asked me.

I was shaking with anger and more than a little fear. Did Reed Taylor somehow have something to do with this? Was he demon bait, too? "The usual," I said, and threw my leg over my bike. "I don't want to talk about it. Listen, Reed Taylor, it's been swell, but I need some time to think. I work best alone. Catch ya later."

He looked hurt, so I quickly pulled my helmet down and started the engine. Demons ran from the house like dark water, flowing toward Reed Taylor and me. The Tracing sizzled and I felt my head start to spin. I couldn't stay here anymore. I needed to bail.

I found myself doing a lot of that lately.

Chapter Seventeen

I left Reed Taylor standing in my driveway and headed to the flower shop on the far end of town. We had a big garden when I was a kid, full of daylilies. I packed the flowers up carefully and hopped back onto the bike. I needed to think. I needed to calm down. I couldn't go in swinging concerning Lydia. As much as I hated it, Reed Taylor was right. If I tore the city walls down brick by brick, shrieking for Lydia, it was only going to hurt our cause. I had to get control first, and there was only one place I could think of to go. It was a good long drive, and it was getting dark when I arrived at the cemetery.

I had been here so many times that I could walk the place blindfolded. I stepped carefully past the tattered flags and broken stone. My boots didn't make a sound on the soft grass. I knelt down by a double stone that had two names carved on it.

"Hi, Mom," I said, and kissed my fingers. I pressed them to her name. "How are things going there?"

I stopped for a second. I wasn't really sure what to say. I forced a smile, just in case she could see me. And it made me feel braver, more confident. The last thing I wanted to do was curl up and cry on my parent's graves. I am not an orphan in a Charles Dickens story. I'm more…Buffy the Vampire slayer. Only not cute and perky. Or very effective at slaying anything.

Hmm. Perhaps I'm more Dickens than I thought.

"Lydia is so big now, Mom. You'd be really impressed. Sweetest little thing. Smart, too. She's a typical Masterson lady, that's for sure. But she's missing. With her demonic mother, and that's no exaggeration. I don't know how to find her just yet, but I will. And Seth…well, he's going through a hard time, but I'll figure out how to pull him through. You know I will."

I gave Mom a daylily, Dad another, and stuck the third behind my ear. This is how we shared flowers when I was young. There was always a flower for Seth, too, but he never wanted anything to do with them.

Daylilies didn't bother him. Dad bothered him.

I sighed. "Dad, I'm not sure what to do. There's this mouthy little demon that keeps popping up everywhere. He tells me things are going down, that they're going to get really bad. My natural tendency is not to believe him, of course, because, well, he's a demon. But there's something about him. His earnestness, maybe. I think he's telling the truth, and I'm not sure what to do about that. Because if things are getting bad…" I snorted. "What am I saying? They are bad." I turned to Mom's side of the grave. "Cover your ears, Mom. This isn't for you." I turned back to Dad. "Sparkles just waltzed in out of nowhere. Said she wanted Lydia, and Seth just lost it, or something. I found him in the bathtub today and he had taken a whole bottle of pills. Sounds like Sparkles took her before Seth did it."

I lay down between them on their grave, my arms behind my head. The moon was large and luminous, and faintly sinister. I couldn't get over the feeling it wanted to lean down and bite me. Perhaps there is evil inside the moon, and has been all of this time, and we never knew about it.

"I don't know what to do, Dad. Everything is so messed up." I paused and bit my lip. "There's a boy, though. A guy. His name is Reed Taylor, and I sort of dig him. Mom, you can listen to this part. He's something special, he really is." I thought about my parents, about their bodies moldering in the ground all of these years. What would be left, really? I closed my eyes to keep myself from thinking that. Things were bleak enough.

"I didn't want to talk about bad things, only. That's why I mentioned Reed Taylor. I wanted you to know there are good things going on, too. Always. Anyway." I stood up and dusted the dirt off of my back and legs. "I love you guys. Just wanted to let you know." I walked away from their graves without looking back. Ever since I had been a child, I never looked back.

I intended to head for my motorcycle, but I surprised myself by taking a turn and walking toward the rose garden adjacent to the cemetery. It was full of peace and beauty, and maybe I needed that right now. Plus Lydia loved roses, and this was a way to feel closer to her while I thought of where to look. I found a white stone bench that gleamed dully in the moonlight. I sat down and pulled my knees up to my chest, content to just look at the sky.

"Beautiful night tonight," Mouth said conversationally.

I groaned and pulled my knees in tighter. "Why did you have to show up? I just want to be alone. It seems I'm never alone anymore."

If I thought Mouth would apologize, I was certainly wrong.

"What do you expect?" he said. He shrugged, not caring. "You're Marked. You're a popular girl nowadays, Luna, and popularity has its price."

"Ugh, the great Tracing that turns me into demon bait. What can you tell me about it, anyway?"

His voice remained level. "I can smell it a mile away. I can feel it in what used to be my bones. It's everything I can do not to throw you down and push into your soul right here right now, and I'm one of the good guys."

I felt my eyes widen.

"Yeah, that Mark you wear is bad news, girlie. I don't think you understand the full implication of it."

I didn't know what to say, so I didn't say anything. I leaned my head back against the bench and smelled the roses. They seemed clean and slightly sultry at the same time. I turned my head toward Mouth.

"Can you smell the roses? Is that something demons can do?"

Mouth leaned back, as well. "Well, I'm not your typical demon, I'll have you know. Most have lost that sense. They've lost most senses. Lost most of their minds. I'm more…intact than they are, I guess you'd say." He flashed his eyes in my direction, and I couldn't read the expression in them. "Yes. I can smell the roses."

"Don't they smell wonderful?"

He didn't move. "They smell like decay. Like a dying thing."

Oh. Well. That was cheery.

Mouth obviously felt like elaborating. "You're just a hunk of meat, Luna. You and everybody you care about. That guy. Your brother. The baby girl. You walk through life, going about your petty little routines, and your bodies are dying all around you. It's disgusting. It's what true horror is. I can hardly abide being near the living."

Normally I would have jumped on that full force, but it had been a hard couple of days. "I'm sorry I disgust you, then," I said, and I very nearly meant it.

He eyed me. "Man, you're in a mood. I can't believe you didn't take my head off for that. I'll have to try harder."

I took the daylily from my hair and held it up so it was centered in the middle of the moon.

"I'll be honest, Mouth. I don't know what's going on. I always say I'll land on my feet, but I'm not so sure this time." I turned the daylily around and around, a delicate moon dance. "Sparkles scares me. I've seen her demon. I had never seen anything like it. I'm worried about Seth because he's always so calm, and that was completely... I don't know what to do. I don't know how to...and the house today..."

I couldn't finish. I swallowed hard and pursed my lips together.

From the corner of my eye, I saw that Mouth was studying me. Normally I'd be embarrassed, but I was too tired to be embarrassed.

"So maybe I'm kind of sorry about taking you to your house today. A little."

I didn't say anything, so he continued.

"I wanted to scare you, of course. I wanted you to see how serious things were becoming. You're always so rebellious and unconcerned, and I'm not sure if that's how you really feel or if it's an act. You need to realize, Luna. I...I don't want anything to happen to you."

I was surprised at how gentle his voice was. I turned to look at him. His smile was crooked. How could I know he had a crooked smile? I stared hard into his eyes. They had a hint of color.

"Mouth! Are you...you're not as transparent as you usually are. Are you becoming fully formed?"

I reached out a hand and grabbed at his sleeve. I felt some real substance there, underneath the air and resistance.

He gently pulled his sleeve away. "It comes and goes. It seems to be stronger when I'm happy and calm."

I raised my eyebrows. "I'm nearly crying my eyes out as I tell you that my life is falling apart around me, and you're happy and calm?"

"Funny, isn't it?"

I closed my eyes, tested my energy level. "I didn't even feel you taking anything out of me."

"I didn't."

That startled me. "You didn't? You managed to form on your own? But I thought…"

He looked weary. "I told you I'm not like everybody else. I don't need to use you like the others. If I'm relaxed enough, I can solidify without even meaning to. Do you know how that feels?" His eyes shone. "To manipulate things in the real world? To actually leave an imprint? That's why everybody's after you, you know. Because you can see them. Because they're finally real to somebody, even if it is a smart-aleck woman."

"Hey."

"You can't deny it."

He took the flower from my hand. I looked at him in amazement. "You're formed enough you can actually touch that?"

He held it in his palm. I almost expected it to wilt in his hand, but it didn't. It held its form and even looked more lovely than usual, if that could be possible. Something serene and beautiful held by something created from despair. It made me want to cry.

"You take this for granted," he said. "You take everything for granted. Life truly is wasted on the living."

He took the daylily and gently tucked it behind my ear. I was reminded of my father. I was reminded of Reed Taylor. I remembered I shouldn't be sitting in the moonlight with a demonic presence. It was dangerous. But I couldn't keep myself from staring at the swirl of color that fought its way up from deep inside of his eyes. His eyes were dangerous and frightening and surprisingly lovely.

"Get some sleep. Be well." Mouth breathed in deeply through his nose. "Oh, Luna. The Mark. You have no idea how your soul smells. It smells like blood and lavender on ice. I'd better leave now or you'll be dead by morning."

This time he didn't just disappear. He stood up and walked away. I'd hate to say he frightened me. I'd like to think I'm braver than that, but as I reached up to touch the flower in my hair, I couldn't control the trembling in my hands.

Chapter Eighteen

I had no desire to go home and see if it was still Demonic Central so I slept on the bench. Of course I was cold and cranky and stiff when I woke up. Not to mention I had dreams about demons and daylilies. I was a little more bitter than usual this morning.

Mouth had given me something to think about, I guess. He was a demon and demons were bad. But he seemed good. Ish. If he could just get over his hatred for Reed Taylor, that is.

The first stop was the hospital. The nurse smiled when she saw me.

"Hello. And who are you here to visit this morning?"

Obviously she hadn't heard anything about me. I gave her my cheeriest grin. "Why, hello, my wonderful and helpful health care provider. I'm here to visit my brother Seth Masterson. How is the sweet boy doing today?"

Her eyes flickered. "Seth. So you're his sister, then."

Ah, she had heard of me.

They directed me to Seth's new room. He was staring at the ceiling when I walked in.

"Hey."

His gaze floated my way. "Hi, Luna."

"Now, you be nice," said the nurse, and she left us. I sighed and threw myself into the uncomfortable chair by the bed.

"So how are you feeling?"

His lips barely moved when he talked. "Better."

I looked at him. His face was gray and his eyes were lifeless. Maybe this was better compared to being unconscious, but it really couldn't be better than much else.

"So tell me what happened." I tried to keep my voice as even and unaccusing as I could. I felt I had done a pretty decent job.

Seth turned his face away from me. "I don't want to talk about it."

Well. Unaccusing be hung.

"You don't want to talk about it? You almost kill yourself, leaving Lydia to Sparkles, and you don't want to talk about it? Well, I have news for you, big brother. You have to talk about it. I can make you! Oh, yes I can, and you know it." I glared at him with what I assumed was my most regal pose. "My will is much stronger than yours."

Silence. And then a strange sound. He wiped at tears in his eyes.

"Oh, Seth, please don't cry. I'm so sorry. I didn't mean—"

He snerked. "I'm not crying, you idiot. I'm laughing."

I peered closer. He was right. I felt my mouth tighten.

"What's so funny?" I demanded. He laughed harder.

"I'm not sure," he said, and then he fell helpless, laughing and shaking and sending the little beepers on his machine completely haywire.

"Shh, you're going to get me into trouble," I said. "Nurse Prissy Pants might be my biggest fear about now."

He laughed for a minute longer, eyes closed, tears streaming. Then he slowly got himself under control. My brother was a mess of hiccups and sniffles. I turned away, resolute in my dignity.

"Luna?"

I didn't want to grace him with an acknowledgement, but then I thought of yesterday. His pale face half in the water. The terror I felt when

I thought he was gone forever.

"What?"

He rubbed his eyes with a thumb and forefinger. "Thank you. I had almost forgotten what laughing felt like."

I moved from the chair and sat on his bed. "Seth, this all happened so fast. I never expected this from you. Not in a million years. You really floored me. I don't even know what to say."

He sighed. "It all feels like it was a very long time ago. Has it only been a day? It feels like it's been an eternity."

"I found you yesterday."

He looked into my eyes, and I was embarrassed by the emotion I saw there. "Luna, I am so sorry. I've been thinking about it all night. What it must have been like to find me. Like when I found Dad. I thought of how Lydia would feel, knowing I did what I did. Feeling like she wasn't good enough to live for."

His eyes were tearing up again, and this time it wasn't in hysterical laughter. I took his cold hand in mine.

"Never do something like that again. That goes without saying. I want to tell you Lydia would have made it through, because we made it through, but you know how it would have been. Seth, you know. Why would you have even thought of suicide, even for a second? How could you do that to her?"

He shook his head. "That's the thing. I have no idea." I growled and pulled my hand away, but Seth grabbed it in both of his. "I'm serious, Luna. You know how I feel about Dad. How I was angry at him for giving up and leaving us all alone. Feeling guilty, feeling we should have done something, been more. But last night, I just felt…different. I felt like I was doing her a favor, almost. I know," he said, when I started getting upset again. "I know it doesn't make any sense, but that's how it felt. Besides, after Sparkles came over—"

"To our house?" Suddenly my antenna was up. Seriously, talking to Sparkles could make anybody want to die. But this was more sinister than that, and I knew it.

Seth took a deep breath. "Yes. Sparkles came over to the house yesterday. She said she wanted to discuss the arrangement with Lydia. And before you interrupt," he said, just as I was about to interrupt, "I told her there had been no arrangement with Lydia. She had bailed out on all of us. I actually gave her a pretty good piece of my mind," he said smugly. "You would have been proud of me."

"Good. And then?" I was getting nervous. The feel of the house. The demons huddled inside like Russian nesting dolls.

"She said she was sorry. She said she had needed time to think, and she realized she really missed me and Lydia."

I snorted derisively. This time it was his turn to yank his hand away.

"Luna, whether you like her or not, she is Lydia's mother. What was I supposed to do?"

I had a few suggestions, but this wasn't the time for them. "And then what did you do?" Please don't say you invited her inside, I thought. My stomach felt like I had swallowed a block of ice.

"Lydia was just waking up from her nap. She was calling from the crib. So I asked Sparkles if she wanted to come up and see her."

That was it. That explained everything.

"So you invited her inside."

"Yes."

And her demon. And effectively broke the seal. And then everything blew apart.

Seth covered his face with his hand. "She saw Lydia. Sparkles seemed delighted, but Lydia started to scream. I picked her up, and then everything became confusing. Sparkles was telling Lydia she was back, that she was here now, and Lydia was going nuts. I started to tell Sparkles to leave, but suddenly I saw how it looked. Here I am, a single man with a dead end job. I don't know how to raise a little girl. I'm looking up Youtube videos to learn how to do her hair. I'm living with my crazy sister who is nice enough, but definitely has her issues. What do I have to offer? What do you?"

The ice I had eaten had grown spines. I licked my lips, but it didn't help to moisten them. "You thought that Lydia was better with her mother."

Seth laughed, and the sound made me wince. "I did. It seemed to make so much sense at the time. I handed Lydia to her. I handed over her pink star blanket. I kissed Lydia on the forehead and told her I loved her very much. And then I filled the bathtub."

I didn't need to hear the rest. I had seen the end result.

"How do you feel now?" I was afraid to ask, but I needed to know. I needed to get a feel for how much internal damage had been done.

Seth stared at the ceiling again. "I feel…tired. And stupid. I can't believe myself because that isn't something I would ever plan to do. But I can't deny it made perfect sense then. If I was right back there, I might make the exact same decision again. It felt so obvious." He looked at me. His eyes broke my heart. They shone with so much pain and torment that I felt my soul twist. "Why is that, Luna? Why would I do that?"

"Do you really want to know?"

He sighed. Hesitated. Then he said, "I don't know. Do I?"

I took his hand again. "Seth, listen to me. Sparkles has a demon attached to her. Or perhaps she's attached to it; I'm not really sure at this point. But either way, they're together. Sparkles was mean to begin with, but now she is crueler and has a depth that would have seemed impossible before."

"Luna," Seth said. His voice had that familiar warning note. It almost made me smile.

"You said yourself that it seemed like the right thing to do, even though it obviously wasn't. It goes against everything you believe in, and still, you tried to kill yourself. Kill yourself. We're not talking about doing something little that is slightly naughty. We're talking about the big Kahuna. Death. Forever and ever."

"I get the picture."

"And ever. Got it?"

"Got it."

"But wait, there's more."

"Oh goody."

"I had done that little spell. Seal. Thing, whatever it was called, that kept the demons out, right?"

"Supposing you're not crazy."

"Yeah, suppose."

"Then yeah, I remember."

I grinned at him. What a good brother. "Well, it kept everything demonic out. Until the seal was broken."

He played along. "All right. So how was the seal broken?"

"You invited Sparkles inside."

He didn't say anything. I hurried on.

"When I went over later with Reed Taylor and that mouthy demon, the house was absolutely full—"

He interrupted me. "You're saying you honestly, truly, one hundred percent believe my soon-to-be ex-wife is possessed by a demon?"

"I do."

"A really bad demon. A demon I invited into the house, which effectively broke the protection on the house that my kid sister had put on it."

"Right."

"And then the demon did something so I felt bad about myself…" He looked at me for help. I was happy to step in and tell him what I know.

"You invited them in, and left the house and yourself wide open. You were too strong for the demon to possess straight out, or else you wouldn't remember a thing. And you wouldn't have nearly died, you would have totally died. Demons can be quite thorough, you know."

"Undoubtedly."

"But she had enough influence that she could suggest things for you to do. Suggest your unworthiness and…what?" I caught the look in his eyes. It wasn't pretty.

"Why would she have this influence? I'm like, super weak or something? My mind isn't strong enough to keep the demon out?"

Dad again. Losing his mind. Again. Seth's worst fear kept popping up in his face over and over and over. Now that I had his attention it was time to set the record straight.

"It doesn't have anything to do with your mind. Not really. Mind and willpower are just kind of, I don't know. They help, I guess, but not much more than that. It's all about heart. Spirit and feelings. And no matter how awful Sparkles was, she was still your wife, and Lydia's mom. She knows your weaknesses, and your weakness is your daughter."

"She used Lydia to make me feel like a total loser?"

"Well, wouldn't you say so?"

He struggled to sit up in the hospital bed. I wanted to help him, but I leaned back and watched him do it by himself. When he finally sat upright, his hair was damp with sweat and his face glistened, but the anger and triumph on his face made my heart sing.

"Screw that woman. She's not allowed to have that type of power over me again."

He was so full of confidence and verve that he shone. It was almost more than I dared hope.

"Do you…do you actually believe me? About the demons?"

Seth's eyes locked into mine. "I spent my whole life trying to explain everything away. The nightmares you had as a little kid. Dad talking to ghosts, and trying to convince us they were real. You were all 'demons, demons, demons' and it was…it hurt my heart, you know? To think you were experiencing the same symptoms as Dad. I tried so hard to be so normal. Afraid insanity was contagious. Maybe a little jealous that it wasn't, because then at least I'd feel like a real part of the family. But the way that I felt in there? Handing Lydia over to a woman who never cared about her, not in the least? Lydia was screaming, Luna. You should have heard her scream. Like her heart was being torn out, and I just hand her over like a good little ex-husband, leave the room and try to die? I don't think so. It's not happening. I don't know how to explain it, except to say something happened there. If you say it's a demon, then, sure, whatever, it's a demon. I've been afraid for too long, and what did it do? It lost me my daughter."

I'm sure my eyes were absolutely starry. They began to feel strange and prickly, and I realized they were filling with tears. Finally, my brother believed me. It was about time.

"Hey." Seth's voice brought me out of my happy little reverie. Seriously, I was lost in a land of bunnies and rainbows, where Reed Taylor and Seth and I held hands and danced around together. It was beautiful.

"Wait, what?" I blinked. "What were you saying?"

Seth's eyes were harder than I had ever seen. "I just handed my baby girl over to Sparkles."

"Right."

His eyes were fairly glowing with their intensity. It was like he had his own little touch of demon. It was absolutely delightful and a little bit terrifying.

"They won't let me out of here. That means you have to go get her."

I stood up. "I'm on it."

Chapter Nineteen

Reed Taylor, I need to talk to you." I was nothing if not polite and gracious on the phone. A thing of beauty. An absolute queen of decorum.

"Uh, not right now, Luna. I'm kind of in the middle of something."

I felt my eyebrows rise. "Really? But Seth believes me and needs our help."

"Not now. This is important."

"What could be more important than helping me get Lydia back?"

He made a sound, and I could tell he was getting exasperated. Was I really being that forceful? Well yes, yes I was. But I needed him, and he knew it. At least, I thought he knew it.

"Reed Taylor?" I asked.

His voice was definitely strained. "Nothing is more important than getting your niece back. That's precisely what I'm trying to do, but I need to deal with this right now, all right? Later, bye." And he hung up.

He hung up, just like that.

I stared at the phone in shock. It looked properly apologetic. "I have no idea why he would possibly act in such a dastardly manner." It seemed like it was trying to say, "I am really most appalled. Please accept my sincere apologies."

A scaly demon shambled in front of me. It stared at me for just a second, licked its lips, and then ambled on. I was extremely relieved. I didn't have the strength to fight all of these little demons, especially if I was going to take on the big one. Besides, I wasn't even sure exactly how to find Sparkles. Nobody knew where she had run off to. She was still listed as living with Seth.

As if.

Truth was, I needed Reed Taylor. I'm a strong, independent woman, but even we strong, independent women need a friend when the going starts getting as rough as this was. Seth couldn't help me. Reed Taylor would have to.

I hopped onto the bike and started for his house. I had been there once, and it was a tiny little thing, more like a box than a house. But he kept it neat and had put stainless steel kick plates on all of the doors so he didn't scratch them when he exuberantly kicked them open with his big boots. It's things like this that made me dig this man.

A large demon zipped in front of my bike. His robes swirled around him like black ink, strangely beautiful yet vomit-inducing. Another demon with big, leathery wings temporarily blotted out the sky. They were both heading in the direction of Reed Taylor's house.

What was up with that? I nervously chewed on my bottom lip and kicked up the speed. I've been seeing an awful lot of demons. Couldn't this just be a coincidence?

It could, but it wasn't. Reed Taylor's immaculate yard was full to bursting with demons. Tall demons, small demons, human-shaped demons, and some that most decidedly weren't. I think I even I saw Cthulhu, but that could just be my inner fan girl coming out to play.

I was pretty sure I'd seen Mouth out of the corner of my eye, but when I turned, he was gone. It was probably just wishful thinking. One demon looks an awful lot like another for the most part. Dark. Bleak. Evil.

My stomach lurched, and I felt the Tracing start to prick between my shoulder blades. If I didn't hurry, this whole thing would launch into full swing, and I'd be in a world of hurt. I remembered the agonizing feel of the Mark tearing my skin apart at my house, and I practically ran up to Reed Taylor's door. I banged on it with both of my fists.

"Reed Taylor, open up this instant! Something is wrong with your house, do you understand me? It's a demonic Mardi Gras."

"Luna," something chanted behind me. Its voice was whispery and mocking. "Luna, Luna, Luna, Luuuuuuna."

I banged again, a bit hysterically. "Let me in! Let me in, let me in!"

Something touched me on the arm, slid its featureless fingers down my back and then up between my shoulders. It pressed gently until it found what it was looking for. "Mmm, the Tracing," it moaned. "The Mark."

Bang, bang, bang! "Reed Taylor!"

The sound of the lock, and then the deadbolt. The door opened and I burst inside, throwing myself into Reed Taylor's arms.

"Something is wrong," I said. I was nearly wild with panic. I could still feel the demon's searching fingers caressing the wound in my back, and I shuddered. "We have to get out of here. We need to find Lydia and see if we can fix this."

I looked into Reed Taylor's face. I stepped back, confused. He looked angry. His green eyes flashed.

"I told you now wasn't a good time, Luna. You shouldn't have come."

"Wh-what do you—" I was interrupted by a voice.

"Luna Masterson? Well, this certainly is a surprise."

I blinked. It was a woman's voice, dripping with sultry charm and disdain. It sounded familiar, but I couldn't get my brain to work properly.

Why would Reed Taylor have a woman at his house? And what did he mean, this wasn't a good time?

Reed Taylor started, and his arms fell from around me. He turned toward the woman, who was entering from the other room. What was back there? The kitchen. The bedroom. She was most certainly entering from the kitchen. She had to be. Right?

"You know her?" Reed Taylor sounded surprised.

The woman laughed heartily. There was meanness in it. The voice had slid by me, but I knew that laughter. My fists clenched by my side, and I gritted my teeth before looking up.

Sparkles.

Chapter Twenty

What are you doing here?" I demanded. I was so angry that I was shaking.

Sparkles laughed. "Oh, darling, you never cease to amuse me. You're always so quick to lose your temper. You realize that's why you're always alone, don't you? Nobody can take your attitude."

"Shut up," I bit out. "Tell me where she is."

She smiled. It was reptilian. I saw demonic appendages waving in her hair and hatred emanating from her skin. She and the demon had become one, all right. I wanted to throw up. I wanted to hit her. I wanted to hit Reed Taylor, who was standing there looking more angry than I had thought possible.

"Whatever are you talking about? Everybody knows you're touched in the head, talking to things that aren't there. Do you really think you see them? Or do you simply lie? Nobody would blame you if you do. What a tragic childhood. What a horrid, difficult girl."

A dark tentacle slid out of her mouth and went up through her nose. Her eyes looked like they were leaking oil.

"Tell me where she is," I said. "I'm not going to ask again."

She ignored me and ran her hand down Reed Taylor's arm. "Reed said he was seeing somebody new. Who could ever have guessed it would be you? My goodness, darling," she said to Reed Taylor, "You do have a little mean streak, don't you?" She laughed again, and my fingernails cut into the palms of my hands.

"Cecilia, knock it off," Reed Taylor said. He stepped away.

Sparkles' eyes shone. "He does have charm, though, doesn't he? I never regretted him. Not for one minute. In fact, I thanked him for taking me away from my humdrum little life. Some women weren't made to be married, I'm afraid. Or mothers."

My eyes were so wide that they hurt.

"No, he couldn't have been the guy who—"

"Luna, meet Reed. Reed, I see you know Luna. How unfortunate."

"How could you?" I spit at Reed Taylor. He turned back to me with his eyes on fire. I matched their flame with my own. "You're disgusting! What, your angel never said anything about the demon wrapped around this woman? Or you just ignored it?"

Sparkles covered her mouth. "His angel? Oh," she said, her face collapsing in mock sympathy, "did Reed tell you he sees things, too? He always does know what to say to put a woman at ease."

"Enough," Reed Taylor said. He was tired and stressed and obviously at his limit. Well, so was I.

My hand snaked for the small knife I always kept on me. I used it for opening packages sealed with too much tape and digging small rocks out of the grooves of my shoe, but suddenly it felt good in my hand. Too good.

Reed cursed, knocked the knife from my grip and kicked it away. "What's gotten into you? Are you insane?"

I snarled and elbowed Reed Taylor in the gut. The sound he made was satisfying. I was already heading for Sparkles.

One good punch landed on her sneering face before Reed tackled and pinned me to the ground. I fought to throw him off.

"Get off me!"

"Luna!" He looked dangerous.

Sparkles whimpered in the background. I struggled, but Reed was using all of his strength to keep me down.

"Why are you defending her?" I demanded. "How could you do this to me? To my brother?"

"Calm down. "

"I'll kill you!" I screamed at Sparkles. "I'll kill you right now if you don't tell me! Where is my—"

Reed Taylor pulled me to my feet and slapped me. He slapped me right across the face. The sound of it ricocheted through the room like gunfire. I went silent and touched my hand to my cheek.

"Get out," he said. His chest was heaving and the muscles in his arms were bunched. "You won't behave this way. Not in my house. Not ever."

I thought I'd cry. I thought I'd rant and rave. I thought I'd give Reed Taylor the tongue-lashing of his life for sleeping with Sparkles and defending her. I didn't do any of these things. I scooped up my knife and tossed my hair back from my eyes. I glared at the monstrosity that was my sister-in-law.

"I will find Lydia, Demon. You'll regret taking her. You'll regret what you did to my brother."

I turned my gaze to Reed Taylor. "And as for you. You're nowhere near the man I thought you were. Having an affair with Sparkles? She left her husband and child for you, and then you start showing up, following me around. Why, so you could report back? I hate you, Reed Taylor. I expected so much more."

He looked stricken, but I didn't care. He reached out for me, but I jerked out of his grasp. I gathered my dignity about me as much as I could, turned on my heel, and walked away.

The demons sniffed and bit and clawed after me.

"Screw you guys," I said and walked on by.

I saw Mouth standing by my motorcycle.

"You knew," I accused him. I threw my leg over the bike.

"I did. I tried to warn you."

"Whatever."

He sighed and leaned on my handlebars. His eyes were glittering beneath his hood. "Listen, Luna—"

"Not now," I said. I revved the bike.

He stepped away and pulled his hand back. "I cleared out your house. You can go home."

I gave a curt nod and accelerated. My tires flipped dirt and gravel all over him and the demons, but I didn't care. I had just lost everything.

Everything.

That night the phone rang. I glanced at it and saw it was Reed Taylor. I took it off the hook. My cell phone rang a few minutes later. I turned it off. I thought about having a hot bath but immediately thought about my brother and the way that his clothes floated around him as I tried to pull him out of the tub. My stomach turned. I walked around the house, made dinner, and then didn't eat it. I went and lay down on the floor of Lydia's room.

Where was she? Was somebody holding her? Was she locked in a closet somewhere? She must be so scared without Daddy and Mama Luna. The poor girl had such a bad go of it, and it was all our fault. She was born into a family of dysfunction. There wasn't anything the girl could do about it.

"My sweet girl," I said. I thought of her pigtails like banners, the sweet way her chubby arms wrapped around my neck. She loved me when nobody else did. She was the only one who didn't think of me as a screw-up.

I got up. I paced. I slammed my fists into the walls and screamed. I cursed Sparkles as vehemently as I knew how. I curled up and sobbed. I raged. Just a disturbed girl going crazy in an empty house. Alone.

As I learned young, the darkness comes when you're alone.

Chapter Twenty-One

Luna." I moaned and threw my arm over my face. It didn't help any.
"Luna. Good morning, pretty girl."

"Mom?"

A snort. "Nice try, loser."

I blinked and sat up. I was still on the floor in Lydia's room. Cripes, I hadn't slept in a normal bed for two nights, and it was starting to get to me. My bones were screaming.

The demon lounged in the doorway. "Time to rise, sunshine."

I yawned and stretched. "What are you doing here, Mouth? What time is it?"

He flowed over and sat beside me. "It's time for you to get cracking. I'm here to tell you to quit feeling sorry for yourself and get your butt in gear."

I frowned. "I'm not feeling sorry for myself." I gingerly prodded at the emotional wounds from the last few days. Missing Lydia, nearly-dead Seth, betraying Reed Taylor. Ouch. Yeah, I was feeling sorry for myself.

Mouthy demon kicked at me with his dark foot. It almost hurt.

"Hey! You're feeling calm and happy again! Look at you, almost fully formed." I dragged myself to my feet and glared at him. "Why do you seem to celebrate my misery?"

He shrugged. "Your misery always seems to be for my gain. Now come downstairs. I made you breakfast."

"You did?" I followed him down. A piece of poorly buttered toast sat on the counter. I poked at it. "Is this it?"

He pouted. "Hey, be grateful! It's harder than you think when you're not fully formed. Taking the little wire off of the bread bag nearly took all of my concentration. And getting the butter out of the fridge? Almost impossible!" He waxed on about the inconveniences of everyday modern life while I chewed.

"Earth to Luna. Come back to me."

"What? Sorry. Guess I have a lot on my mind."

He sat beside me next to the bar. "I guess you do. That's why I'm here."

I looked at him, sitting in the early morning sunshine, hanging out in my kitchen. Making me toast. Offering his aid.

"What do you want from me, demon?"

He looked irritated. "We're back to that again? You should know better by now."

I looked away. "Yeah, I thought I knew Reed Taylor better, too, and look where that got me."

He shook his head in agitation. "Look, I tried to tell you about him. You didn't want to listen, which is totally your prerogative," he said when I shot him a withering glare, "but you can't say I didn't try. I'm on your side."

If only that were true. But...

"You're a demon."

"And you're a lunkhead. Let it go already. Sheesh."

I looked around the house. "So where did all of the other demons go?"

He looked around, too. "I told you I cleared the place out. It wasn't hard, not really. They all followed Sparkles back to Reed's house."

Another early morning ouch. "Oh."

"Yeah. About that."

I shook my head. "It's still too early to talk about that."

"No. It isn't." He reached out and put his hand on mine. I could almost feel it. "We need to discuss it now."

I pulled my hand away. "Why are you always so bossy?"

He grinned. "I am a demon of authority. It carries over."

I finished my last bite of toast and studied him. Clearer features, happy demeanor. He was getting more and more solid by the day.

"You're not like all of the other demons," I admitted.

"It's about time you realized that. You have the hardest head of anybody I ever met, you know? Like a brick wall."

Normally I'd refute him, but what could I say? He was right. This wasn't necessarily a bad thing. It got me where I am today.

"So, Mouth. Tell me why you're different. Tell me how you became a demon."

He quickly averted his eyes. "You don't want to hear all that."

I leaned back. "I do, actually. I'm interested. Whaddya have to say?" I hopped off the stool and got myself some juice.

He sighed. "We really should be coming up with a battle plan. You know this."

"This first. I need the distraction."

"There's not much to tell. I had a lot of anger I held onto. I couldn't get rid of it."

"But to become a demon?"

He made a popping sound with his mouth. "See, Luna, you see things in black and white, and it isn't always that way. You act like it's always a very deliberate choice. It wasn't like, hey, I'll wake up this morning and turn to a life of darkness. It was more like, hey, I'm really mad that things aren't going how I wanted. Oh, still mad. Still fighting mad. Then one day

I realize I'm still hanging around the place. I haven't moved on. Being mad was pretty much all it took, for me."

I raised my eyebrow. He rolled his eyes.

"It's true. You've hung out with me. Do I seem like the kind of guy who likes to cause mischief? Torture babies?"

"You sure hate Reed Taylor."

"Well, can you blame me?"

I took a deep breath. "I still can't believe that. About Reed Taylor. I can't believe he'd sit there listening to me go on about Sparkles and this guy she ran off with, and never once say, 'Hey, you know that guy? The one who completely wrecked everybody's lives? It was me.' I mean, how could he date me after that? Seriously?"

Mouth lifted one shoulder in a half-hearted shrug. "I dunno. Maybe he's totally screwed up inside. Maybe Sparkles got her claws into him and he became his own type of demon. Can't tell you."

"And you don't necessarily want to tell me, do you?"

"Can't say I do. Besides, maybe he didn't realize you considered your weird relationship dating. Seems to me like you were happy to take him when you wanted him, but you brushed him off whenever you didn't. Most guys don't go for that type of action."

I stood up. "Thanks for breakfast. I'm gonna go take a shower now, finish waking up."

"See? That's exactly what I'm talking about. Eat my toast, but the second I…"

I didn't hear the rest of it. I was too busy stomping up the stairs.

Chapter Twenty-Two

The shower was always a place where I could think. It was the one place where I was truly alone, except for once when I caught something peeping out at me from the bathroom mirror. Seth had come running when I had screamed and assured me it wasn't a demonic presence, but only a particularly bad case of bed head. As if.

I let the water cleanse everything away. The leftover malice, the hurt and despair. I tried to imagine the water had healing properties that could wash away all of the misery. But really, I simply had to push it all to the back of my mind. I couldn't afford to waste my energy feeling crushed. It was time for action.

I dried off, got dressed, and combed my hair. I stepped out of the room to see Mouth leaning against the wall, waiting for me.

"Hello, Mouth. You're being particularly stalkerish and creepy this morning."

"Really? I thought I was always this way. Maybe you're just ultra-sensitive."

"Shut up."

He followed me down the stairs. "You look kind of different without your makeup on."

"Dewy and ethereal?"

"Maybe that. Less likely to take a bite out of anybody who crosses you."

I laughed. It sounded a little harsh. "I'll definitely swipe on the eyeliner before I tackle demonic Sparkles, then."

"I think you'd better."

I sunk onto the couch. He followed suit. I swear I even felt the couch shift under his weight, he was becoming so tangible.

"Okay. So what are we going to do?" I asked, then thought for a minute. "Besides murdering Sparkles, maiming Reed Taylor, re-kidnapping Lydia, and busting Seth out of the hospital?"

Mouth's eyes were on mine. They looked like they were made out of silver, but every now and then I thought I caught a faint blue sheen.

"I think you'd better leave the planning to me, Luna. All of those options sound…well, they sound pretty stupid, actually."

He had me there.

I put my bare feet up on the coffee table and leaned back. "All right. Shoot."

He leaned back with me. It seemed like an endearing gesture. "Well. You ran into Sparkles, and that didn't work out so well. She's not going to tell you where Lydia is."

"Think Reed Taylor knows?"

He caught my eye. "Wanna ask him?"

Ah crap. The guy was good. "So how else do we find her? Ask the cops? Find a lawyer?"

The demon wiggled his toes. He actually had toes. He must be enjoying this. "I doubt they'll give you any information, especially after you pulled a knife on her last night."

"How did you know—"

"I know a lot of things."

I'll admit it; I was slightly embarrassed. "I wasn't going to hurt her.

Not really. Not super bad, anyway. Maybe just go for her demon. Make him tangible and slice the crap out of him."

"It's not that easy," he said. "It's going to be almost impossible to damage the demon without damaging Sparkles at this point. They're too intertwined."

"I'm not afraid of damaging Sparkles." The bitterness in my voice surprised me.

Mouth turned to me. "Hey, I know this is really tough for you, but you have to pull yourself together. Don't lose yourself in all of this."

"Maybe I don't mind losing myself."

He clicked his tongue. "Yeah, but what would the consequences be? When they haul you off to jail, what are you going to say? 'I'm sorry I killed Sparkles, but she was bellied up to a demon, and I couldn't get one without getting the other'? Don't forget there are consequences in your world. Besides, there's more than being locked up and having the key thrown away."

He had my interest. "How much more?"

His eyes met mine. "I don't think you realize you're in danger of becoming a demon yourself."

My mouth dropped open. "You can't be serious."

"I am. Noticed how the Mark is getting easier to bear?"

I thought about it. "Yeah. I guess. It isn't really bad unless we're in Demon Utopia, or something." My gaze sharpened. "Why is that?"

Mouth was examining his fingers. Five. Five fingers, almost completely solid.

"It's a desensitization thing. When the demon marked you at the fish and chips restaurant, he basically shoved what was left of himself on your skin. Into your soul as much as he could."

"I think I remember it," I said dryly. "Hurt like—"

"The Devil? Sin? Hell? It was supposed to. That's exactly what it is."

I was irritated. "So he puts little bits of demon around my soul in order to…what? It seemed like some big beacon. Suddenly I'm a demonic blue plate special. What's that all about?"

"Let me look at it."

I jumped. "What, the Mark? Are you serious? No way! Back off, you sicko."

He rolled his eyes. "Luna. Chill. Let me see it."

I slowly turned my back to him and hiked my shirt up. I wasn't sure what I was doing here, sitting in my abandoned house and showing my deliciously delicious demonic Mark to a pervo demon, for crying out loud. Had I lost my mind?

He ran his fingers over it, spreading them until they fit neatly into the still tender holes. The coolness of his misty hand felt good on the freezing heat of the wound. I sighed in relief.

Yep, I had lost my mind.

"You feel that?" he said. "Can you feel my fingers? They're directly on the Tracing."

I wrapped my arms around myself and leaned forward. I was equal parts uncomfortable with the intimacy of the situation and grateful for the soothing relief his fingers gave.

"Yeah."

"You don't have to sound so resentful."

"I'm not resentful," I said resentfully.

"You're already beginning to turn. I bet that felt good."

I pulled away from him, regretting the sensation of itching annoyance that came back when his fingers left my skin. I tugged my shirt back down.

"That's what I wanted to show you, Luna. You were right when you said it was like a beacon. It is. It's a stamp on you, proclaiming you as some sought-after demonic entrée, if you will. Your soul emanates like blood in the water."

"So I'm chum."

"Yep. You're chum."

I frowned. What a completely degrading concept. "So why has it been feeling better as of late? I mean, it still hurts. And it itches something fierce, but generally it isn't the driving-me-to-my-knees, blinding agony it was before." I looked at him, worried. "Is this a bad thing?"

"Yep."

Oh, okay. He certainly didn't spend any time softening the blow, now, did he?

He leaned forward. "Let me explain. It's bad because you're used to it. You've become used to our presence. There was always a demon or two around, and that didn't really bother you too much. Irritating, sure. Creepy? Yep. Still, what's one demon, right? But four or five? Six? Suddenly they're everywhere, right, and you don't really care. They've become part of the background. Unless there is a whole slew and suddenly you're on the ground trying not to puke on the carpet."

"So it isn't hurting because I've become used to demons?"

His eyes shone. It was quite disturbing, actually. "Right. The Mark doesn't have to draw us like it used to. We're already there. We're skittering across the top of your soul and you don't even bat an eye, for the most part. What I did there, with my hand? Don't you ever, ever let another demon do that, do you understand? They're not as strong as I am, and they won't have your best interests at heart, not at all. They'll slide right under the surface of your soul in a second, and there won't be anything you can do about it. Got it?"

My teeth started to chatter. I hadn't even realized I was cold. No, I wasn't cold. I was scared.

"But I don't have to worry about you?"

Mouth's sigh was full of longing. "I'll never take your soul, if that's what you mean. Without your permission."

I couldn't help it. I laughed. "Without my permission? That's a good one. Like one day I'd be all, 'Take my soul, please.' Sure."

"You don't have to believe me, but that's how it happens sometimes."

I snorted. "Right. People just walk up and hand their souls over."

"Sparkles did."

Suddenly it didn't seem the least bit funny. Sparkles was bad news. She'd always been bad news, but it still seemed extreme to just offer yourself to a demon. You'd think that anybody would know better. Even her.

"So why would she do it?" I asked Mouth. I couldn't look at him, at this creature from Hell sitting right there next to me. I should be running or screaming. Instead I was chatting it up like we were meeting for tea.

"People come to us for different reasons. Despair. Revenge. Some do it unintentionally, like me. Sparkles was different. She wanted the power. She wanted the deviousness. She's a different breed, that girl." He looked around the house. Everything was neat and orderly. The furnishings were modest and sensible…for the most part. I stuck screwy things here and there to lighten the place up, but Seth's warm and conservative style still shone through.

"What's a nice guy like your brother doing with a woman like Sparkles, anyway?" he asked.

"I dunno. She seemed nice at first. And Seth wanted a family so badly. Maybe he wanted to rewrite the past or something with his new and improved home life. Still, I was surprised when they hooked up. Maybe she was Seth's one chance at being wild and crazy for a minute, who really knows?" I stretched. My muscles felt better after the shower, but they were still eons away from being loose. "So enough of this. Nice little chit chat and everything, and I appreciate you explaining the Mark, but we have a lot of work to do. It's time for action. What do you propose?"

He smiled. "It's killing you to sit still like this, isn't it?"

"Don't you know it," I said. My fingers were practically twitching in anticipation of the violence I expected to ensue.

He stood up. His tangibility had diminished somewhat. "Okay. Let's go, then. I suggest you wear something that makes you feel particularly tough. Like that black jacket and maybe your combat boots."

"Why's that? You think I'll manage to intimidate the enemy with my swell fashion sense?"

He was already rummaging through the closet for my jacket. "It's worth a try, isn't it?"

I slipped the jacket on and opened my mouth to say something scathing, but he was already zipping up the stairs. Presumably after my combat boots.

"I can dress myself," I shouted after him.

He didn't answer, but I was pretty sure he was laughing at me.

Men. Demons. Whatever.

It occurred to me I'd better turn the phones back on in case the hospital tried to call about Seth. No sooner had I done so when it rang. I grabbed it automatically.

"Hello?"

"Luna, thank goodness! I've been trying to get a hold of you all night."

"I don't have anything to say to you, Reed Taylor." I slammed the phone down. It felt really good. I picked it up and slammed it down again, two more times.

"I'd hate to be on your bad side," Mouth said. He walked over to me with a pair of socks and my boots. "Throw these on and let's go."

"Don't be so sure you aren't on my bad side," I said to him.

He shook his head. "You're a prickly woman."

"Get bent."

The phone rang. I soundly ignored it. My cell phone started to buzz. I looked at the screen and turned it back off.

"Ready?" Mouth asked.

I nodded. "Ready." We headed for the door. "So, where exactly are we headed?" I asked him. I felt like I was walking blindly into the situation. 'Cuz I was. Luna Mama is no idiot.

"A house. A dark house. It's complicated," he said slowly.

I shook my head as I yanked the door open. "Ain't it always."

Chapter Twenty-Three

We ended up at a house on the far side of town. I expected a crazy, broken down, dilapidated place that screamed "Haunted!" and "Demonic!" and "Hello, I'm your worst nightmare!" But this was a normal stucco house standing shoulder to shoulder with its normal stucco neighbors. There was even a kitschy little lawn gnome in the garden.

"Who lives here, the Stepford Wives?" I eyed the neat hedges rimming the cheery yard. "Is this house going to kill me?"

"No. It's just a house. It can't hurt you."

Mouth was standing ramrod straight. Calm and happy he was not. He was wispier than I had seen him in a while.

"Mouth. You're freaky nervous. Tell me what's going on."

He didn't say anything, which was unlike him. I wanted to kick him, but my foot would just go right through.

"Mouth?"

He turned and grasped my hands in both of his, but I didn't feel anything besides a rush of cold air.

"Luna," he said earnestly. "I can't go in there with you. I wish I could, but it's…it's not allowed. You're going to have to do this alone."

He must have seen my horror because he ran his misty fingers through my hair. "If it's any consolation, I'm pretty sure you'll survive."

I wanted to say something dripping with sarcasm, but my tongue wouldn't work. The demon smiled. It seemed incredibly forced. Something in that thin smile reminded me he was a demon, and demons weren't my friends. I took a step away from him.

"So I'm going into the gingerbread house to...what, exactly?" The Tracing stung like a hive of wasps. There was definitely activity inside, and I was traipsing in alone. This was so uncool. There wasn't any other way to explain it.

"There's a chance Lydia might be inside. Or if not, maybe something knows where she is."

"Something."

"Or somebody."

I narrowed my eyes at the pleasant looking house. "I think I'll stick with 'something.'"

"That's probably much more accurate. This place it's...it's a portal, of sorts. A Nexus. It attracts and houses the worst of the worst."

"Right here in this cute little subdivision?"

He shrugged. "This is where it is now. Who's to say where it'll turn up later? It's wherever darkness gathers."

"Cheery."

"That's my motto."

I reached for the comfort of the tiny knife in my pocket. It didn't make me feel much better.

"The worst of the worst, huh?"

The ink of Mouth's robes flickered.

"I can handle it," I said with more bravado than I felt.

"Sure."

It was an awkward moment. I stared at the pleasant looking house and took a deep breath. Demon or no demon, I reached out and squeezed Mouth's hand. It flashed tangibly in mine for just a second, and then it was smoke again.

"All right, then. Wish me luck." I took a step toward the house.

"Wait!" He flowed up to me, grabbed my face with his misty hands and stared directly into my eyes. "You're going to see some things in there. They might be wonderful. They might be horrible. You need to know they're not fully real. Do you understand that? They're tricks. Deceit. This place plays with your mind. You need to stay conscious of what truly exists and what doesn't, got that? No going nuts in there, Luna Masterson."

He pulled me to him and pressed his mouth to mine. I tasted anger and misery, a shadow of cool air. Then he stepped through me and disappeared completely.

The demonic bossing me around. Telling me not to go nuts when I felt most ready to. Story of my life.

Chapter Twenty-Four

My stomach lurched when the doorknob turned easily under my hand. I expected the door to creak, but it opened silently and I stepped inside.

Hazy light filtered through the windows, making it difficult to see the sparse furniture and filthy red carpet. It looked like the carpet had been ripped up, snapped out by a giant hand, and left to lie where it fell.

"Hello?" I called. I didn't expect an answer, but it seemed abnormal to simply saunter in unannounced. My mama didn't raise rude little girls. That's what I told myself, anyway. Honestly, I was trying to restore some sense of order to the place. Maybe it would keep me from flipping out.

Stop. Get a hold of yourself. I released the breath slowly and realized my fingernails were digging into the palms of my hands. The sound of water echoed, a sickly trickle that inexplicably filled me with thoughts of taint and decay. I was as drawn to the sound of the water as I was repulsed by it. My imagination was already starting to run away with me. A gigantic, grotesque fountain? An undead demon with a river of human blood pouring from its mouth? Sweet Lydia drowning in a bathtub, just like her father?

That last thought nearly broke me. The paralyzing fear that kept me hovering near the front door was nothing compared to the vivid picture I had painted in my head. I nearly flew over the rumpled carpet, following the liquid noise.

"Lydia?" I called. "Baby girl?" I didn't care who heard me; I just needed to get to her. The despair and panic clawed its way up my throat. I tripped over a wrinkle in the carpet and nearly fell, but quickly righted myself. "It's Luna Mama, sweetheart. I'm coming!"

A faded red curtain hung over a doorway leading to an adjacent room. The weak sound of trickling water came from behind it. Now a cautious Luna would take a second and think about her options. She would silently approach the curtain, listen for sounds of movement, and then warily peek through to see if it was safe to proceed to the other side.

Cautious Luna had been thrown by the wayside the second I saw Lydia's pale, cherubic face in my mind. If something happened to her, I wouldn't want to live. I'd yell at my brother for being selfish and hogging that suicidal bathtub when he should have shoved over and given his horrible sister some room to do herself in, as well.

I finally saw the water and stopped abruptly.

It wasn't Lydia. It wasn't Lydia.

I sagged against the wall, waiting for my heart to start beating again. My eyes were full of tears, which surprised me, and I wiped them on the back of my leather jacket. This newfound fragility was irritating. I scowled and did a quick scan of the room for any sign of life, but I couldn't see anything except for the bizarre sight in front of me.

In the center of the room, resting on the disheveled red carpet, sat a large fish tank. It was tilted heavily to the side, and water was running out of the top and soaking into the carpet underneath. I looked down at my combat boots and raised one foot. The carpet was soaked. It had absorbed far more water than the tank had would have been able to hold. Strange.

My eyes caught a flash of color, and I carefully stepped forward. The floor was littered with starfish. All sizes. All colors. I reached down and tried to pick one up, but it adhered to the carpet. Still alive.

With a sharp plop, a starfish vaulted from the fish tank and landed on the carpet. I blinked and felt my mouth twist. There was something so off and vicious about the movement. Was it escaping? Was it being tossed? Starfish are charming little things, but seeing it do something that shouldn't be physically possible was making my hackles rise.

The tank vomited out another starfish, and I had to look away.

Enough of this. Get in, find out if anybody knows where Lydia is, and get out.

"Keep it together, Luna."

I wished Reed Taylor was here.

The thought struck me right in the face like a fantastic left hook. It nearly dropped me to the floor, too. Why on earth would I be thinking about Reed Taylor when what he had done was so unforgivable? Man, I must be freaking out.

I shook my head. Stepping over the silent starfish, I made my way to the cracked fish tank and peered inside. The smell that emanated from it was unholy and disturbingly familiar. Sweet with a slight metallic tang. My instincts demanded I run, but I only straightened up and turned my face away, my eyes still focused on the water. It wasn't a fishy smell at all. I struggled to place it. Then I had it, and my stomach dropped.

"It's blood."

Almost like my words had conjured it, the clear water turned cloudy. The unceasing water began to run red, and the thick, sticky blood was quickly swallowed by the carpet. The starfish on the ground lifted themselves like spiders onto their legs and struggled to crawl away. The starfish in the tank began to scream. One sailed out of the bloody water and smacked into the side of the tank. The glass cracked and the starfish slowly slid back into the depths, leaving a bloody trail behind.

My breathing was coming much too fast. I should sit down and put my head between my knees, but couldn't bear to touch the damp carpet. Was it always red, or had the blood simply stained it this color? Blood pooled around my foot as I shifted my weight, and I thought I was going to be sick right there.

I had seen demons my entire life, but this was something beyond that. There was something going on in this house that was more twisted and evil than anything I had ever experienced. I needed to be strong if I was going to overcome it. Suddenly I understood Mouth's angry and despairing kiss and, for the first time, I realized I genuinely might not make it back out.

Chapter Twenty-Five

There wasn't anything else I wanted to see here. I stepped over the shrieking, crawling starfish and headed deeper into the house of horrors. What was it Mouth had said? This house was full of illusions and deceptions. Starfish didn't scamper around like that. Water didn't turn into blood. This wasn't real.

Still, I wasn't going to chance fate by standing around and declaring shenanigans. I was here to find Lydia, and that's what I was going to do.

Blood wet my boots with every step. The carpet was no longer merely soggy but was drenched with more liquid than it could hold. The place smelled like a slaughterhouse. I pressed on.

There were two doors on the back wall. One was painted yellow and one was painted blue. I hate yellow, quite honestly, so I reached for the blue door.

"I wouldn't do that," said a voice. I whirled around.

"Who said that?" I demanded angrily. I couldn't see anybody.

"It's a trap. Both doors lead to Hell."

A small girl appeared out of the gloom and stood before me. Her eyes glowed in her dirty skin. Dried blood was smeared across her face like bruises.

Part of me wanted to sweep her into my arms and run with her out of this house. But the saner part of me pressed myself against the wall.

"Who are you?" I asked. I felt my eyes narrow.

When she spoke, her lips didn't move. "I am just someone. I am not to be feared, not like the others in this house." She cocked her young head to one side and a pink ribbon flopped into her eyes. "Don't touch the doors, Luna. You'll regret it."

She knew my name. I shouldn't be surprised. I also didn't see another way out except the way I came in. "So what am I supposed to do? I can't just leave."

"Yes, that's exactly it." Her strangely glowing eyes were earnest. "Leave. Go outside and breathe the fresh air. Leave this place and its evils alone. You're not supposed to be here. It's unsafe."

I snorted. "Like I don't know that? Listen, creepy little girl, I appreciate your help and all that, but I can't just run, you know? I need to save my niece. Do you know where she is? Her name is Lydia. She was taken by a woman named Spark…er, Cecilia. Cecilia has a demon, and—"

Suddenly the little girl's nostrils quivered, and her eyes widened. "You have…the Mark? I can smell it on you." Her eyes went wild, which was even more disconcerting because her pale mouth didn't change expression at all.

I pressed my back closer to the wall and looked around for something to use as a weapon. I was afraid this was going to go badly.

The girl closed her eyes and sniffed the air again like an animal. When she looked at me, her eyes seemed to be smiling. "Ah, you are not alone. He doesn't come with you, I see, but still he is here. This is good."

I reached behind me, groping for the doorknob. "Okay, Miss Child of the Corn, I really don't have the time to chat. I've got some demon to fry."

The girl looked sad. "I wish you could win, Luna. For his sake more than yours."

I bristled. "What do you mean? Of course I'm going to win. This," I said, drawing a circle around my face with my hand, "is the face of a winner. And don't you forget it."

I thought the girl nearly smiled then, but it faded quickly. She rolled her eyes to the ceiling and was quiet for a second. I didn't dare look away from her, but I felt behind me for the doorknob again.

Her shining eyes pinned me against the wall, and her words were loud in my ears. "They know you're here." Her voice was heavy with sorrow. "I so wanted you to have a chance." She started to tremble and then went into full-on convulsions.

"Hey. Hey! Are you all right?" I reached out to grab her, but her skin was hot, like flaming metal, and she burned my fingers. I gasped and yanked my hands back. The girl fell to the ground, and I knelt down beside her on the bloody carpet.

"Tell me what I can do to help." I tried to touch her again, but her clothes were starting to smoke and flame. I scooted away and covered my face with my hands. This was too much. It was too horrible.

"You give up too easily."

I jerked my head up at the sound of the girl's voice. Her body was charring and melting in front of me, but her voice was just as calm as it had been when she had first spoken to me. I looked around, but I couldn't see any other source for her voice.

"How are you speaking to me?" I looked away from the tiny smoldering body.

I practically heard the voice shrug. "I am here. In this place. I didn't want to scare you so I chose the body of a young girl to speak to you. You humans are all so fragile."

I surged to my feet. "You what? You chose to look like a little tiny burning girl? What are you, some kind of sicko?" My hands were on my hips, and I was ready to give this disembodied voice a piece of my mind. The voice interrupted me mid-rant.

"There's no time. Check my body."

My mouth dropped open. "Check your body? There's no way I'm going to get close to that thing! Are you insane?"

The house shook, and I nearly dropped to my knees. The voice sounded angry.

"The body. Now."

"Bite me."

"Don't you want your little niece back?" the voice cooed. "I thought that you would do anything to save her. Perhaps not."

"Wait," I said. The desperate hope in my voice shamed me. "Is she here? Do you know where Lydia is?"

"I'm trying to help you. For her sake as well as yours, please do as I've asked."

I crawled over the bloody carpet to the smoking body. The smell made me a little bit hungry, and that just made me sick. "Ugh, I'm disgusting!"

"Luna."

"All right, all right."

I gingerly rolled the bones and tatters of material over until I saw what I was looking for. A shiny blue stone hanging from a chain around her neck. "This?"

"Put it on."

"Not a chance."

"Do you want to find the girl or not? I can't help you if you don't wear the pendant."

"What does it do? Shine with a holy light or some crap? I don't steal jewelry from dead girls. Just isn't my style."

Suddenly I heard them. Lydia's screams. They came from inside the room and out, looping round and round like terror itself set on repeat.

"Baby girl!" I looked around, but of course she wasn't there.

Her screams became louder and nearly drove me to my knees. Over her wailing, I heard the disembodied voice of the burning little girl.

"You're killing her! You're killing her! Quick, the pendant."

I snatched the chain and ripped it from around the corpse's neck. I put it on and tucked it under my shirt.

"Okay. Now what?"

Lydia's screaming stopped abruptly. The silence rang uncomfortably in my ears.

"So fragile," the voice said, and the chain around my neck tightened.

I gagged and clawed at it with my hands. It had seemed like such a delicate thing, but I couldn't manage to break it. I was hyperventilating but no air would come in.

I was going to die like this, here in this room. No Lydia. No Seth. No Mouth and no Reed Taylor. This made me infinitely sad.

I fell to my knees, my hands tearing ineffectually at the necklace.

"You don't know how you smell," the voice said. It was right by my ear. I felt something slide down the back of my neck and come to rest on the Tracing. "It's absolutely divine, and we don't get a lot of divinity in this place." I felt pressure on the Mark increasing as the voice probed the area.

Oh no, it di'n't. That kickstarted the rebellion in me. I swiped at the air and connected with something that offered a familiar resistance: demon. No demon was sticking its dirty finger into my soul; not if I could help it.

I needed a way out. My vision was going spotty and my initial panic was starting to die down into a dull haze. I was sitting right next to the blue door; the one the demon had initially stopped me from opening.

If the demon wanted me to stay away from the door, then there must be a reason for it. I grabbed the doorknob and pulled it open.

"No!" gasped the demon, and the chain pulled even tighter around my neck. I was already out of air so what did it matter? I pulled myself to the door, saluted, and dragged myself over the threshold.

Then I was falling, and everything went black.

Chapter Twenty-Six

I woke up with something long and leggy skittering over my mouth. I sat up, spitting and sputtering, and the dark thing faded into the darkness. There's nothing like tasting demonic viscera when you're coming to. My life rocks.

The hateful necklace of death was charred, blackened, and crumbling around my neck. I tore it free and threw it against the wall. Whatever that thing in the other room had been, it apparently didn't have any hold here. Whether that was because the prize truly was behind Door Number One, or because there was something even scarier in here, I had to find out. I staggered to my hands and knees, still unable to get to my feet. My head was killing me, but the frantic pounding in my chest hurt even worse.

The room seemed quiet enough. I squinted through the dim light, taking in the small room packed to the gills with junk. Old bureaus and broken chairs were covered in so much dust that I instinctively covered my nose and mouth with my arm. Several mirrors reflected my pale face. One of the reflections was smiling. I looked away.

I looked at the filthy palms of my hands, grimaced, and wiped them on my jeans. Didn't look like this place had been cleaned in twenty years. Fan-frickin'-tastic. Especially since this whole area of town hadn't been built until five years ago.

I climbed to my feet and leaned against the wall. I still felt like I couldn't get enough air, so I practiced breathing in and out while searching the shadows for movement. Besides the tiny creeping demon and my sinister reflection from a few minutes earlier, I didn't see anything else, but the room was strangely silent, and I felt immense pressure in my ears.

"So what am I supposed to do?" I said aloud. The sound of my own voice calmed me. It made me feel less alone.

Funny, that's what crazy people think.

Something glinted in the ghostly light. My boots didn't make a sound on the grimy floor as I crept closer. It was a framed picture, and it felt strangely warm in my hands.

A man sat on an oversized chair with a child on his lap. They were reading a large, colorful book. I blinked.

Not a man. My father.

My hands shook. I gritted my teeth and willed myself to be still.

A shadow oozed from the wall and swirled into the corner of the room. I ignored it. Tears wet my lashes.

"Daddy?"

He looked young. Handsome and strong. Not tormented. Not like a man screaming into insanity.

Something ghosted over my back, slid its dry resistance between my shoulder blades. It settled on the Mark.

"Uninvited," I said, my eyes firmly glued to the picture.

The pressure increased, and the demon's translucent hand began to feel firmer, more solid. Its coolness felt good against the sting of the Tracing.

"Uninvited!" I screamed and wrenched myself away from the demon. I spun to face a creature with a long horse face and four fingers instead of hooves.

"Lunaaaa," it hissed, and my stomach twisted at the human language that obviously didn't come easily to its tongue. "I waaaaaant—"

"Yeah, yeah, you want the Mark. My delicious soul. You know what, demon? You ain't getting it." I stepped forward until we were face to face. The demon looked uncertain, but I was so angry I could have lit it on fire with my eyes.

"Look, I'm busy here," I said, brandishing the photograph. "I'm sick of you, do you understand? I'm not here for you. Now be gone, or I'll call Demon Patrol. I know a guy who knows a guy. Got it?"

The demon hesitated, and I pushed my face into its misty snout.

"Get out of here!" I screamed and bared my teeth. The demon faded away into shadows. I sighed and looked back down at the picture. I ran my fingers over my father's face. The little boy was frozen in time, but my father adjusted his glasses and smiled at me.

"Hello, Luna."

Chapter Twenty-Seven

The picture fell from my hands. I heard glass shatter as it fell to the floor, but I was busy trying to keep myself in check. Was this it? Was I finally going crazy like my father? Was Seth going to find my body next, just as he had found Dad's?

I heard my name again, slightly muffled. I closed my eyes, but it was distinctly my father's voice.

The demonic me grinned from the mirror, reaching a hand from the glass, almost brushing my hair with groping fingers.

What was a demon compared to my real fear? Demons were nothing, just sad beings who had it in for the living. But the things that lurked inside my own brain were what scared me the most. My outer toughness was a lie. It was a shell. I was horrifyingly vulnerable underneath.

I looked down at the shattered glass around my feet. The shards glistened like stars. I had never seen anything more beautiful.

"Luna!" My father's voice was a sharp command, and it brought me back to myself.

Demonic Me had stepped from the mirror. Her eyes were black and inky, no whites in them at all.

"Well, aren't you pretty." I reached for my knife, but the idea of slicing what looked like my face made me wince. "Now why don't you hop on back into Wonderland and leave me alone?"

She didn't say anything but took a deep sniff of the air. She smiled, and there were way too many teeth for her face.

"I'd like to be you," she said. Her voice sounded vaguely like mine, but it was twisted, contorted. "I'd like to be you very much."

"Sorry, babe. The job's taken. Uninvited."

I felt her reach for me, searching for my strength. The Mark burned between my shoulder blades, and I gasped.

"Listen, lady," I snarled, grabbing her wrist. I was surprised she had solidified so quickly. I needed to be careful. "I don't have time to play. I'm looking for a little human girl, preferably one who won't burst into flames. Seen her?"

Her tongue flicked out of her mouth. It was forked. Now that was just disturbing.

"Why should I help you?" She reached toward my face with her other hand. I instinctively ducked away, protective of my eyes.

"Careful, Luna," my father warned. "This one has an especially bad disposition."

"What a coincidence. So do I."

Demonic Me lunged forward, her toothy mouth wide. I grabbed her hair, slammed her face into my knee, and then banged the back of her head on the floor. I stomped on her once for good measure.

The demon groaned and faded away.

"And she had such a lovely face."

My father's grin looked exactly the same as it used to. It made me want to grin back. I wanted him to brush my hair away from my eyes and tell me that everything was going to be all right. I had always believed him when said that. I wanted him to reassure me now.

"That's my girl. You seem to be taking this fairly well," he said.

I shrugged. "Yeah, well, I'm taking it with a grain of salt. Either I'm absolutely bonkers or you're some alternate reality conjured up by this place. Mouth said I'd see a lot of weirdness in here."

"And who's Mouth?"

"He's a..." demon, friend, pain in the neck, informant. "Guy," I finished lamely.

"A guy?"

"Something like that."

"A guy who has some information about this place."

He had me there. I sighed. "He's a demon, Dad. For some reason, I think he wants to help me, but I'm not always sure. I mean, he hasn't done anything to hurt me so far, but he's, well, you know. A demon."

"And demons are always bad." My father looked wise.

"You tell me. You saw them, too."

He looked away from me then, his lips twisting in a way that seemed completely unlike him. Mouth's warning sounded loud in my ears: I may see things that are wonderful or horrible, but they're illusions. This isn't my father. I had to remember that.

If I'm to believe the words of a demon, that is. This was confusing.

The look of disgust disappeared from my father's face, and he looked like his old self again. Interested. Concerned. "What are you doing here, Luna? This isn't the place for you."

I played with my earring while I studied the picture. I was hungry for my father, for his face and his voice and his words. "I'm here to find any info on Sparkles and her demon and to get Lydia back. I might be here to start the demonic apocalypse, I don't know. I just want to take Sweet Baby Girl home. That's it."

"Why isn't Seth here with you? Why would he expect you to get Lydia without him? What kind of father did he turn out to be?"

My stomach jolted.

"He's…kinda having a bad day. He wasn't able to come. That happens sometimes, you know."

My father's eyes changed to concern. "A bad day? Is Seth all right?"

Well, he isn't dead. I realized my definition of all right had changed drastically in the last few days.

"All right enough. He'll be fine once I get Lydia back. Is there anything you can tell me about Sparkles and her demon? Where they are? How to take them on?"

My father eyed me, his expression very grave. He looked down at the boy perched on his lap. He met my eyes again and for the first time he closed the book. "Sparkles has aligned herself with a very powerful demon. It's higher in rank than those you usually come in contact with. More stealthy, more seductive."

"More seductive? Have you seen that monster with its demony tendrils sliding their way up Sparkle's nose? What can possibly be seductive about that freak?"

He smiled and shook his head. His hair flopped over his face just like I remembered. "Some things never change, sweetheart. You always were quick to jump to conclusions. Very quick to judge."

I felt my back stiffen. "I am not quick to judge. I'm open-minded and tolerant. In fact, I'm the very pinnacle of…why are you laughing?"

Tears were running down my father's face. It was disconcerting. "Oh, Luna. You do know how to make your old man laugh. You, tolerant? Not quick to judge? Ha, ha, ha."

I felt my mouth turn down into a frown. This wasn't going the way I expected it to.

"Now hold on a minute here, Dad. What is so freakin' funny? For real?"

He chortled. "Don't you have a demon to catch?"

My frown deepened, if such a thing was possible. "In a minute. This is important."

He wiped his eyes on his sleeve. The frozen boy on his lap seemed unperturbed by Dad's mirth.

"It's been a long time since I laughed like that, sweetheart. Thank you. You don't know how much it means to an old man like me."

I was getting angry. "I don't see what's so funny. And I don't like being laughed at."

"I'm sorry, sweetie. It's just that, well, look at you. It's all so black and white. Sparkles is evil, Seth is a worrywart—"

"Sparkles is evil! We've already established she's tethered herself to a powerful demonic entity. And you can't deny Seth is overprotective. What else have you got?"

He blinked innocently. "Reed Taylor is of the devil…"

I stopped short and narrowed my eyes. "How do you know about Reed Taylor? I didn't mention him."

His smile was sly. "You didn't have to. A father knows these things."

I smiled back, equally as sly. "My father didn't know things like that, though. He wasn't savvy when it came to feelings. He was easily befuddled. You've given yourself away again. Who are you?"

"Why, dear heart, I'm your father."

"You're not my father." I was surprised at how sad my voice sounded. Even though I had known it from the beginning, known the dead don't speak to us out of old photographs, it still made my heart hurt. I swallowed hard and brushed my fingers down the side of his face. "It isn't you."

My father's eyes went wide, full of pain. "What are you saying? You're breaking my heart."

I flicked his shoulder and he winced. "Stop it, demon. I know what you are."

He looked crafty. "Why would you say that?"

I shrugged. "Dad knows why Seth isn't here with me because I told him at the grave. And just because you look like him doesn't mean you feel anything like him. Dad always felt warm and safe. You feel like a nutcase. You're just an imposter. Like everybody else around here." I leaned against the wall. "Does it kill you guys to be straight up? Is there a reason you always have to slink around and lie?"

He almost looked sorrowful. "It's in our nature, Luna. We can't change who we are. Would you…like me to show myself in my true form? Would that be easier than seeing a demon wear the face of your father?"

I was touched. Almost. But perhaps his true form has twenty heads with dagger teeth. "No thanks. I'm cool with you looking like Dad. Besides, it's nice to see him, even if it isn't really him, you know. If that makes sense." I looked around. "It's nice to have something familiar in this place. This is one screwed up house you have here."

The demon nodded. "That it is. It's a place of horrors, as I'm sure you've discovered. It really isn't very pleasant for us here, most of the time."

"So why stick around? Do you get out much?"

A strange emotion surfaced in his eyes. It unsettled me and I had to look away.

"Not a lot, no," he answered, and the subject was closed. He didn't want to talk about it, and I didn't want to see that twisted regret and rage in his eyes anymore. Especially not while he looked so much like Dad.

"So what now? Are you going to eat me? Burrow into the Mark like a parasite? Pretend you're my father again and sing me a lullaby?"

The demon grinned. "Your father was absolutely right. You do have a smart mouth. No, Luna, I'm not going to do any of those things. I'm going to help you."

Chapter Twenty-Eight

I had to admit I was taken aback.

"Help me, huh? That's a new one. And why would you want to do that, demon? Picking up some brownie points for the afterlife?"

He snorted. "That's a good one. It would be nice if I could do that, but no. Truth is, I was a friend of your father's."

Now it was my turn to laugh, but it sounded ugly to me. "A friend, huh? I'm sure you were. You were all lovely friends, weren't you? Hanging around Dad until he couldn't stand it anymore. Taunting him and luring him until it was easier to take his own life than to listen to you any longer. Some friend. No thanks."

I dropped the picture on the ground and turned away. Although I was loathe to head back into the room with the burning girl and the two doors, at least it was better than being here with this nutcase who claimed to pal around with my father. Ho, ho, that's rich.

"Luna," he shouted from the floor.

In his desperation and fury, all former trace of my father's voice had disappeared. The demon's voice was unfamiliar and sounded strangely strained. Good, let him be upset. He deserved it. I stepped on the picture with my heavy combat boots for good measure and grabbed the doorknob.

"Nice seeing ya, loser," I said, and turned the knob.

"I know the demon's name! Sparkle's demon's name."

I stopped short, my hand still on the knob.

"I'll tell you. Luna, come back. I'll tell you the name."

I turned around, my fingers lifting from the brass of the doorknob.

"You really know it?"

"I did know your dad, you know. We really were friends. Why else would I be here?"

I sat down cross-legged and picked the picture back up.

"This isn't the time to be screwing with me, demon. I'm in a fragile emotional state. I have anger management issues. I'm likely to get mad and, oh, I don't know, rip you in half or something. Got it?"

He was quiet for a minute, looking off into the distance.

"Your father saw beings of darkness, but he also saw beings of light. You knew this, yes?"

"Yeah."

"It was harder for him, I think, seeing both. Next to something so beautiful, a demon becomes even more twisted, even more horrific. You compare a demon to a human and there's not much of a difference."

"Hey."

"Well, there isn't, really. But you compare it to an angel, and that's when you see how low and pathetic demons really are."

I wanted to tell it not to be so hard on itself. I also wanted to tell it to hurry up because I had demon butt to kick, but I forced myself to sit quietly. Believe me, it wasn't easy.

"There are few people who can see us, Luna. Much fewer than you'd think. And something about your father…was special. Can you see that?"

I knew he was special. He didn't have to tell me.

The demon used my father's eyes to look into a distance I couldn't see. "He was a good guy, through and through. He talked to me like I was something more than the damned, even when I was blight compared to these beings of light. That matters. I enjoyed talking to him. I missed him after he died, believe it or not. Me. Missing a human. But there was nobody else to talk to. Nobody living who would listen. And the dead and damned, well, our conversations tend to be a bit dreary."

That's it. I was tired of walking through memory lane. Besides that, my legs were starting to cramp up.

"Hurry it along, demon. A little less talk and a lot more action. You were saying you have a name to give me?"

He wagged his finger at me. "Hasn't anybody ever taught you to respect your elders, Luna?"

I shook the picture with both hands. "And don't you understand I'm running out of time? I have to get Lydia. The name. Give me the name."

He closed his eyes. When he opened them, they shone with a color I had never seen before. I caught my breath. The air seemed too still.

"The name is Tsofea."

As soon as he said the name, the walls shimmered like a mirage. I thought I could see through to the other rooms. Flaming corpses. Starfish clambering around blindly.

"Sophia? Really? I know two girls at school named Sophia. Come to think of it, they're probably both a little demonic, too."

"No, not Sophia. Tsofea." He spelled the name out. "And it isn't something you want to mess with."

The floor trembled slightly, and I adjusted my footing. "I really don't want to mess with it, but I have to. It will be easier now with a name." I swallowed hard. Why was this so hard to say? "Uh, thanks. For that. For the name, I mean."

The demon wearing my father's face smiled at me. It was full of sorrow. "I was dearly hoping I could be your friend, too, Luna. I watched you grow up, you know. You saw me many times when you were a child. I was one of the ones your father never chased away. There were two of us he allowed around his family, as long as we kept a respectful distance."

I didn't like the tone of his voice, and the air seemed to suck out of the room, but I couldn't leave just yet. He wasn't my father, but he had known him. And he was kind. Something good in this place of desolation.

"So if you're not such a bad guy, why don't I see you around more? Come stop by the house or something after all of this is done."

He smiled for real, then, and it was beautiful. Suddenly I caught myself thinking that if I were ever to see an angel of light, it would have to look like this: the face of somebody I loved looking so delighted.

"Oh, you sweet girl. You don't know how happy that makes me. You don't know how it feels. It almost hurts. Yes, it does hurt. Thank you, but I can't."

"Why can't you?" I knew the answer before I even asked.

I've heard despair before, but I've never heard a voice created from it. My body grew cold. I wanted to kick the door down and run screaming from the bowels of the house.

"Because I'm trapped here, Luna. We're all trapped here. This is where we go when we misbehave. This is where we stay until we are dealt with. I was sent here for befriending your father. Now that I have given you the true name, my torment will come quickly."

His hair fluttered, and I realized my hands were shaking. "Can't you take it back? Pretend you didn't tell me?"

"Of course they already know. You can see what's happening. They'll be sending somebody for me immediately. You need to leave."

The edges of the picture began to blacken and curl. I dropped the picture reflexively. My father's eyebrows shot up.

"They've come. Run!"

The picture burst into flames and I watched in horror as the little boy began to burn on my father's lap. The book charred. My father's face melted and distorted, his mouth opening in a scream I knew I'd remember until the day I died, and probably even after that. I leapt to my feet and tried to stomp the flames out.

"Go, Luna!"

It was no good. The flames ran across the carpet like they were following a trail of gasoline. They zipped up the walls and the curtains began to burn. I threw my arms over my face and backed toward the door. The wretched screaming finally cut through the panicked fog of my brain, and I realized I couldn't save him. I couldn't save my father when I was a child, and now I couldn't save this creature who was wearing his skin. I'd like to blame it on the heat and the black smoke that was making me cough, but my eyes were full of tears when I finally ripped the blue door open and ran outside.

Chapter Twenty-Nine

There was no longer a charred and burning little girl in the room, and I was undeniably grateful for that. I was still trying to get over seeing a charred and burning demon-father in the last room. Mouth was right: this place was awful. I wanted nothing more than to get out, and burn this place to the ground. Seemed like there was an awful lot of that going on.

"Hey," said a voice. I dashed for the yellow door. The knob turned easily in my hand, but the door itself was stuck.

"Hey, Luna. I've been looking for you everywhere." The first voice was back.

"I'm not listening," I shouted and braced my combat boot against the wall. I pulled on the door as hard as I could but it still wasn't opening. Unreal.

"Luna, let me help you," the voice said and a hand rested on my shoulder. I whirled around and slapped it off.

"Don't touch me, demon," I shouted. I was surprised to find tears rolling down my face, but I was too angry to care. Reed Taylor's gorgeous green eyes looked shocked, and then concerned, but I'd seen enough in this house to know it wasn't him.

I gave the door a good kick, then another and another. I dug my feet into the floor and yanked on the doorknob with all of my weight, leaning back while I did so.

The door stuck for another second, and then swung smoothly open, spilling me onto the ground. Reed Taylor reached to help me up, and I smacked his hands away.

"Don't touch me. I don't want you ever to touch me."

He stood back and shoved his hands into his pockets. "Luna, I think…I think maybe this place is too much for you."

I slowly climbed to my feet, wiping the dust and grime off of my jeans while I tried to calm myself down. It wasn't working.

"You think this place is too much for me? Really? This place is Hell, in case you haven't noticed. And I don't know what you did to be sent here, demon, but I'm almost sorry for you. I just saw what happened to my father—no, he wasn't my father. But I think he wasn't lying when he said they were friends." I was talking to myself, now. That's it. I'd lost it. It wasn't a big, scary demon that had done it, either, but the sight of the demonic wearing the faces of two of the men I had loved the most. Next I'd see Seth coming after me with an axe. My shoulders slumped.

"Luna," Reed Taylor said, and pulled me close. He even smelled the same as the real Reed Taylor, and that made my eyes tear up again.

This is most likely the last time I'll ever be so close to Reed Taylor. And it isn't even him, it's something else.

I leaned my head against his shoulder and took a deep breath. Then I stepped out of his arms.

"Luna, are you all right?"

The punch to his jaw took him by surprise. His hand flew up to his face. I kneed him in the groin then, and he doubled over with a sound that would have made me cringe if he had been a real human. I kicked him in the head, and he curled up on the ground.

"Wh-what…" he asked, but that was all he was able to get out.

Hey, you don't grow up with a crazy dad and not learn how to take a few swings on the playground. "If you ever pretend to be Reed Taylor again, I will find a way to kill you, demon. You should have stuck with the burning girl."

"Luna," he whispered, and I kicked him in the stomach one last time for good measure.

"Leave me alone."

I turned my back on the crumpled body that looked like Reed Taylor. My eyes were dry now. I stepped resolutely through the yellow door and locked it behind me.

Chapter Thirty

Man, kicking Reed Taylor Demon in the head felt good. It revved up the anger in me, and I had a feeling that anger more than anything else was going to save my life today.

The room was different than the others. It was large and cavernous, made completely of stone, both the floors and the walls. A mist blew through it like we were down at the dock. Come to think of it, it smelled alive, like forest and trees and something older than time.

I didn't like it. I didn't like it at all.

There was a chuckle that made the hair on my arms stand up. I recognized it immediately.

"Mmm, Luna," the voice purred. This was my least favorite demon trick ever, I swear. It got old, fast.

"Mmm, Sparkles. Where are you hiding, you coward? Are you saying you're afraid to face little ol' me?" I batted my eyes. "I'm flattered. I didn't realize I was such a powerhouse."

The voice laughed, and I had to admit it was creepy. It bounced off the stone walls with a sick echo that made me want to drop to my knees and cover my ears. It knew this, I was sure. Demons know all of the tricks. They know all of our human reactions, but I wasn't going to give her what she wanted.

"Listen," I said, and sighed dramatically. "It's been a long day. I was attacked by mutant starfish and a necklace that would most likely turn my skin green if it didn't suffocate me first. I've been staggering around in this little funhouse of yours and, really, I just want to go home and get something to eat. Seriously, I'm starving. So let's get the show on the road already. Come be vanquished, or whatever. Or just hand Lydia over nicely. I have things to do."

It felt like the ground moved under me. It didn't shake like an earthquake, but it felt something more like…water. Like something swimming beneath the surface. My eyes narrowed.

"What makes you think I'll give her up?" A voice whispered in my ear. It was genderless, emotionless, but somehow I could feel the loathing and hatred spreading under my skin like a disease. I jumped and spun toward the sound, but again there was nothing. That was ticking me off.

"What reason do you have to keep her? You never loved her. Just give her back to Seth and everything's cool, yeah?" My eyes slid over the stone walls. There was a shadow in the far corner that looked a little darker than usual. Could she be hiding there? Did she have Lydia? It was tough to see through the mist. And what is mist doing inside a creepy horror house, anyway?

Oh yeah, being creepy and horrifying.

Silence. Which was also creepy and horrifying. I couldn't wait to bound away from this place as fast as my legs could take me.

"You've gotta admit that being a mom sort of cramps your style." No answer. I slid one foot ahead of me on the unstable floor. I swear it sank under me slightly like I was walking on mud. I kept my eyes firmly on the corner. "I mean, how boring is it to be married, right? A husband. A yowly baby. Why not let her go and then you can go away? Go back to…" I swallowed hard. "Reed Taylor or whoever it is that you want to go back to. I won't fight you for him, you know. In fact, I just kicked his lookalike's butt out there in the other room. He's yours, if you want him."

There was something in the corner, I knew it. The knob on the yellow door behind me rattled back and forth. There was a pounding on it, and I heard the demon using Reed Taylor's voice scream angrily through the door. I nearly had to close my eyes, but I kept inching ahead into the mist.

"See, Sparkles? There he is, now." Another muffled shout, and some vehement cursing through the door. My salty old grandfather would have blushed at the words coming out of his mouth. "And he's sounding delightfully demonic. You two will be perfect together. Now give me my niece!"

The ground roiled. That was the only way to put it. The stone rolled like waves on the sea, and I was knocked completely off my feet. This was an alarming development. It felt solid enough that it forced an angry sound out of me when I landed, but when I tried to scramble back up, it was like trying to walk on water.

"Sparkles!" I was alarmed to hear how unhinged my voice sounded. "Quit playing and give Lydia back to me."

"You'll never get her back."

The same chilling, whispered voice. It wasn't Sparkles.

It was her demon.

"What do you want with her, demon? She's just a little girl. She has nothing to offer you. Besides, you have Sparkles, who is certainly the most evil person I've ever met. What more do you need?"

The ground bobbled again, and I fell down, knocking my chin on the hard stone with a crack that I felt more than heard. Lights danced in front of my eyes. I held onto the floor and tried to ride the wave out until I could stagger to my feet.

"The girl means nothing." The voice sounded much louder, and I pressed my ear to the cold floor. Was it coming from beneath me?

"So why not give her back?"

"She quiets the mother."

The floor slid under my feet, and I realized what was going on. Whatever I was having a conversation with was literally swimming underneath the stone. How could this be? But then, why would I even ask such a question? I stood up, careful to keep my balance.

"The mother? Sparkles?" I snorted. "That's a good one. Like she cares."

Now that I was watching for it, I could see a long, serpentine shape coiling and writhing under the rock as it traveled from one side of the room to the other. The thing looked huge. Enormous. My mouth went dry. How was I supposed to conquer this thing?

"You know not our ways, human. You are nothing."

I was tired of hearing that. "Listen, keep Sparkles but give me Lydia. She doesn't quiet the mother. The mother is a selfish cancer who exists only to make others miserable. Congratulations, you snagged yourself a real winner. Lydia has no part in it, so hand her over."

"I shall not."

"Do it, demon."

"Do not command me!"

The ground sank dangerously under me, and I was buffeted by waves of stone. I covered my head with my hands, but I still got clocked in the temple hard enough to leave blood running down my face. Was that going to scar?

All right, that did it.

"Demonic entity Tsofea, I call you by name. I command you, using your true name, to give me back the child."

There was a roar that sounded like it was being wrenched out of a thousand tortured beings. The serpent under the floor rocked and contorted into shapes bizarre enough to twist my stomach, but still it didn't break through the stone. The mist became thicker, more dense, coating my body with a layer of fog. I had to pull it from my mouth and nose as if it were made of spider webs. The coldness pierced my bones and made me shiver, but the fire in my eyes kept me warm enough to keep yelling. I felt an intense pressure on the Tracing, which nearly floored me, but I wasn't going to give in without a fight.

"Tsofea, give me the child. I command you!"

It screamed, a surprisingly high and piercing shriek that jammed into my ears like somebody had kicked a pencil through them. I fell to my knees, clasping my hands to my head, my own scream torn from my throat in agony. It joined with the thousand other voices of the bellowing demon, blending alongside the many souls it had captured. This unexpected intimacy enraged me so much I ground my teeth together to muffle the sound until I finally managed to stop screaming. I pulled my hands away from my ears and saw they ran red with blood.

The demon still convulsed, making it impossible to stand, but I saw that the shadow in the corner of the wall was actually a small hole. The shrieking and bucking of the floor brought a few broken stones tumbling to the ground, and the hole widened. I crawled across the floor, thrown here and there, cracking my head and knees and elbows on the rock. I was scraped and bruised and bloody, but I was almost to the hole. I could see darkness outside. I could hear the snarling and howling of what sounded like wolves. And even more importantly, I could hear faint cries that I was certain were Lydia's.

Chapter Thirty-One

I wasn't stupid enough to think I could shout out the demon's name a time or two and have it collapse at my feet. But it was certainly hurting enough that I could scramble through the ragged hole in the stone and escape that ancient room. Their names have power. Exactly how much, I wasn't sure. But it was enough, at least for now.

I used both hands to pull my body through, and then I got to my feet on the other side of the hole. The ground still heaved and hoisted under me, but I leaned against the wall while I got my bearings.

"Lydia?" I called. "Sweet Girl?"

The cries were faint, but they were definitely her. I looked around in shock. Instead of the nice, postage-stamp sized backyard I had expected, I was standing in the middle of what looked like the Black Forest. Not to mention it was suddenly the middle of the night when it should have been closer to 3:00 p.m. How could this be?

I needed to stop thinking about it before my mind broke. Demons liked the dark and dreary, anyway. My priority was Lydia. Nothing else mattered.

I ran toward the sound, my hands out in front of me to protect my graceful self from running headlong into branches. The trees were spiny black shadows in the darkness. Great, even the trees look like demons here.

"Lydia, it's Mama Luna! I'm coming for you, sweetheart."

I was going to kick Sparkles in the face when I found her. Then I was going to knock her down, sit on her chest, and punch her in her bitter, twisted mouth until I was too tired to punch anymore. Then I'd spit on her. When I was done, I would start all over again, and then take Lydia and go home. Sparkles won't be more than shreds of meat by the time I'm through with her. She'd never come after Lydia again.

The Mark pulsed and seared with my thoughts. It almost felt good. It did feel good.

In the back of my mind, something that strangely sounded like common sense was warning me that physical assault might not be the best way to go about this, especially if Lydia ended up with her biological mother due to my family's questionable mental state. But I never was big on listening to that certain part of my mind. Get bent, common sense. I have some revenge to wreak.

I was almost there. Lydia sounded only a few feet ahead of me. The thick night was getting even blacker, and the tiny sliver of moon disappeared behind a cloud. Fantastic. I couldn't see a thing, freezing in the paranormal fog, and I was getting more creeped out by the second. The Mark on my back ached even more, growling like an angry stomach.

They're here.

Something zipped past me in the trees, zig-zagging its way easily through the brambles and branches that repeatedly caught me up. Something else rustled the leaves overhead. I knew they weren't birds or innocent little woodland animals that would come cuddling up to wayward princesses and dashing princes. They were dark and sinister and evil. They were attracted to the Mark, and I was afraid they were also attracted to the innocence that was Lydia.

My legs pumped harder. I was racing disaster in the woods. If I got it to her first then everything would be okay, I kept telling myself. I needed to believe it.

I found Lydia in a little clearing. She sat on the dead, leafy floor, her pigtails haphazard and her face covered in dirt and tears. Her yellow sundress looked out of place in the menacing, freak-of-nature woods. She looked like goodness personified. She looked like bait.

"Lydia," I called out, and her head turned my way. She held her pudgy arms out to me. They were covered in filth or blood, I couldn't tell, and the sudden surge of anger I felt made me want to snap my teeth on somebody's throat. I didn't care if it was a trap. Didn't care what the darkness was planning. I needed to get to my sweet girl.

"Lydia, I'm here."

A dark shadow that smelled of must and sweat darted in front of my legs. I actually stumbled on the darn thing. If it was that close to physical form, I'd better be ready for anything.

"Get back, demon. You can't have her."

It grinned at me, its teeth wrapping most of the way around its head, and then it dropped to all fours. It ran awkwardly, and then the gait straightened into something smooth and loping. Its ears pulled back and its toothy face opened into a snarl.

A wolf.

I shuddered as I realized the implications. I had never seen a demon change into another form, and I was scared beyond anything I could remember. If it could do that, what else could it do? I thought I was so knowledgeable, but I didn't really know anything about them, did I?

Isn't that what Mouth kept trying to tell me?

The demon barked, its guttural voice several octaves too low for it to belong to a real wolf. It was a terrible thing to hear, and my mouth went dry.

It was headed straight for Lydia.

"No!" I screamed, and grabbed a rock from the ground without breaking my stride. I threw wildly, and it hit the rump of the wolf with a thud. "Leave her alone."

The wolf shrugged off my attack and padded up to Sweet Girl. It huffed hot air on her, blowing her hair back, and I felt the blood flow out of my face. It felt like dying slow.

"Please, don't touch her," I begged. I stood stock still, trying not to scare it, trying to think clearly. If I ran at the wolf, it would give Lydia a few seconds to get away. Before I'm torn apart and the wolf went after her, that is.

I didn't know what to do. I was terrified and alone and Lydia didn't have anybody but me. The poor girl was in big, big trouble.

The wolf nipped the tender white toddler shoulder, drawing blood. Both Lydia and I shrieked at the same time. That's it. If it wanted a fight, it'd get a fight. I snarled and darted forward.

The wolf opened its jaws wider than I would have thought possible, but its lips didn't move. The voice that came from its canine vocal chords sounded strained and broken. It was absolutely terrifying.

"Stop or I will kill the girl."

"Looks to me like you plan on killing her, anyway." I slowed to a careful walk, but I didn't stop moving toward Lydia, who was screaming and trying to crawl to me. The wolf snapped its jaws inches from her face, and the shrieks started anew.

"Do not assume you know my intentions."

"You're a demon, therefore your intentions are evil. I know your kind. I know what I'm up against."

The wolf laughed, a terrible sound, and I wanted to curl up into a ball right there.

"You have no idea what you're up against."

It was true. I was completely in the dark, and I knew it, but what was I supposed to do? I was less than ten feet from Lydia and her terror made my heart pound. I needed to clean the wound on her shoulder. I couldn't imagine that demonic wolf bites could be good for the soul. I needed to snuggle her and bring her back to her daddy.

Two more wolves materialized behind Lydia. One hadn't finished changing shape correctly and still wore the sharp teeth that wrapped most of the way around his head. I'd be seeing that grin in my nightmares for the rest of my life, I knew it. I just hoped the rest of my life lasted longer than two or three minutes. There was still so much to do. The thought of giving up here made me sad.

"What…what do you want in exchange for the girl?" I asked. The pressure on the Mark intensified suddenly, making me gasp, driving me to one knee. It felt like a giant claw planted firmly between my shoulder blades, as though the demon who cursed me had never really left. Perhaps he never had.

"What makes you think you have anything to exchange, girl?"

The pain was so severe that I saw comets. I wasn't going to pass out, I just wasn't. I raised my head as high as I could, meeting the wolf's eyes.

"Demons are all about want. You're created by want and need. She'll never be enough for you; you'll always want more."

"Perhaps," the alpha wolf said. "All I know is need. Desire. The pressure to take and have and destroy." His eyes glittered. "Your soul for hers."

His jaws were held impossibly wide, and I thought, with horror, perhaps they would split open from the force. I anticipated the sound of his jaws breaking, the bone splintering, and I imagined what that would look like, how Lydia and I would be forced to watch it. I wondered if she'd remember, if it would come to her in her dreams, or maybe when she was older and getting ready for school. It was too much for me. I turned my head to the side and threw up.

"Selfish," the wolf said, and made a strange clicking noise deep inside his throat.

The deformed, toothy wolf moved faster than I thought possible. He bit down hard on Lydia's foot, and I heard a crunch that sounded like gravel being poured in a bag. Lydia's eyes bulged and her mouth opened in something too painful to be a scream.

"No! No!" I shouted, and tried to crawl forward, but the agonizing pressure on the Mark pushed me further to the ground. I was on my belly, scrabbling through the dead leaves and rotted refuse as I tried to claw my way to my broken Lydia.

The second demon wolf dove in, and a sickening fight ensued. The screaming stopped, and I heard the sound of snarling wolves and the tearing of flesh and clothes.

"Yes! My soul for hers! My soul for hers!" I twisted and fought, screaming and writhing toward Lydia with everything I had. My boots scraped in the dirt, my fingernails broke and bled while I struggled against the unfathomable power that pinned me to the ground.

Lydia wasn't moving. She wasn't moving. One wolf lost interest and wandered away. The toothy wolf played with Lydia's tiny body a while longer, dragging her along the ground by her shattered leg as I watched. Lydia's eyes were open. Her tiny starfish hands were white and still.

"Mmm, the blood of the innocent. It makes me hungry." The alpha wolf turned toward Sweet Girl's broken body.

"You can't have her," I screamed, and I went wild again, fighting just as fiercely as before, even though I knew there was nothing left to save, that I had failed, that Lydia was gone, that part of my heart had been torn apart alongside her.

Chapter Thirty-Two

I thought I had experienced despair before. Finding my father swinging inside of our very own home nearly broke me. Finding Seth in the bathtub drove me closer to the brink than I had ever been. I didn't think it could get any worse than that. I thought a mind had a threshold, and once you hit it you were somehow immune to the horror. Like the universe would somehow say, "Congratulations, my dear, you have officially hit your allotment of misery. Now destruction will pass you by."

I thought if I was tough enough, and dealt with everything well enough, and kept a positive attitude, well, as much as possible, then somehow I would be rewarded. Everything would end up all right. Evil would fall and good would prevail, and there would be some glorious shining prize at the end of this terrible game, something that made it worth the constant struggle we call life.

But I was wrong. There is no light at the end of the tunnel. No reward for living a good life. There's just death, and more misery, and tiny little girls who become caught in the middle of it even though they did absolutely nothing wrong.

I couldn't save her. I tried my best and I failed. Miserably. The terror and pain Lydia had gone through in her last moments…I couldn't think about it. The struggle and the fight went out of me. I couldn't find the strength to care about protecting the Mark from the demon who currently prodded around, testing the strength of my soul. It didn't matter anymore. Nothing mattered. This was misery, and despair. This was Hell.

I curled up on the ground and cried. I had never sobbed so hard. Even when I felt the cool fingers of the demon slide over the Tracing, I didn't move.

"I win, Luna," the demon said and laughed and laughed and laughed.

Chapter Thirty-Three

L una?" Somewhere in the back of my mind, I heard my name. I didn't wonder who it was. I didn't care.

"Luna, tell me what's wrong."

A warm hand slid through my hair, over my scalp, down my arms and legs. Checking for broken bones. Checking for damage. It slid over the demonic Tracing and I heard a hiss as it pulled away. I almost missed its chilling touch. It cooled the nearly unbearable heat between my shoulders.

"Luna. I need you to look at me. Can you sit up?"

I couldn't remember how to speak. Something to do with my tongue and moving my lips, but then I thought of the demon speaking through the wolf's cavernous mouth like an old record being played on a phonograph. I began to shudder. I was quickly pulled into a seated position, held close to somebody's warm chest.

"I'm here. I have you. You're safe."

The wolf demon stood close by. It snorted and I winced. "You're never safe, Luna. We always know where you are. We always know what you are doing. We will follow you until the end of time." It grinned.

I blinked, wiped my face with my sleeve. Looked up.

"Reed Taylor?"

His gorgeous greens tight around the edges with worry. One eye was starting to blacken, and his lips were cut.

"It's me. Try not to kick the crap out of me again, will you?"

The wolf demon growled, padded right up to Reed Taylor. Its ears laid back and it bared its teeth. Reed Taylor's eyes narrowed and he leaned forward, searching the air in front of him. He and the wolf were nose to nose. I forgot how to breathe.

"I know you're here, demon," Reed Taylor said. His voice was unusually rough, and he held me with hands that were no longer gentle. I was too tired and stunned to squirm out of them. "I want you to know you don't scare me. How do you feel about that, hmm? I'm not afraid of you."

The demon pushed his muzzle even closer. They were only a few centimeters apart.

"I know who you are, mortal man," the demon spat. I jumped and Reed Taylor held me closer, his eyes straining to see a threat that was currently invisible to him. "I know you well. You have earned your place here in Hell."

He growled, and then huffed. The hot air ruffled Reed Taylor's hair. Reed Taylor's mouth tightened, and I sat frozen in his arms. This demon had the power to hurt him physically. I hoped Reed Taylor knew that. I was certain he did.

"Luna," Reed Taylor repeated, his eyes still not on me. "You're crying. Tell me why."

He hadn't seen Lydia's body. My throat closed up, and my tears began anew.

Reed Taylor grabbed my face in his hands and searched my eyes. "Tell me. I hate being left in the dark."

I couldn't say the words, so I just pointed. I turned my face away and pointed at Lydia's small corpse, still being guarded by the deformed, toothy wolf. I couldn't make myself look at her. I couldn't see her like that again, her adorable yellow sundress stained with blood.

"What are you pointing at?"

My gaze shot up to Reed Taylor's. Was he kidding? Surely he couldn't be this cruel. Was he going to make me say the words?

"L-l-lydia," I stuttered, and gestured wildly to her body. "They killed Lydia! Right in front of me. They made me watch, and I couldn't get to her..."

I was going to go hysterical, and now wasn't the time for that. I took a deep breath, squeezed my eyes shut.

"Lydia?" he said, and his voice nearly made me cry again. He said the name with such love. I had almost forgotten what a monster I thought he was.

"Sh-she kept screaming, and the wolves, they tore her apart. I tried—"

"Here?" He said, and pointed. Lydia's bloody legs. Her tiny broken feet.

I nodded.

"Baby, there's nothing there."

I blinked at him. Nothing there?

"What do you mean?" I asked. My brain was working too slowly. I couldn't process what he was saying. If it was a joke, it wasn't funny, and I'd hold him down and make him pay for it later. But I knew he wasn't joking. His beautiful green eyes were calm and serious.

"Luna, there isn't anything there. I don't see a thing. Do you see Lydia right now?"

I looked at her, bit my lips. I nodded.

"She isn't there. She isn't real. Whatever you saw didn't really happen."

Could he be right? Was it true? Had I finally gone crazy?

Reed Taylor pulled me close, nuzzled his nose into my hair. "Luna, if it really was Lydia, I'd be able to see her. It must be an illusion. Look closely. "

I felt it, the barest glimmer of hope. It felt like water on parched roots.

It gave me the strength to lean out of his arms and really study Lydia's body for the first time. The woods had disappeared; Lydia's body lay on the beige carpeting of the cookie-cutter house. Her wounds and gashes were horrible. The dark bruising on her cheeks filled me with dread. But I took a deep breath and looked harder.

Lydia's eyes weren't Lydia's eyes at all. They were crafty, watching. They were eons older than the earth, older than time. Lydia's cherubic lips parted.

"Your terror was delicious," the demon said, its dark voice terrifyingly out of place in Lydia's body. "I could dine on it for weeks." Lydia's lips stretched in a smile far too wide for her face.

I shot to my feet.

"How could you?" I shrieked. "How could you?"

They didn't answer, but laughed that bone-chilling laughter. Toothy demon pranced close to me on its deformed feet. Too close.

My hand flashed and caught it by the throat. It gurgled in surprise.

I pushed it down and pinned it with my knee.

"I'm gonna cut that smile off of your face." My voice was calm and steady. I felt strangely in control as I reached for the small knife in my pocket.

The demon's distorted grin faded. The others leaned forward, eyes glittering.

"Yes," Alpha demon encouraged. Toothy demon whimpered and tried to dissipate and wriggle away. I pushed my essence into it, forcing it to stay solid.

"Oh no," I told it, running the blade of my knife underneath its eyes. A thin line of blood appeared and I heard Lydia demon moan in lust. "None of that. This way it's going to hurt more."

"Luna!" Reed Taylor's voice. "What are you doing?"

A quick thrust with my knee against the demon's, and the joint busted. It screamed and gibbered.

"Legs aren't supposed to bend that way, are they, demon? That'll teach you not to pull your little tricks when it comes to Lydia."

"Luna, you need to stop it. Do you hear me? This isn't like you."

This was exactly like me. This was exactly who I wanted to become. The blood and the power and the hate sang through my veins. The Mark hummed and purred high on my back. It was pleased.

It was pleased.

This realization made me wrench myself back in horror. The demon whimpered and tried to scrabble to three legs. It fell down again, landing heavily on its wounded limb. A sliver of white pushed through its skin and I nearly retched. Reed pulled me to my feet and slid the knife out of my grasp.

"Let's go," he said.

Alpha wolf leaped forward and ripped out toothy demon's throat. I stepped back from the snarling, yelping carnage in front of me.

"Such a pity. You were so close," Lydia Demon said, still in form. Alpha wolf licked its bloody lips, grabbed her by the neck and dragged her into the closet. It shut with a neat click.

Toothy demon's body disappeared, and I turned to face Reed Taylor.

"They're gone," I said. I could feel the expression of anger on my face. I was certain it wasn't pretty.

"I'm worried about you."

I ignored that. "What are you doing here, anyway?"

He shrugged. "I followed you. I wanted to talk to you about Cecilia, and then I saw you dart into this place."

I paled. "So that really was you, earlier? In the room?"

He grimaced and took a step back. "You have a mean swing on you. I didn't expect you to still be so angry, or I would have been more prepared. Worn a cup or something."

I turned away, put my hands in my pockets. "Yeah, well, sorry. I didn't think it was you. I thought it was—"

"A demon? Yeah, I guessed that when you kept calling me 'demon' and telling me to shut up. This place sounds like a nightmare for you." The concern in his eyes nearly touched my heart, but I didn't think I was ready to feel anything yet, so I looked away. "What are you doing here, Luna? What is this place? Why do you have to be somewhere that feels so wrong?"

I sighed and held my hand out for the pocketknife. He handed it back. "It's a long story, Reed Taylor, and although I'm grateful you helped me realize that wasn't Lydia, I'm still not sure I trust you enough to tell you right now. I'm sorry, but that's how I feel."

The wind blew my black hair around my face. The blue tips reminded me of doing my hair while working on Reed Taylor's, and suddenly I wanted to change my hair more than anything. Cut it off. Dye it blonde. Change it in a way that didn't have anything to do with this man I realized I loved, and who confused me more than anyone else on earth.

Reed Taylor nodded. He put his hands in his pockets, his stance mirroring mine. "All right, then. We'll talk. But not right now. Let's get out of here first. This place creeps me out, and I can't even see most of it."

Shiny eyes followed us as we walked through the deceptively cheery house. Neither of us said another word until we were outside on the front steps, walking away from the house of horrors.

Chapter Thirty-Four

Mouth flowed up to me as soon as I was off the property.
"Luna, I'm so glad to see you." He ran his eyes over me, lingering on the cuts, scrapes, and the blood. "You made it out."

"Barely." I doubled up my fist and swung right for his face. My hand passed through, and I batted harmlessly at the air.

"What's your problem?" Mouth didn't even sound like himself. "I feel horrible you had to go in there alone, but I hoped you'd understand that once I go in, I can't come back out. I couldn't…and then this troublemaker shows up." He jerked a thumb toward the beautiful redhead at my side. "Here, of all places. I would have kept him out if I could've, but…"

I swung at him again. Anger is so much safer than pain. "You sent me into a frickin' nightmare. I saw such horrible things, and for what? Nothing. I'm still no closer to finding Lydia. I hoped she'd be there, but she wasn't even in that awful house."

Mouth suddenly looked sick. I didn't think that was even possible for a demon, but he seemed to surprise me every day.

"She wasn't in there?" I looked away from him and spit on the ground. Mouth studied me, and then he turned his attention to Reed Taylor.

"Where's his entourage, anyway?"

I nudged Reed Taylor too hard with my shoulder. "Mouth wants to know where Demon Patrol is."

He shrugged. "I don't know. He's been missing for a while, now."

"Ever been gone this long before?" the demon asked. I repeated the question.

"Nope. And I have to say I'm worried. It feels like something big is going down, and I don't have a clue as to any of it."

I glared at Mouth. "You know anything about this?"

He looked worried. "No. Maybe. Nope."

"You're lying."

His eyes cut to me. His voice cut, too. "Why, because I'm a demon, and demons always lie?"

I met his fiery gaze with fire of my own. "No, because I know you and I know you're lying. Stop being so defensive."

"Stop telling me how to be!"

"Stop arguing," Reed Taylor said, and sighed. He rubbed his eyes. "It's tough being with you two, you know. I only catch one side of the conversation, which is probably a good thing because you two go at it like cats and dogs. But knock it off for now, okay? I wasn't even in there very long and the house got to me. Besides, I'm sure it gets a kick out of your fighting."

The demon's mouth went ugly for a second, and then he took a deep breath. Funny. I didn't know demons needed to breathe.

"The idiot's right," he said grudgingly. "The house thrives on negativity."

"So it's probably eating this conversation up with a spoon," I said.

He glared at Reed Taylor, who was studying my face like he was memorizing it. "That's why I was so ticked off when Clueless here showed up. That house is a tinderbox and this guy's a spark. I'm surprised the whole place didn't go up."

I knew it was a figure of speech, and he meant it didn't go up in a vortex of evil, or an inferno of damned souls or some such thing, but I thought of the burning girl and the demon with my father's face.

Reed Taylor took my arm. "You look sad. Are you still thinking about Lydia?"

Mouth was eyeing Reed Taylor's hand on my arm, but at the mention of Lydia, his eyes flicked up to my face.

"Luna?" he asked. "What did you see?"

Starfish crawling in blood. Something writhing under the stone. The destruction of a thing that looked like my father. Little girls burning and being ripped apart by demonic wolves.

"Nothing," I said fiercely and yanked my arm away from Reed Taylor's grasp. He put his hand in his pocket. I whirled on the demon and stared him down. "I didn't see a thing in there. Nothing that matters."

Demons aren't the only ones who lie, but I couldn't make myself talk about it, at least not yet. I'd seen enough to last me the rest of my days, and yet it wasn't enough. There was going to be more. I'd walked in there in order to find some information on my niece and maybe even bring her out, and I was standing here empty handed. What good had it done?

No good. Nothing had happened. I'd nearly been destroyed by a couple of dark things playing around, and I had nothing to show for it. No Lydia. No repentant Sparkles.

Mouth reached up with transparent fingers to wipe away the mascara that had run and pooled under my eyes during my torrential crying. I couldn't even feel his touch. Happy and calm he was not.

"I tried to warn you, but there's no way to prepare you for it. This place messes with your mind. You'll see things that aren't real. It vomits misery, and strives to create it. I am sorry, Luna."

I was tired.

"I've got to get out of here," I said, and pushed my way to my bike. I strapped on my helmet and roared off, leaving them standing silently side by side, watching me.

Chapter Thirty-Five

I didn't think I had a destination in mind, but soon I found myself parking my bike near a rocky cove near the water. The sea always calmed me. Its homicidal anger made me feel like I was mellow in comparison.

I climbed down the rocks, careful not to slip and knock myself out. The way my day was going, that was a fairly likely scenario. Something reached out with a soft, black tentacle, and I kicked it with my boot.

"Uninvited," I said. It withdrew.

Mom had also loved the sea. It's one of the only things we had in common. She was soft and delicate with a quiet, gentle voice, not like me at all. She was everything I wished I had been.

She had died when Seth and I were still pretty young. Cancer. It didn't creep up on her like you always hear about. It came hard and swift and took her almost before we realized it. So fast she didn't have time to harden. She just wilted like a flower without enough water. Strangely beautiful and tragic at the same time.

Something pressed against the Mark. My shoulder blades drew in automatically.

"Uninvited," I said again with more force. "How many times do I have to tell you?"

"You're a prickly one, Luna. That's for sure."

I glanced up, watched Reed Taylor scrabble down to sit beside me. His hair caught the setting sun like flames. The sound of the water had masked his footsteps.

"I came out here to be alone," I told him pointedly. "I need to…process."

"I know you do, but you and I need to talk. You didn't let me get a word in edgewise back at the house. You just came in with both barrels blazing."

I should defend myself, but I was too tired. Too sad. I watched something swirl around in the water like ink. Like I said, lots of activity in the sea. It never stops.

"So what do you want to talk about?" I wasn't going to make this easy. Then again, I never do. I felt my frown deepen.

"Cecilia. Sparkles. We need to talk about it."

"I don't want to talk about it."

"Tough, Luna. We're talking. I hate that you're mad at me, but I hate it even more that you think I'd lie to you about Cecilia. I didn't know she was married when we dated. She told me she was a single mom, that there was no guy in the picture. And I didn't realize Cecilia was your Sparkles. She never called herself that, and you never called her by her real name."

"She doesn't deserve to be called by her real name."

"This bitterness isn't becoming."

"Screw you."

He reached out, put his arm around me. I tried to pull away, but then I leaned my head against his shoulder.

"I don't think you're a bad guy, Reed Taylor. In fact, I think you're one of the good ones. But you and Sparkles just blew me away."

"I know. And I'm sorry. I didn't realize what the problem was until you flat out told me before you left. I felt sick when I figured out I was the guy you were always talking about, the guy you hated so much for moving in on Seth's wife. You have to understand that I would never, never do something like that on purpose. I don't know a lot about family, Luna, but I value it. I wish I had one. I wouldn't go after somebody else's."

"So why did the two of you break up, anyway?" I wasn't sure I wanted to hear anything about his days with Sparkles. Maybe I'm just a masochist. Maybe I deserve to be punished for being a rotten person. Maybe I want to prove that I can take the lickin' and keep on tickin'.

"There were a few reasons."

"Hit me."

He tilted his head, listening to the sound of the waves. "I didn't like that she wouldn't let me come to the house. Of course I understand that now, but it seemed strange to me. I didn't like that she had a kid and I never even met her."

I blinked. "You never saw Lydia?"

"Not once. And that was cool for a while, you know. I mean, you don't want to go around introducing every guy you meet to your kid, and all that. It could get confusing for them. But to never meet her at all? Cecilia spent an awful lot of time away from home without her daughter, and that bothered me."

This wasn't as bad as I thought. I could get used to hearing Reed Taylor bag on Sparkles. "What else?"

He looked at me. "Look, we had our issues, but I don't think Cecilia is as evil as you'd like her to be."

I bristled. "Not evil? Did I describe the demon that has wrapped itself around her closer than even you did, my friend? I'd call that the epitome of evil. What, your angel never mentioned it?"

He pulled away. "Sorry, Luna, but I'm not gonna rise to the bait."

"I'm not baiting you." I was baiting him.

"Sure you are. That's what you do. I can roll with it; it doesn't bother me too much, but don't deny it. Cecilia isn't pure wickedness and you're no white knight. You two are much more alike than you realize."

My laughter startled a seagull perched nearby. It couldn't get away fast enough.

"Alike? How are we possibly alike? Besides our fine taste in men, of course."

His eyes were emeralds. "You both like to hurt. You're also the loneliest women I have ever met."

I pulled away. "I am not lonely."

"Not only lonely, but you're thorny. You keep everybody at a distance. You don't even call me by my first name."

The sun was starting to set. Maybe in another life it would have been romantic, but in reality it made my heart drop. The night would be stark. The activity would kick up. Reed Taylor wouldn't be able to sense any of the demonic hijinks. The thought made me feel more alone than ever.

"So are we cool?" he asked me. It was said nonchalant, but I could feel the tension in the muscles of his arm. He cared. What I said mattered. That's what made it so hard.

"No, Reed Taylor. We're not cool. I…I'm not sure if I can do this anymore."

He pulled back, looked at me. I turned my eyes away from his gorgeous greens.

"Because of Cecilia?" His voice was tight. "Because I was a user? Because I'm not good enough for you all of a sudden?"

Something ghosted past him, slid its misty form toward my face.

"Uninvited!" I screamed, and Reed Taylor and the thing both jumped.

"You didn't even sense that," I said dully. It was a statement, not a question, and I didn't like the weariness I heard in my voice.

"No. I didn't."

I took a deep breath, leaned back and looked at the stars that were appearing over the water. "That's the problem. We literally live in two different worlds. I'm dealing with this junk all of the time, and it's not even there for you. Do you know how frustrating that is?"

He snorted. "You think I don't know? There are two angels that have been following you ever since you parked your bike. In fact, that's how I found you. Sitting there and there." He pointed. "And you act like I'm the one who doesn't have a clue?"

Ouch. He had a point. "Is Demon Patrol one of them?"

He shook his head. "Haven't seen him around in quite a while. I was worried, to tell the truth, but now I wonder if it isn't time for him to go. Maybe he never planned to stick around forever, I don't know. I miss him, but I'm getting used to the idea. I thought, maybe it won't be so bad as long as I have Luna." He turned his blazing eyes on me and I couldn't get out from under them. "But I don't have you anymore, do I? You just don't know how to say it."

I didn't realize a tear had rolled down my cheek until the sea breeze chilled it. I wiped it away with the sleeve of my leather jacket. "I love you, Reed Taylor, and I know you realize how hard that is for me to say. But it isn't going to work. You see angels. I bet they're beautiful. But I see devils. They can hurt you and torment you, and you wouldn't have the slightest clue about what's going on. I mean, Sparkles. She's the worst of the worst, and you were in love with her. At your house, if you could have seen her…" I took a deep breath. "I have a lot to do right now. Save Lydia. Defeat Sparkles' demon. Protect my brother. And you're only getting in my way."

I wish I could say he looked stricken. He didn't. He went completely dead. "I'm in your way."

"Totally. I can't worry about myself and you, too. I don't have the energy."

"So you're breaking up with me because I can't see demons like you."

I frowned. "It sounds so stupid when you say it. It's totally reasonable in my head. It seems noble and responsible."

He stood up, stuffed his hands in his pockets. "It's stupid any way you look at it. But whatever, Luna. I'm done chasing after you. I can only take so much."

He turned and climbed up the rocky slope. I listened to the engine of his bike start and speed away. I felt the chill on my cheeks again, dashed the tears away.

The dark mist drifted my way again, drawn to the scent of the Tracing.

"Uninvited," I said firmly, and the harshness of my voice sounded horrifyingly cruel to me. I wondered if Reed Taylor was right, and there really were angels watching after me. If they weren't frightened away by the ugliness of my words, that is. "Uninvited" was getting far too easy to say, even to the ones I love most.

I rested my forehead on my knees and spent the rest of the evening trying not to cry.

Chapter Thirty-Six

So?" Seth said to me. He looked better than he had the last time I'd seen him. They must have slipped some perky meds into his breakfast. Now if only they'd give him some pants, things would be almost perfect.

"So I had a showdown with Sparkles' demon, but she wasn't there. And Lydia wasn't there, either."

His face fell. "You didn't see Lydia at all?"

I chose my words carefully. "Well, I thought I saw Lydia, but it turned out to be a demon instead. Wearing, you know, Lydia's form."

Seth's face went red. I wanted to smile because it was something that used to happen to my father, and Seth hated that it was passed on to him, but I wisely abstained. This girl has some brains, I tell you.

"Tell me what happened."

"Trust me, big bro, you don't want to know."

"Tell me."

His voice sounded like rusty metal, sharp and dangerous. I told him with as little detail as I could. It still made my voice shake and my hands clench, however. I watched Seth turn red and white in quick succession.

"You saw her die."

"But it wasn't really her."

He spit out a word then that I had never heard him use.

"Did you call an ambulance? The police? Where is she?" He started scrambling out of the bed. His IV caught and he snarled, pulled it out.

"What are you doing? I told you it wasn't really Lydia, just a demon who shape shifted to look like her. There's no need…" Then it hit me. "You don't believe me, do you?"

"Where are my clothes?" Seth yanked the stickers off of his chest. The machine next to the bed went crazy. "They have to have my stuff here somewhere." He started to rifle through cupboards.

"After all of this, you still don't believe me about the demons. You think I'm lying."

Seth turned to me, exasperated. "I don't think you're lying, Luna. I think you're unstable. My daughter is missing and you see her body lying on the floor of some house, and you just walk away? I don't care," he said, and I knew better to interrupt him, "that you think it wasn't really Lydia. You saw her, and I need to make sure my little girl isn't dead. Okay? Okay? Get it?"

I got it.

This wasn't the time to have hurt feelings. I started punching buttons on the monitor until the beeping stopped. "We don't have time to find your clothes, Seth. Just hold yourself closed. Let's go."

He grabbed the back of his hospital gown and I hurried him toward the door. We hustled down the hall until we passed the nurse's desk. I was hoping it would be unmanned, but no such luck. I put my arm around Seth like I was supporting him.

"Hi," I said brightly, strolling by. I gave the nurse my cheeriest grin. "Just taking him for his daily walk. I'm so glad you guys suggested walking around the floor. It's really helping his recovery."

"It does that," she said and smiled back. The phone rang and she turned to it.

"This way," I whispered, and Seth and I darted down a back hall toward the stairwell.

"This is so very unhygienic," he complained, grimacing at his bare feet as we thundered down the stairs. "Think of all the things that go on in the stairwell of a hospital."

"Shut it," I commanded. "I'm still furious at you right now."

"You know you'll forgive me later."

"Not hardly."

We burst out of the hospital. A security guard on a Segway eyed us suspiciously. Seth looked ready to push him down and speed away on his laughable machine if he tried to stop us.

As much as I cheered Seth's newfound fierceness, now wasn't the time.

"Excuse us," I said. "Tom here needs a cigarette in the worst way. They said he couldn't smoke inside the building, and I know we can't hang around the doors. Could you kind of point us…"

"That way," the security guard said. He nodded toward the parking lot.

"Thanks, man," Seth said. The guard nodded and zipped away.

"'Thanks, man?'" I asked. "Is that how a guy jonesing for a smoke talks?"

He glared at me. I shrugged and led him to my bike. He caught the helmet I tossed and climbed on behind me.

I did a double take. "Aren't you going to hold that gown closed? What, you're going to flash the entire city with your blinding skin?"

"I need both hands to hold on. I know how you drive."

A minute later we were on the road, my brother safely ensconced in his hospital gown and my leather jacket. Hopefully that would be enough to keep us from being pulled over for indecent exposure.

"How close is this house?" he yelled.

"Not too far. Relax. I'll kick up the speed."

I heard a shriek as I gunned the bike. I was still angry enough that it gave me a smug sense of satisfaction.

When we arrived at the house, he took a few shaky steps toward the front porch before he broke into a full run. He reached the door, and then spun to me, his face pained.

"It's locked," he said.

"Locked? No way," I answered, but he was already peering through the windows.

"It looks empty."

"There weren't any humans in it, if that's what you're asking."

"Close enough." He used his elbow and broke the front window.

"Hey! Watch my jacket," I said. My irritation was getting the better of me. He ignored me and cleared the broken glass away as best he could before crawling inside.

I took a deep breath before climbing in behind him, steeling myself for what I was going to see. My eyes adjusted to the dim light and I turned to find…nothing.

There wasn't anything here. No monsters, no blood, no disembodied voices. It was just a simple house with beige carpet. Not horrifying at all.

"Where was she?" Seth asked. His body was tensed like a predator before a strike.

"Here. She was here." My boots ate up the ground as I strode to the back room. The place was small, harmless. It was almost adorable. I threw open the closet and it was clean. Empty. "This was it."

Seth dropped to his knees, examined the carpet. "You said there was a lot of blood?"

I nodded. "Definitely. Here, and she was attacked over here." I moved to the center of the room. The carpet was pristine. "This whole area was saturated."

Seth sighed with relief and let his head fall to the floor. "The carpet isn't damp. There's no way somebody could have got the blood out so completely in such a short time."

I crossed my arms over my chest. "Oh, what? I wasn't lying?"

He slowly stood up, and I realized he was trembling. He had been terrified and here I was, acting like a jerk. Whether they were physically here or not, the demons were getting their hooks into me.

I stood in the center of the room and began to shout.

"Why are you doing this? What can you possibly gain from toying with me, you hateful, hateful things? Oh, it's fun to torment the sick girl, isn't it? It's fun to see if you can drive her mad."

"Luna." Seth grabbed my arm but I shook him off.

"I'm tired of your stupid games. You're a bunch of cowards, taking a little girl and then hiding away when I come after you. When I find you, I'm going to destroy you, do you hear me? I'll take you apart one by one, and you'll be sorry you ever messed with us."

"Stop, Luna. Just stop."

My fists were clenched, my chest heaving. I wanted to tear something to shreds with my bare hands.

Seth looked exhausted. From worry for Lydia. From dealing with me.

"Seth, I—"

"No, forget it. You're crazy with worry over Lydia. I am, too. We'll find her. I promise."

We rode home in silence. At least I comforted myself with the thought that things couldn't get any worse.

As usual, I was wrong.

An unmarked and a black and white were pulled into our driveway. Seth climbed off the bike, looking utterly ridiculous in his I-Just-Sprang-Outta-The-Hospital garb.

"Busted," I whispered. "The Segway security guy must have ratted us out. Man, that hospital takes its policies way too seriously."

"Are you Luna Masterson?" The detective didn't even flick an eye at my brother, but the officer looked him up and down.

"Sure am. What can I do for you, o' fine enforcers of the law?"

"We need to ask you a few questions. Do you know where Cecilia Masterson is?"

"Sparkles? Nope. I've been looking for her myself."

He looked grim. "She's been reported missing."

That got my attention. "Missing? But I just saw her. Where's Lydia?"

"I know you saw her, ma'am. An altercation was reported between the two of you."

Cripes. They didn't know I had actually hit her, did they? Or, and this was even worse, had gone after her with a knife? I felt myself pale. Reed Taylor was right: I had gone absolutely out of control back there. Was he the one who turned me in?

The detective's expression never changed. "We're going to need to ask you some questions, ma'am. Here or at the station, it's your choice."

"Here. Come in, guys." Hope there isn't anything incriminating lying around. Body parts, for instance. Demon bits.

I opened the door and led them inside. The officer turned to address my brother, his brown eyes narrowed.

"For crying out loud, put on some pants. There are minors in this neighborhood."

Seth's eyes met mine. They were full of worry. "I'm sure Lydia's fine," I told him. I grinned, but I didn't feel it. If even the police didn't know where Sparkles was, where was Baby Girl?

Chapter Thirty-Seven

They grilled me forever. Then they grilled Seth. Being the estranged ex of a missing woman made him a natural suspect.

"I'll answer any question you have," he said, dignity rolling off him in waves. "Just let me fetch some pants first."

After they left, I grudgingly headed to work. I wanted to call out more than anything, but Seth was taking an involuntary leave of absence from his job and the medical bills were gonna start rolling in. Besides, working with needles might soothe me.

Yeah, that was a nice thought, but stabbing didn't make me feel any better. I was kind. I slid the needle under my client's skin with grace and decorum.

It sucked. Literally.

I wanted to stab something good and hard. I wanted to find a demon, knock it to the ground, and demand it take me to Sparkles. As soon as I got off work, I was going to do some sleuthing of my own. I'll track her down, show up on whatever doorstep she was haunting and kindly ask for Lydia back. Who could resist my sweetness? Failing that, I would find other ways to be persuasive.

I was cleaning up my workspace when a shadow fell over my hands.

"What's up?" I said, looking up.

Nobody was there.

Suddenly my stomach flew around inside like lightning bugs. "Demon Patrol? Is that you?"

No answer, of course. Not that I expected any. But still, Demon Patrol was the only angel I could ever sense, and if he had stopped hanging around Reed Taylor, maybe it wasn't too far-fetched that he'd swing by to see me for a minute.

"Demon Patrol, if that is you, Reed Taylor has been missing you horribly. I broke up with him. I'm mad as sin at him for Sparkles, and I want to keep him safe and it seems like the right thing to do. It's… complicated. It's also making me miserable. I can't find Lydia. And I caught a glimpse of Sparkles' demon, and it was the biggest, darkest thing I've ever seen. And Seth nearly killed himself thanks to Demonic Sparkles."

My voice cracked, and I pulled myself together. I glanced around to see if anybody noticed me talking to an empty space in my office. Not yet. I lowered my voice.

"And if you aren't Demon Patrol, sorry. I don't really know how to deal with angels." Or people, for that matter. Only demons, and I don't even do that particularly well. If that isn't pathetic, I don't know what is.

The shadow didn't move. Neither did I. I just sat there feeling stupid. That'd been happening far too much for my liking lately. Where was the confident Luna who would just waltz into any situation and shoot off her mouth like a Fourth of July firework? I didn't know where she had gone. I missed her.

"I think I suck," I confessed to the shadow. "I used to be full of smart aleck swagger, and now I'm just full of loss. I was even thinking about knifing Sparkles, did you know that? Do you know what kind of person thinks about that sort of thing? Not me, that's for sure."

The shadow quivered in excitement or agitation, I couldn't be certain which. But it was most likely an angel, and angels were the good guys, so I chose agitation.

"Don't worry, I won't do it," I said in my most soothing and reassuring voice. It was my Good Luna voice. My Everything Will Be All Right, I Won't Slaughter Those You Love voice. "I totally won't knife anybody tonight. I promise. There. Feel better?" If I had cupcakes, I would have offered them to my agitated guest. It doesn't get any sweeter or nicer than that.

Blood. I thought. The image of something red and sparkling ran down the walls of my mind. The immediacy of the thought nearly made me gag. Blood. Blood.

"You can not be Demon Patrol! What kind of sicko angel are you? Uninvited, I say! Uninvited!"

Blood, blood, blood, blood, blood.

"I'm telling your mother," I admonished, gathering my things together. "She would be so ashamed of you. Bad little angel. Bad."

I stood up and put on my jacket. Ed, my boss, appeared behind me, silent as the night except for his heavy breathing.

"Luna, we have one more draw. Latecomer. Can you take him?"

The shadow shivered behind him. I sighed.

"Aw, Ed. I just closed my station. Is anybody else open?"

His red cheeks wobbled when he shook his head. "Nope. Just you. Do you mind?"

Of course I minded. I was stuck in a tiny office with a bloodthirsty angelic presence.

"Don't mind at all. Send him in."

"Thanks," he said. He dropped the paperwork on my desk. I slid out of my jacket and sat back down to look it over. "I appreciate it."

Ed was being decent today. Not lascivious or bug-eyed. The world has officially gone insane.

"Not a problem, Ed."

"Listen, since we're the last ones here, I wondered if you wanted to—"

"Bradley Guzman!" I bellowed out. "I'm ready for you right here. Come and get stuck."

"Right then," Ed said, and stepped out of the tiny room. I leaned my head back and closed my eyes.

Blood, blood, blood, blood! Blood! Blood, blood!

Cripes, welcome to crazy town! I felt somebody sit down in front of me, and I automatically smiled.

"So you must be Brad…" My voice trailed away. The tiny man had dark hair and a beautiful smile. He also had a demon wound around his neck.

"Hello," he said. His eyes danced. I nearly vomited on the floor.

"So, um, looks like a standard blood draw. Ain't no thing," I said, and forced my hands to steady as I reached for the alcohol and wipes. "Roll up your sleeve, please."

"Okay." The demon slithered its tongue in and out of Bradley Guzman's ear. I forced myself to breathe normally.

"How's your day going, Bradley Guzman?" I asked. I slid the needle easily under his skin. He didn't bat an eye. The demon glared at me once and then turned its attention back to its host.

"Pretty good, I guess," he said. I filled one vial. Two. I was nearly done, and then I spontaneously reached out for a third vial. It filled easily.

"Awesome to hear. Apply pressure here, please." I labeled the vials, taped the cotton pad over the tiny wound. "Good to go, my friend. Have a glorious day."

"Thanks. You, too." He left. The demon raked its claws through his hair. I held the three vials of blood in my hand.

Why had I done that? It had never happened before. What was I going to do with an extra vial of blood? And what would I tell Ed? "Whoops, I was just having so much fun watching his demon flirt with him, I could have gone on filling vials all day. Thank goodness I came to my senses, ha, ha, ha."

I'd have to dispose of it. I ran the two vials to the fridge, and surreptitiously slid the third into the pocket of my jacket. Suddenly I felt a purring sensation, and this time it wasn't the Mark reveling in my underhanded behavior.

Blood, the presence seemed to titter inside of my mind. I felt a twinge of emotion, both happiness and a sense of relief. Blood. Blood!

"Okay, you little savage," I muttered under my breath. "I could get fired for this. There had better be a darn good reason you have me siphoning from the demon horde. Angel has some 'splaining to do."

Blood. The presence disappeared.

I drove home carefully. I couldn't stop thinking about what type of woman would carry around a stranger's blood in her pocket. It wasn't comforting.

Chapter Thirty-Eight

I was sitting at the kitchen table staring at my ill-gotten vial of blood when the phone rang.

"Hey," Seth said. "I made a few phone calls today. I think we've been going about it all wrong. We'll never get Lydia back this way. We're going to have to make some changes to the plan."

I tossed the dark red vial from hand to hand. From the look of things, Bradley Guzman had an iron count that would make Tony Stark blush. He also needed to hydrate more, but it didn't seem in my best interest to track him down and let him and the demon know.

"What plan? The fight at OK Corral plan? Where I heroically find Lydia and snatch her away from the jaws of Demonic Sparkles?"

He sighed. "Yes. That plan. How's it working for us so far?"

I growled.

"Exactly."

"So what does the new and improved plan entail?"

He suddenly sounded very weary. "We have to look as stable as possible. Can you do that? Act like a fine upstanding citizen? I'll try not to kill myself and you don't act crazy."

I eyed the vial suspiciously. "I can do that." I think.

"Good. I'll be home in a few. Then we can talk."

I slid the phone back into my pocket and groaned. Of all the times to turn klepto about bodily fluids.

"What are you so down about?"

I shot upright, wrapping my fingers around the vial and hiding it from view.

"What are you doing here, Mouth?"

He flowed over, sat in the seat beside me.

"Hello to you, too."

Whatever. I still hadn't forgiven him for sending me into Hell House. I'd see Lydia's mutilated body in my mind's eye until the day I died. You don't just get over something like that.

"What do you want?"

He went even wispier than usual, but I didn't care.

"You don't sound very happy to see me," he said. The jauntiness was gone and he sounded hurt. Do demons even feel hurt?

"I'm not. I have a lot on my mind. I'm trying to act as perfectly normal as possible, for some mysterious reason that Seth will elaborate on later. That doesn't involve talking to you when he walks through the door, so say your piece and get out."

"You should be nicer to me." Simple words, but his tone made my breath catch. It sounded like ice and fog and darkness. It sounded like the voice of a demon with authority.

It made me afraid. I was tired of being afraid, and that just made me downright mad.

"Listen, you," I hissed, and jabbed my finger toward his chest. It was encased in the surging blackness that was building up around him. "I don't like being threatened, got it? Especially in my own house. I don't trust you." I jabbed him with my finger again. "I don't like your kind," jab, "and right now I don't like you. If you have something to say, then say it. If you don't, then leave. You aren't welcome here."

Mouth surged to his feet. He was taller than usual, black and angry. My instinct was to shrink back, but I countered that by standing straighter and putting both hands on the table to brace myself.

"You forget yourself, Luna. You forget who I am. You forget what I am. Do not anger me, human. I have more power than you."

"Get out," I yelled. The rage in my voice surprised me. "Just get out of here. Uninvited!"

The darkness blossomed out of him like a burst of pollen from a deadly flower. It filled the room and then receded back to his body, a sickly halo.

"I was going to tell you how to get Lydia back. It goes against everything I stand for, breaking every oath I took. I was going to do it for you. But you're not worth the eternity of torment that would have ensued. I can't believe I was so foolish. I'm only glad I realized it now."

The Mark seared between my shoulder blades and I dropped to the floor. The pain was so intense that I couldn't even pull myself to my knees. I gritted my teeth together to keep from screaming. The vial of blood fell from my hand and rolled across the linoleum.

Mouth looked at it and smirked. "Clever," he said. He shouted a word in a strange language and the vial shattered, spraying blood in a small circle on the floor. I closed my eyes and turned my face away, praying I didn't get any on me, that it wouldn't work its way into my mouth or my eyes.

"Look at you," the demon said, and the disgust in his voice hurt my stomach. "How could I have possibly thought you were worth it?"

He flowed backwards and through the door. The pain of the Mark and the terror was too much for me. I threw up on the floor, twice, and curled into a shivering ball.

The door opened again. I cringed, unsure if I would be able to stand another attack.

"Cripes," Seth said, dropping several grocery bags onto the kitchen floor. He surveyed the scene and blew out a breath. "I tell you that we need to act normal, and this is what I get?"

Chapter Thirty-Nine

Normal is as normal does.

The very next day I was sitting on a carefully neutral couch, staring into the face of a carefully neutral woman.

"What are you thinking?" Sheila the Counselor asked me. Her voice was, no surprise, carefully neutral.

I was thinking that I hated this place, and it was a shame to spend my lunch break doing something so banal. I was thinking that Seth's idea of playing by the rules totally bites, especially since it meant meeting with a counselor to see if we're crazycakes. I'm thinking that this broad could use a little pizazz, like some bright lipstick or highlights in her hair. That made me think of Reed Taylor, which made me think that I hate myself a little bit. And that made me mad, which made me hate everything else. A lot.

"I was thinking about how my motorcycle is in the shop, and how grateful I am to my kind brother for letting me borrow his car today. He's so caring and responsible."

I tuck my combat boots neatly together and smiled demurely at the woman. She almost smiled back, but not really.

"Luna, you know why we're here."

"Yes."

"Why don't you tell me in your own words?"

Be normal, be normal, be normal.

"You're here to determine if my brother and I are stable enough to parent Lydia."

She blinked her eyes at me. I blinked back.

"Do you think you are?"

"Yes."

The clock ticked. Inaction makes me fidgety. Personally, I like my idea better, which was to track Sparkles down using dogs or dark denizens of the night, and then beat her to a bloody pulp with a baseball bat.

"What are you thinking now?" she asked me.

"Well, Sheila, I'm putting together a shopping list in order to make a healthful, nutritious dinner. I'm heading from here to work, and then to the store. I find it useful to multitask."

After wreaking vengeance on Sparkles, I'd drop Lydia off with Seth. While he was busy packing so we could flee, I'd take out Reed Taylor's mailbox out of spite. Maybe get a hit or two on his bike. Following that, I'd whisper sweet things to Mouth until he was calm enough to be happy and fairly substantial. Then I'd break his legs.

"And what is on your grocery list?"

My eyes gleamed with sincerity. "Broccoli. It's versatile enough to work in several meals and robust enough to last in the fridge. And I could use the iron. I'm a little deficient."

While Mouth cursed my existence, I'd head over here and knock Counselor Lady's block off. Take out all of the windows and definitely that wolf-howling-at-the-moon picture. I mean, seriously? Who decorates like that, for real?

"Tell me about the time you and your brother found your father's body."

The mental me immediately ceased all carnage and dropped her baseball bat. The literal me gaped from the couch.

"Wow," I said. "Way to go for the jugular."

The counselor arched her brow. "We weren't getting anywhere with the nicey-nice talk. Iron deficiency? Please."

I bowed my head. "I concede defeat, my valiant foe. It seems I underestimated you."

She laughed. "Most clients do. It's this cursed beige room. There isn't anything I can do about it. Anyway, tell me about that time, Luna. We won't have time to get into a lot, and this is just an initial assessment, but I sense that gaining custody of your niece is very important to you, and you don't seem the type to waste time playing games. Do I have you pegged?"

"Completely. Tell me what I can do to hurry this along."

"Tell me about that incident."

I didn't want to, but I didn't want to lose Lydia, either. I described it tersely. Seth screaming for me. Him holding onto Dad's legs to support him while I climbed the chair, stood on tiptoes, and sawed at the rope tied around his neck. The letter pinned to his chest, calling us both by name and telling us he was sorry.

The counselor listened carefully. "Surely you have formed some theories as to why your father chose to end his life. Do you feel comfortable sharing them with me?"

"No. Will it help me get Lydia back?"

Sheila smoothed down the arm of her already smooth chair. "Transparency and honesty always work in your favor. If you're resistant and secretive, others will often wonder what you have to hide."

I cursed inwardly. This was hitting far too close to home.

"Dad...thought he saw things. Angels and demons." I chose my words carefully. "I think it eventually became too much for him."

"Do you believe there is any credibility to these visions of your father?"

This was it, the moment of truth. Do I say, "Heck no, my father was completely bonkers." It hurt me to even think the words. But the second I said, "Why, sure, I see demons, as well. In fact, your receptionist seems to have a couple locked securely into the back seat of her car," I could kiss Lydia goodbye.

I thought back to what Seth had told me this morning. "I love you," he said, and this admission shocked the words out of me. He looked me in the eyes. "Please come across as normal, Luna. It's the only way I'll get my daughter back."

I faced the counselor firmly. "I believe he thought he saw the things that he told us. I don't think he was lying. But actual beings from another realm?" I shook my head, and felt my heart break inside. "I love my father very much, but I think he was unstable."

Sheila's eyes were piercing. "How do you feel about your brother?"

I laughed, but didn't sound like myself. "Seth is the most stable guy I know. A real 9 to 5, by-the-book type of guy. He doesn't deal in hallucinations. He took a couple of different jobs in order to support Lydia after Sparkles left. He would do anything for Sweet Girl. He adores her."

"Why do you think he attempted to end his own life?"

I felt my face change. It felt like steel. "Sparkles came to see him right before. She physically took Lydia away, and told Seth he wasn't a good father. I think he wasn't strong enough to handle her on his own. That woman," I said honestly, "is absolutely demonic."

"Harsh words."

"Harsh woman. Seriously, I don't think she has a soul."

The counselor blinked owlishly. "And why would you say that? Has she ever mistreated Lydia?"

I picked at my black fingernails. "Mistreated? No. More like ignored. Lydia simply didn't exist to her. If Sweet Girl was hungry or scared or needed changed, Seth did it. Sparkles brought Lydia out every now and then to get a discount at a store, or look good to somebody, but the second she couldn't get anything more out of her, Lydia was dropped off with her daddy. Seth was knocking himself out, trying to support the three of them and be a full-time parent. It devastated him when Sparkles left, but I think maybe he was a little relieved, too."

"Why do you think he might have been relieved?"

I hate biting my nails, which is why I polish them. It didn't stop me, though. "Sparkles feels…she feels like a storm, right? A big, heavy storm that's going to blow through and rip everything apart. She's always building up to a meltdown. And when she was gone, I think maybe Seth could breathe a little. Now he only had to worry about Lydia, not deflecting Sparkles. Does that make sense?"

She didn't answer the question. Counselors.

"And this is when you moved in? To help Seth care for his daughter after Sparkles left?"

Suddenly I saw myself how she must see me. Dark smudged eyeliner, black hair with streaks of color. I was wearing torn jeans, my favorite pair of boots, and my AC/DC t-shirt. I looked like some ragamuffin from the '80s. I didn't look like I could parent anybody.

"Listen," I said, and I sat up straight. I wrapped my hands tightly in my lap to hide my bitten nails. "I know I don't look like much. I come across like some smart aleck wayward child, and I get that, I do. But I love Lydia. I love her more than I ever thought it was possible to love anybody. I may not be the best at cooking and, I don't know, doing those crazy little girl French braids that all of Lydia's playmates have, but I do my best. I haven't seen her in a long time, and I miss her. It freaks me out knowing Sparkles took her. I don't know if she's left in a dark room somewhere when Sparkles goes out, or if she's getting enough to eat, or if Sparkles knows she likes to have three songs before bed. Three." I held up my fingers.

"Which three songs?"

I dashed tears from my eyes with the back of my hand. "Sleep Tight. It's one my father used to sing to Seth and me when we were little. And then Twinkle Twinkle Little Star. And then How Much Is That Doggy In The Window. All three, in that order. And she's scared of the dark, so she sleeps with a flashlight. I mean, how is Sparkles going to know that? It's not like she called to ask. It's not like Lydia can tell her. I bet she just throws her on the sofa or something and calls it a night."

"Talking about this is making you emotional."

I sniffed, hard. The counselor handed me a tissue. I took it grudgingly.

"I'm sorry."

"There's nothing to be sorry about."

"I don't usually cry."

"Crying is not a weakness."

"Sure it is."

"Did you cry when your father died?"

I pursed my lips together. "Are we back to this? Didn't I just bare all with Lydia? Can't we talk about my lovely nutritious, broccoli-rich dinner that I was telling you about before?"

"What is your main concern with Lydia?"

I stopped and thought. Did I think Sparkles was really going to physically hurt her? Normally I'd say no, but that glance at her demon made me want to scream and hide under the floorboards. She was unpredictable. She could hurt Sweet Little Girl. I could never see her again. She wouldn't understand what was going on, why I never came for her.

"I never had a chance to say goodbye."

"And this concerns you?"

"I don't want her to think Seth and I just abandoned her."

"Like your parents abandoned you?"

"That's different."

"Tell me about your best friend."

"Wha—" This broad made my head spin. What was she getting at? "Best friend? I don't have one right now, I guess."

"I see. Somebody that you're seeing romantically?"

"Kinda. We just broke up."

"Who initiated the breakup?"

I eyed her. "I did."

"I see. No friends at all?"

I didn't like where this was going. Did I not sound like I had a strong enough support system? Was I not sounding stable enough?

"Well, I do. Have friends, you know. Acquaintances. And one was pretty close for a while. His name is Mouth, but then, uh…" I looked at the floor. "I sort of drove him off."

Her lips barely curved, but I saw it. "Has it occurred to you that perhaps you hold people at bay because you don't want them to leave you? That perhaps you abandon them before they have the chance to abandon you?"

I blinked. "That doesn't sound stable at all. Am I totally jacked up? Did I screw up Seth's chance to get Lydia back?"

"Take a deep breath, Luna."

I shook my head. "No, listen to me. Yes, yes, abandonment issues, okay? I know how it feels to be left behind and Lydia will never, ever feel that way, not if I can help it. I'm a mess, whatever. But just tell me what I need to do. Dude, I'm already coming to therapy. I'll tell you about my childhood, I'll take prescribed zombifying drugs. I'll even move out of the house if Seth is better off without me. But please, let me show you how stable I can be. I love Lydia more than life. I'll do whatever it takes to make her happy, and if that was with Sparkles, then I would leave her there. But that's not where she belongs. She belongs with her daddy. Tell me how to bring her home."

I looked at my nails again. Ragged. Torn. Bitten down to the quick except for the right pinky finger. I hadn't worked my way there yet.

The counselor was smiling, this time genuinely. "I think that was a very honest, sincere expression of your feelings. It didn't sound unstable at all."

"Yeah?" I studied her face and leaned back in my chair. I arched my brow. "You totally pinned me down. I'm not used to that."

"You mean I called you on your crap?"

I grinned. "Yeah, well, I've been told I can be a bit resistant to criticism."

She looked wry, and suddenly I saw how she might have been in her youth. Somewhat rebellious, somewhat knee-jerk. Somewhat like me.

"Resistance isn't necessarily a bad thing," she said. "You don't want to change for everybody that suggests it. But it's like the old saying about the wind in the trees. Sometimes you need to know when to bend."

Chapter Forty

Therapy must be good for you. You hardly look homicidal at all."

"Ha ha, big brother."

I threw myself into an empty chair and tossed the car keys to Seth. He was crouched over the kitchen table, doing his ceaseless paperwork. Filing for custody, filing to see Lydia whenever she was found, doing whatever he could. Truth was, I was feeling pretty good. I wouldn't say the counselor was playing for Team Luna, per se, but she wasn't running around with the demonic hordes. That was a step in the right direction.

I looked at Seth. "Don't repeat this, and if you do I'll deny saying it, but I think that things might eventually turn out after all."

"I wouldn't count on it."

I was out of my chair so fast that Seth nearly fell over. Papers scattered everywhere. "What's wrong? What's going on?" he asked.

Mouth was standing in the doorway. He looked equal parts grim and angry.

"What are you doing here?" I asked. My hands were balled against my sides. "Planning to tell me how worthless I am again? Because I'm warning you, I'm not in the mood."

"Chill," he said and glided to the table. He eyed Seth's papers. "Still doing things the good old fashioned way, huh? Playing by the rules.

How noble."

"Get out."

Seth's head snapped back and forth. "Who are you talking to? Who's here?"

"Cute," Mouth said and yawned. He put his ghostly feet up on the table. "Your brother thinks you're losing your marbles right in front of him. Better calm him down before his heart explodes from the stress."

I rolled my eyes. "Seth, this is Mouth. I've mentioned him before. I kind of hate him at the moment. But sit down. I'll let you know if there's anything to worry about."

Seth trembled a minute, then sank down in his chair, looking defeated. I glared at him.

"He's as real as you are." I turned to the demon. "You've got brass, coming back after your threatening 'I am a demon of authority' gig last time. Got something to say? Say it, and then get out."

"Can it, princess. I'm not here to talk to you. I'm here for your brother."

"You're…what?"

"Knew that would get ya."

"You want to talk to Seth?"

Seth's jaw fell to the floor. "It wants to talk to me?"

Mouth shook his head. "Are you two dunderheads finished acting related? Because this is important, and we don't have much time. Luna, you're going to have to translate. Ol' unbeliever here gave up his chance at hearing me out a long time ago."

"Seth, he says that…huh?" My gaze snapped onto Mouth. "What do you mean, gave up his chance?"

"Gave up my chance for what?" Sweat was beading Seth's face now, and Mouth's prediction for Seth's exploding heart didn't seem too far off.

"Hey, calm down," I said, and put my hand on Seth's shoulder. "Listen,

I'm mad at Mouth at the moment, but I think I pretty much trust him. For the most part. Kinda. Like, for a demon." Maybe not as reassuring as I had hoped to be. I rubbed my eyes and tried again. "He's cool. If he wants to talk to you, I'd do it." I spoke without looking at the demon. "What do you want me to tell him?"

"Tell him this whole thing has just gone up another level. Lydia's in danger."

"How much danger?"

"Tell him."

I swallowed hard, looked Seth in the eyes. "Mouth said Lydia's in danger, that everything is stepping up."

Seth cleared his throat. "What do I do?"

"Tell him there has to be a showdown. It's going to be hard and it's going to be ugly. He has to be there for Lydia during this. More than that, he has to be there for you."

I nodded. "Tough showdown. You have to be there for Lydia and me." I glanced over my shoulder at the demon. "What else?"

His lips were tight. "He has to be strong. Tell him that. He has to be stronger than he's ever been. It doesn't matter how sorry he is. That isn't going to be good enough. He needs power built out of strength, not guilt. Got it?"

"Sure. No guilt strength. But sorry? Sorry for what? It isn't his fault Sparkles—"

Mouth's darkness blazed around him, blasted across the room like a bomb. "Just deliver the message, Luna!"

"Okay, okay! Geez, Mouth, you don't have to be such a... All right, Seth. Mouth here says you have to be strong, and it isn't good enough to be sorry. Or whatever."

Seth's face was a horrifying shade of white. "Sorry for what?" he whispered. "What should I be sorry for?"

I shrugged. "Beats me. Mouth?" I turned toward the demon again, but he wasn't in his seat. He was half an inch from my face, staring at Seth intently.

"Holy crap, you scared me, you twist!" I shrieked. "And you're freaking Seth out. Stop being cryptic and just tell me already."

Mouth slowly turned to me, and his eyes were unreadable. He seemed to be struggling, but not necessarily with himself. He made a choking sound.

"Hey. Hey, are you all right?" I reached for him but there was nothing firm to grab onto. He was all wisp and night mist, gagging on his words and shivering like he was having a difficult time holding himself together. By the way the darkness flowed from him like blood, I think that was exactly the case.

"Tell him…he needs to…"

The shivers turned into convulsions. I grabbed at his arms, tried to cup his face in my hands. "Mouth! What can I do? Tell me what to do."

"T-tiptoe…" I repeated as the demon spit it out. Something started scratching at the corner of my memories.

"Tiptoe?" Seth sucked in his breath, but it barely registered. The shine of Mouth's eyes told me that they were rolling back in his head. Can a demon have seizures? Can they kill him?

"Mouth!" I screamed, and I was done. Done with the anger and the hurt and the grudges I was holding. I wanted him. I wanted him back and on my side. "Don't leave me. How can I help you? Tell me, please."

"Make him tell you…Tiptoe Shadow." He was fading. His black robes were turning gray.

"Tiptoe Shadow. Why does that sound…? Got it. He'll tell me. Just hold on, okay? I'll find a way to take care of you. I'll figure something out…"

A crash. Seth was passed out cold on the floor. I reached for him, and the remaining demon mist disappeared like fog.

I vaguely recalled teeny tiny feet. Whispers in the dark of night. That, mmm, laugh.

Seth's breathing was loud in the silent room. I nudged my brother gently with the toe of my boot. He didn't budge. My hands felt horrifyingly empty where I had tried to hold onto Mouth.

I was alone again.

The darkness comes when you're alone.

Chapter Forty-One

It took Seth about sixty seconds to come to. I was ready.

"Tell me about this Tiptoe Shadow."

He moaned, touched the back of his head where he had hit the floor. "I want a drink. Do we have anything to drink? Whisky? Vodka?"

"Since when have you touched a drop? Stop stalling and tell me about this shadow. Now."

His face was dangerously white. Part of me said to stop riding him so hard, and the other part said to heck with it, press the guy until he squawks. I don't know what exactly was going on with Mouth back there, but it had been major. And it had been ugly.

"Did…did this demon really say to tell you about the Tiptoe Shadow? I mean, did it use that name?" He turned huge eyes on me, and suddenly Seth seemed decades younger. It scared me.

"Yes. That name exactly." I watched him carefully.

He sighed, and it was such a hollow, broken sound. Chilling, really, especially from Pulled-Together Seth.

"Hey, are you hungry?" I asked too brightly. "Want some popcorn while we talk about this?"

Nervous energy had me moving about the kitchen. I grabbed the popcorn and stuffed it unceremoniously into the microwave. I tapped my fingers on the countertop as I waited for the bell to ding.

"Listen, Luna, I have a story to tell you. It…it isn't easy. Will you hear me out?"

I was almost irritated. "Of course I'll hear you out! I've been trying to drag it out of you ever since you woke up from your fainting spell. How's your head by the way? Need an aspirin?"

It was like he didn't even hear me.

"When I was little, and you were just a baby, something used to creep into my room," he said. I stopped my pacing and relentless finger tapping. He had my attention.

"Something like what?" I asked him. I didn't realize I was holding my breath.

"Something dark. Something hunched over that came on its tiptoes."

I was chilled. This was familiar but I was pretty sure I had never mentioned my old nightmares to Seth. "Did it have a face?" I asked carefully.

He looked at me with those too big eyes. "You know it didn't."

The microwave dinged heroically, but I didn't move toward it. I leaned against the counter and crossed my arms over my chest.

"You actually saw him."

"I actually saw him," he agreed. "Every night. He'd come in and say things. The most horrible things, in the strangest, most bizarre way. His voice was like air. Like someone breathing cold. I tried to tell Mom, but she said it was a nightmare. Too many scary shows, and so we stopped watching TV at night."

"Did you ever mention it to Dad?"

Seth snorted. "Of course not. Mom said it was nothing. And Dad? He had enough to worry about, you know. He didn't need to know his son was…"

"Crazy."

He flinched when I filled the word in for him.

"Yeah. That."

I took a big breath of the festive, popcorn scented air. It didn't make me feel any better. "I didn't know you could see him, Seth. I thought I was the only one who could. But not until later. I don't remember him until I was about four or five."

"You were four. Four years old. Far too young to deal with the things you had to deal with. But even then, you were stronger than I was. I knew you could handle it. At least, I hoped you could handle it."

"But why didn't you tell me you saw him, too? It would have been such a relief to talk to you about it!"

His eyes darkened. "I couldn't see him by then. Things had changed." When he looked up, his gaze was intense.

"We had a pond in our backyard. Do you remember?"

I shook my head.

His words came out in a rush. "You were pretty young. The Tiptoe Shadow used to mention that pond every night. Saying there was magic in the water, that I should go put my face in there and look. I didn't like the way he leaned close. Remember how he leaned close?"

"I remember."

"And one day I finally just begged him to stop, that I'd do anything if he'd leave me alone. He looks at me all serious, and he says, 'You'll do anything? Give me anything? How about your sister?'"

My arms chilled. My mouth went dry. The microwave chirruped again, but I couldn't move.

Seth rushed on. "I told him I couldn't give up my sister. I loved you, you know? I mean, who knew where he'd take you, what he'd do? And he starts to laugh in that way of his. Do you remember? Where there's sound but no sound, and it makes you want to throw up?"

I couldn't say anything, so I nodded.

"He laughs and he says he won't take you away, that it's more fun to have you here to feel things and smell things and hear things. He said he'd tell you all kinds of things, and he'd leave me alone if he can visit you."

I was torn between wanting to throw my arms around Seth as this scared little boy, and punch him in the face. "You didn't. Make an arrangement, I mean. You couldn't. Trade me for you?"

His face told me everything I need to know. I turned away.

"He told me there were more of them, Luna. More than just him. He said they'd all come, that they walked and flew and rode the currents and had legs…"

I whirled back around. "They do. And tentacles and they scream and sometimes they laugh and they even sob. They're in the water. They're outside. They came into the house and they're always frickin' here. Are you telling me I didn't see them before, that I wouldn't see them at all if only you had been a braver boy? Or loved me more?"

"I did love you." He jumped up, tried to grab my arm but I pulled away. "I loved you more than anyone. Still do, except for Lydia. But I'm not strong enough, Luna. Even when you were smaller than me, just a little girl, you were stronger. More courageous. I knew you could handle it better than I could. I mean, look at you. You're practically a warrior."

"Did it ever occur to you that I don't want to be a warrior?" I was yelling now, but I didn't care. "I have to be this way, Seth, because I spend my whole life being attacked from all sides. Yes, even you," I said, when he tried to deny it. "You threw me to the wolves when I was just a kid. You were my big brother and should have protected me. And then," I said, my voice getting even louder as realization hit, "you acted like you didn't believe me when I tried to tell you about the demons. You had me thinking

I was crazy, when you knew they existed. You knew. How could you?"

"I'm sorry," he screamed back. His intensity matched my own. "I don't know how to fix it. I don't know what to do."

"I have to get out of here." I stormed outside. Great, my bike was in the shop, and I'd left Seth's car keys on the table. I stomped down the road. Seth ran after me.

"Wait! It's the middle of the night, and it's going to rain. You can't go."

"Watch me," I said.

"We need to figure this out."

"Forget it," I said, and the look I shot him stopped him in his tracks. "Stay away from me, Seth. I don't want to talk to you."

He looked stricken, but I didn't care. I blew through a pack of demons without even thinking twice. They blinked benignly after me.

I almost hate you for this, I thought to my brother, and I felt the Mark burn.

Chapter Forty-Two

Seth was right about the rain. It started when I was about half a mile from the house. I could feel the anger on my face and my mascara was surely running. I had to look like a lunatic.

I snorted. The irony of it was that I had been trying so hard to be normal. Not just lately, but always. Life isn't kind to outcasts, and nobody is on the fringes more than the Demon Girl. And Seth knew? Had caused it.

I couldn't think about it anymore. My head would explode, and I would murder my brother. Besides that, Seth was the only person in the world I had at the moment. No matter how angry I may have been, I still loved him.

Although there are different levels of love, and he'd just dropped down a few hundred pegs. Bottom rung love. Subterranean love.

A demon wisped by. It had the body of human and the head of a dog. Great. Just what I needed: another reminder of demonic Lydia's wolf murderer. Like that scene hadn't already played itself out in my head a zillion times today.

Mouth did try to warn me, I thought, and suddenly I knew what I had to do. Wandering around in the cold rain wasn't going to do me or my temper any good. I had something better in mind.

"Hey, Anubis," I shouted to the demon. It turned its strange canine eyes on me.

"Yeah, you. I have a question about something that happened to a friend. Think you can answer it?"

It drifted close. Too close. Rain dripped off its muzzle and ran down its fur. I wanted to pull away and give myself some space, but I didn't want to appear intimidated, so I glared instead.

"Why would I help you, Luna? You are so disdainful of my kind."

I sighed. Of course it knew me. They all knew me. I was a dark superstar.

"Not all of your kind, dog-face. I actually want to help one of you. I think he may be in trouble."

"And I care because?"

"Uh, because demons of a feather must stick together?"

He barked, showing yellow teeth that made my breath catch in my throat. Hopefully he couldn't hear it under the rain.

"I don't think so." He closed his eyes, sniffed the air. "Mmm. You smell delicious. Perhaps I should do all of us a favor and put you out of your misery."

That gave me an idea.

"Really? Delicious? How delicious?"

He whimpered, more dog than man.

"That delicious? What if I told you I have the Mark? Your precious demon Tracing?"

His tongue ran around his chops. Gross.

"What if I also told you—"

"Yes?"

"That if you give me the information I need, I'll let you feel the Tracing?"

His eyes snapped open, pupils dilated.

"But," I said, and held my hand up, "only for five seconds. If you don't back off in five seconds, we're going to have a problem. Got it?"

His face was sly. "Oh, five seconds will be more than enough."

So he thought. He wasn't counting on my willpower or my anger.

"Let me see it," he whined. "Let me see the Mark."

"Uh, uh, uh." I wagged my finger. "Information first. Do we have a deal?"

He sneezed. "Deal."

Talk about making a deal with the devil. I pushed my soaking hair behind my ears. "Okay, so here it is. My demon buddy was in the middle of giving me DL on something, when—"

"DL?"

Oh yeah. This guy was more into Ra than the Urban Dictionary. "He was giving me the down-low. Some advice. A tip. Whatever."

"All right." His eyes were half closed. He was in La-La Land, deep in fantasies of possessing my soul and riding around in my body until it fell apart like the piece of meat that it was. I'd be lying if I didn't say that chilled me.

"Hey, Fang, I'm onto you and your little doggie desires. But no info, no Marky Mark, dig?"

"I understand."

"Okay. So anyway, in the middle of telling me this information, he started to really have a hard time. Struggle. Couldn't get the words out. And then—"

The demon interrupted. "He physically couldn't get the words out? As if he was choking?"

"Yes! And then he started going into convulsions. It was absolutely terrifying. What can cause that sort of damage to a demon?"

He shook his head, water flinging everywhere. "I would rather not say."

"But you know."

"I suspect, yes. But it is not something I care to share. Least of all with a human."

I shrugged nonchalantly. "Hey, no skin off my nose. I was just curious. See ya later. My deliciousness and I will take ourselves elsewhere."

I turned to walk away.

"Wait!"

Right on cue. I paused, looked over my shoulder. "What?"

"The Mark."

"No go. I said you could touch the Tracing if you gave me info. You didn't give me a thing. Now back off before I call the pound."

I started walking again, my boots splashing through the puddles. I knew what he was thinking. Obviously he didn't want to tell me what he knew, but the draw of the Tracing between my shoulder blades was too strong. And if he could slide his fingers in there, he'd most likely be able to take over my soul, so he thought. More than that, he'd be able control my body. He didn't know I knew how to resist him, that I was stronger than he suspected. That would come as a nice surprise.

I stretched exaggeratedly, the muscles rolling under my skin. I popped my neck, and yawned. Oh, to be able to do such things. Oh, to walk down the street and have normal, everyday people see him. Oh, the power.

"I'll tell you what you want to know. I need the Mark. I have to dig my claws into it."

"Spill," I told him. "What was happening to my friend?"

He chuffed, his black nose quivering. "He didn't happen to be telling you about another demon, did he? Somebody more powerful than he?"

I thought. "He was telling me to ask about someone called the Tiptoe Shadow. Do you know who he is?"

His long ear flopped in irritation. "How am I supposed to know? You humans and your silly names. That isn't important. What's important is that he was obviously betraying one of the Others."

This had my attention. "The Others?"

He growled. "The Others, the Builders, the Elders. Older than time, creators of all of us. You can't betray the Others. It's—"

"What, a sin? Don't make me laugh."

You never want to feel the full hate of a demon's glare. I was experiencing it now. "Tread carefully, human. You know not of what you speak. There are laws, and they must not be broken."

I nodded grudgingly. "Gotcha. So betraying the Others. Betraying them how? He just wanted to me to learn about this guy, that's all. How can that be such a bad thing?"

"We do not speak of those higher in our line. It is forbidden."

I started. "In your line? Like, you guys are sired or something?"

"Merely soldiers. There is a rank. We do not challenge or betray those who come before. There is a strict penalty."

I grew cold, and it wasn't from the rain. "What kind of penalty?"

"I have said too much. The Mark, Luna. Do not forget we made a deal."

I wasn't going to get any more out of him, but this was enough. I was pretty sure I knew where Mouth was. And I wasn't looking forward to going after him. And honestly? I wasn't looking forward to this impending scuffle with Old Yeller here, either.

I shrugged out of my leather jacket, turned around and pulled up my shirt. He moaned and ran his hands over the throbbing wound between my shoulders.

"I keep my promises. And don't you forget you only have five seconds, or I'm gonna get real angry. Got that? Go."

His fingers dove into the Mark with such violence that I was taken by surprise. I hadn't expected him to turn solid so quickly. He pushed me down to the sidewalk, his knee in the small of my back.

"Hey," I tried to shout, but couldn't get the word out. I was choking on the rainwater that ran in streams down the sidewalk. This wasn't going how I had planned.

"Your soul, it's so inviting. It wants to be taken, don't you see?" He did his dog-moan again, and I struggled against him. I felt the top layer of my spirit peel away. How had he gotten through so fast? Why were my defenses so thin?

"Enough! Your five seconds are up." He didn't move, but leaned into the Tracing with his full weight. I screamed. Another layer of soul was rent. I felt anger and desire and a terrifying sense of need fill my body. Those weren't my emotions. They were coming from him.

"Uninvited!" I shrieked. "Uninvited." I was panicking. I didn't expect to be pinned underneath him; that changed everything. How was I supposed to fight my way out of it when I was stuck in a vulnerable position like this?

"What a wonderful surprise you're turning out to be," he murmured in my ear. "After all of these years, who knew I would have a body again? And you were so willing to hand it over. It really wasn't a struggle at all."

Another layer of soul tore apart, shredding like fabric. I could almost hear it. Nobody had ever dug down this deep. I bucked, tried to yank him off of me, but he was too heavy. He was panting, his breath hot and steaming in the weather. I felt a wildness build up in me, his personality merging with my own. I wanted to sink my teeth into warm flesh until blood ran across my tongue.

"That's right," he said. "That's what we'll do. Who first, Luna? Shall we find a store with strangers? Shall we go back to your house and lap the blood from the throat of your brother?"

I closed my eyes in want. That sounded so good. So good.

"Ah, I see he has betrayed you. It is time to even the score, yes? Time to go on the hunt. Think how the taste of his flesh will fill you. And after the blood of your blood, who shall we pursue?"

Reed Taylor. My stupid boss. Sparkles.

"Yesssss," he hissed, and burrowed down even deeper. "All of them, one by one. Or in a pack. And then we shall go for the softest one, yes? Tender. The pup. The child. Think how her skin will rend, how she will fill our jaws nicely, how her tiny body will feel as we shake, shake, shake her, and bury her bones in the soft dirt. The child. Let us go for the child."

The child? Lydia. He wants to hurt my Lydia.

He licked my ear, but my scrambled thoughts were righting themselves.

"The child?" I asked. I laid still on the concrete, water running over my split lip and broken nose. The dog demon leaned closer.

"The little one. Little ones are so tender, and the sound they make as they die..."

He didn't have time to finish. My elbow cracked up into his sensitive snout. He grunted and rocked back. I flipped onto my side, bending his arm painfully, and punched him in the snout again.

His fingers ripped from the Tracing, and I was disgusted to find I missed the feel of him, missed the rush of heated emotion that pulled from me. Disgust and horror gave me strength. I rolled on my back and kicked him, once, twice, in the head. My boot connected solidly in his ribs, and he sprawled backwards, howling. I clambered to my feet.

"You won't touch her," I spat out between kicks. "She is not for you. I may be flirting with darkness myself, and think horrible things, but I would never, never, never," I accentuated each word with another kick, "hurt her!"

He curled into a ball, whimpering. I realized I should have felt sorry for him, but the anger humming in my veins felt too good. With each passing second, he was fading away into mist, and I wanted to hurt him for as long as I possibly could. Make him feel it. Break his legs and make him limp home, sorry he had met me. Sorry he knew my name.

Blood flowed from his snout, dark and red, and the thick heat of it burned in my throat. Could demons bleed? Is that even possible? I took a step back from him, breathed deep, and really looked.

One eye was swollen shut. He was breathing quickly, shallowly, his tongue lolling from his mouth. His skin was slick with rainwater and blood.

Blood. It reminded me why that vial of demon's blood had been so important to Demon Patrol. Obviously he knew something I didn't. I needed to talk to Reed Taylor, see if he had any answers.

I swallowed hard and wiped my mouth with my hand.

"You'll never touch her," I said uselessly.

He was fading away now, nearly translucent. I wanted to look away from his ravaged body, at the things I'd done to him, but I couldn't make my eyes do what I asked them to. They ran over his bloodied muzzle and his trembling hands.

I never thought I would go this far, but maybe Seth knew. He was too delicate to handle the demons, but maybe he had seen a monster in me that I hadn't known was there. I could see why he had made that trade, after all.

Anubis spat at me. "You can't hide what you are. Your bloodlust is apparent. You only make things easier for us."

"But I don't normally—"

He laughed, the sound jarring and unnatural coming from a twisted animal's maw. "You don't know who you are anymore, Luna. But I do."

He turned away from me, and faded out of view. I stood there in the rain, watching the water wash the thin stream of his blood from the pavement.

I had lost myself. Again.

I spun on my heel, striding as fast as the bumps and bruises would let me. This wasn't going to end here. I had to do get some help. I had to save Mouth. I had to save Lydia. Perhaps by doing this, I'd save myself.

I burst into the house with my usual grace. Seth was sitting with his head in his hands.

"Luna!" He ran over, threw his arms around me. "I'm so sorry. I know I can't take back anything I've done, but I—"

"Can it. You're forgiven. Listen, I need some backup to keep me from turning into an animal. I'll be back soon."

He blinked. "It's the middle of the night. Where are you going?"

I felt my face harden. It hurt. "To speak to Reed Taylor. Give me the keys to the Pinto. Now."

Chapter Forty-Three

My thoughts were going wild as I drove to Reed Taylor's house. Anubis had very nearly stolen my soul as well as breaking my face, and I was still cursing myself for that. I had misjudged him. I thought about Seth's confession about the Tiptoe Shadow and my eyes narrowed. I had misjudged everything.

Well, if I was so great at misjudging, perhaps I had misjudged the endgame. I had always assumed I'd end up on top.

I pulled into his driveway and felt like pulling right out again. His house was perfect. His lawn, although overgrown more than I had ever seen it, was a thing of beauty. The flowerbed bloomed flowers and... wait, are those actually weeds? Real weeds dared to invade Reed Taylor's yard? I remembered what he said to me once, about being fanatically tidy, and to call for help if I ever saw a weed. Suddenly every sense was alert. I slammed the car door and scanned the area. Something creepy and relatively harmless hovered around the backyard, yes, but that wasn't alarming. But weeds? And the too-long grass? For such a cool, laid-back guy, Reed Taylor usually kept things surprisingly tidy.

Something was wrong.

I walked to the door as casually as I could, splashing through the puddles. I couldn't forget I was still trying to present a normal front.

Perhaps he's just so torn up about the end of our relationship that he doesn't really want to mow the lawn. Or maybe he's dead, stabbed with a knife or lying with his head cracked open in the garage. What if he's dying right this second, weakly calling for help, and I'm out here like an idiot?

"Reed Taylor," I yelled, pounding on the door with my fist. "Open up right this minute or I'm coming through the window, do you hear me?" I waited a second, turned and noticed a pale face pressed against the window in the neighboring house. I forced myself to smile, my split lip cracking in the process. "Uh…please?"

A sound from inside the house. Was that a muffled shout? A groan?

"Seriously, Reed Taylor, I need to know you're not dead, okay? If you don't get to this door in the next thirty seconds, I'm coming in after you. And I'm not paying for damages."

Maybe that didn't sound super stable, but at least it sounded concerned. The panic in my voice frightened me so I cleared my throat.

"Be cool, be cool, be cool," I whispered. I relaxed my shoulders and popped my neck. Waited.

Forget being cool. I raised my fist to pound again when a voice suddenly purred in my ear.

"Mmm, Luna is all alone."

I jumped. I'd been so absorbed in the moment that I'd failed to notice something dark and unbearably thin had slithered close. Too close. I yanked myself away from its probing hands and positioned my back firmly to the door. Great. A snake with arms. Fantastic.

"Uninvited," I snarled.

Snakey demon grinned, and I felt my stomach turn at the malice I saw. "Uninvited? I think not. I think," it said, sliding its fingers over my cheek and into my hair, "that perhaps you aren't as strong as you hope, yes? Oh, you didn't think I could touch you, did you?" It smirked as my eyes widened. I felt behind me for the handle to the door and tried to turn it. Locked, of course. "You thought," the fiend continued, "that you'd shout your little catchphrase and everything would go away, yes? Well, fragile one," Snakey said, and a horrifying red light blazed from its eyes, "that isn't how it works, is it? Not now. Not anymore."

"Reed!" I shrieked. It was the first time I had ever just used his first name. "Reed! Open the door." I pressed against it, trying to protect the Mark from the demon's probing fingertips. It burned. It stung. My stomach twisted, and I turned my head to vomit off the side of Reed Taylor's porch.

"You had forgotten, didn't you?" The demon sneered, and suddenly grabbed both sides of my face with its hands. Sharp nails dug into my skin. "You'd forgotten how strong we can be. You think that since you've seen one of the major demons—"

"Back off, demon."

"—the rest of us are nothing, is that right? I'll show you nothing, Luna Masterson. I'll show you what it's like to suffer."

It grabbed me by the hair and slammed my head against the door. Twice. Three times. I scrabbled uselessly at it, trying to get some purchase. It slammed my head back again, turned it so pain exploded on my ear and cheekbone with the next assault. I screamed.

"I like the sound of that," the demon said, and the side of my face hit the heavy metal door again. My body sagged, and the demon turned me around, yanking one arm up behind me as it crashed my face against the door. I shrieked as I felt my nose crunch and my lip split. I tried to kick at it with my feet, but I was having a difficult time staying upright.

When the demon spoke, I felt its breath on my good ear. It was cold, and the desolate sound of it brought more tears to my eyes than the broken nose did.

"Where are your friends now?" it asked. A sob caught in my throat, but I wasn't going to give it more than that. "Where is your demon protector? Where is your Reed Taylor? You chased everyone away and where has that gotten you?"

I ran my tongue over my newly chipped teeth. My vanity and humiliation stoked my anger, and it felt good. I spit out the blood that was running from my nose.

"One day, demon, I'm going to find out exactly how to vanquish you. And I'm going to enjoy it."

The demon hissed. "Say hello to your father," it said and plunged its fingers into the eager, waiting wounds of the Mark. Darkness flooded my soul. I threw my head back and screamed.

"Enough!"

Reed Taylor stood in the doorway, shining with rage. His green eyes were frightening.

The demon spat and grudgingly withdrew. "We'll finish this later, shall we?"

I sank down on the porch. The demon was right. One way or another we'd finish this. I didn't have the strength to do anything else.

Chapter Forty-Four

O h, Luna," Reed Taylor said, and squatted down beside me. I was too dazed to move. I noticed the blood running from my face and soaking into the porous stone steps. Nice color, good body. I wasn't as iron deficient as I had told the counselor.

"Sorry," I tried to say, but the word came out funny.

Reed Taylor cupped my face gently, turning it tenderly this way and that. I closed my eyes.

"I haven't seen you attacked on the street like this before," he said finally. I missed his hands when he pulled them away.

"They usually don't..." I stopped talking, tried to touch my mouth. The mere thought of my own searching fingers made me cringe, and I blinked tears out of my eyes.

Reed Taylor stood up. "You need to go to the hospital. Is Seth home? I'll give him a call, tell him to pick you up."

"Can't...you take me?"

My words were slurred. I suddenly felt very tired, and cold. I shivered and Reed Taylor looked away.

"I can't," he said. "And I can't have an ambulance come here." He yanked a phone from his pocket, punched in a few numbers.

"Seth, hey. It's Reed. Listen, your sister is here and..."

I didn't want to listen to the rest of the conversation. My face hurt. My head hurt. My body was one big ache and pain, but more than that, my heart was being squeezed until I thought it would simply give up and stop beating. Reed Taylor didn't want me here at all. I was lying in a bloody pool outside his house, and he was focused on getting me out of his way. Had I hurt him that badly?

"Hey. He's catching a ride with a buddy. He's on his way."

I didn't say anything. I didn't want to jar anything by nodding. I didn't want to open my mouth because I'd say the wrong thing. Like why are you acting like this? And did you stop loving me so quickly? And obviously I need your help. I can't do it without you.

Silence.

I opened my mouth, worked my jaw. "This sucks," I said.

"Completely. Did you tick that demon off in an earlier life, or what?"

I struggled to sit up and he took my hands.

"Don't," he said. "I don't think you should move. Your face looks like hamburger."

"No, this awkwardness sucks. Forget the demons for a second. I'm more worried about you."

He laughed, and it was good to hear it. "Me? You're the one who's heading to the ER."

"I came to apologize. I need you, Reed Taylor."

He sighed, got to his feet. Disappeared into the house and came back with a wet washcloth. I shied away.

"I'm not coming anywhere near your nose, babe. But I'm gonna mop you up a bit so your brother doesn't have a heart attack as soon as he sees you. You're terrifying. Now listen to me," he said, dabbing at the blood that had run down my chin and neck. "I get what you were saying, Luna. About me holding you back. No, I really do," he said, when I tried to interrupt. "You can see demons and I can't. It's a major setback. At that house, when you were freaking out? I couldn't sense a thing. You were going bonkers, screaming about Lydia's body in the closet, and there I am, standing there like stooge realizing that you're either crazy or genuinely lost in world I can't touch. It's true. It does suck."

"Reed Taylor," I began, but a strange car screamed into the driveway.

Reed Taylor grinned a lopsided smile that I hadn't seen before. It looked brave and sad and it scared me.

"That, babe, is your brother."

Seth leapt out and ran to us. He saw me and stared in horror.

"You look terrible!"

"Thanks, big brother," I said sarcastically and tried to stand up. Both Seth and Reed Taylor reached down to help me up. Standing up made everything throb anew, and Seth supported my weight.

"Her nose is broken, but she's too stubborn to be really hurt," Reed Taylor told him.

"You're not coming?" Seth asked. His eyes narrowed as he fully took in Reed Taylor for the first time. His mouth tightened and he nodded. "Of course you aren't. Well, thanks for the call."

"Goodbye, Seth. I really hope things work out for you. Both of you."

The two men shook hands, and the finality of it made my heart sink. This was it.

Reed Taylor turned to me. "I appreciate that you came by. I know it couldn't have been easy. But don't stop in again. I won't be here." He paused, and then leaned forward and kissed an unbloodied spot on my hair. "Goodbye, Luna. I'm sorry. You won't see me again."

He closed the door, and I heard the lock click.

Seth's eyes cut to me. "Are you crying because you hurt or because you miss him?"

"Shut up," I said, and he hugged me for the first time I can remember. Then he stuffed me into the front of his Pinto of Death.

"This hospital better start issuing us Fast Passes, we're going there so much. So what are you going to say happened? If the words 'demonic attack' come out of your mouth, our bid for stability goes out the window. The same with 'bar fight' and 'mugged by an army of ninjas.' How are we going to explain this?"

I leaned my head against the cool car window. "I'll think of something. Give me a second, will ya?"

"Sure."

We drove in silence. Suddenly I said, "That sounded pretty final back there. Is he going to do something stupid?"

Seth didn't take his eyes off the road. "I'd say he's already doing something pretty stupid."

I peered at him through my swollen, blackening eyes. "What do you mean?"

He shook his head. "Nothing. Forget it. We'll talk about it later. What's your hospital story?"

"Maybe I turfed it on my bike. Bailed and smacked into a tree, or something. Does this look like I smacked into a tree?" I tried to smile.

"Looks like you smacked into a thousand trees and they all smacked back. Okay, we're here. Ready?"

"Ready."

I tried to push Reed Taylor to the back of my mind. I'd have to get used to doing that, I guess. But I couldn't help remembering the dangerous look in his eyes when he told me goodbye. When the doctor reset my nose, the tears in my eyes had very little to do with the pain.

Chapter Forty-Five

The sun was starting to rise by the time we bailed out of the hospital. "I am so tired," Seth told me. He yawned as he got into the car. "I can't wait to go to bed."

"Spill," I demanded. "You said I wasn't astute about Reed Taylor. What was I missing?"

"Cripes, Luna. You sure you want to do this? You'll be wound up and we'll never get any sleep."

I grabbed the lapels of his shirt and yanked him halfway out of his seat. "Seth Masterson, if you don't tell me right this minute, I swear I'll…"

"He was high, okay? He was high. Or coming down from it. That's why he couldn't bring you in or risk the ambulance. They would have known."

My fingers went slack. Seth pulled himself gently out of my grip. "Listen, maybe now isn't the time to talk about it. We already have a lot on our plates, and there's nothing you can—"

"He's using again."

"Looks like it."

"After being clean for so long."

"It happens. I'm sorry, Luna."

"Because I broke up with him?"

He shrugged. "Maybe, but that's pretty extreme behavior for a breakup, you know."

"Something isn't right, Seth."

"Obviously."

"No, it's…" Something was tugging at my brain. Something so close I could nearly taste it.

Seth eyed me. "I don't like that look. It usually means trouble."

"I'm figuring something out."

"That's exactly what I'm talking about."

"Why wouldn't he let me in the house?"

He shrugged. "I dunno. He didn't want you bleeding all over the carpet? You were pretty gory."

"That's exactly it. I was being attacked right there on his doorstep, but he still didn't let me in. He came outside. The demon left and…" Realization. The thing I was searching for, the ephemeral thought that kept wisping away. I finally had it firmly with both hands.

"Your eyes just lit up," Seth complained. "I don't like it."

I poked him hard in the chest. "That's it. Reed Taylor came out, told the demon off, and it left."

Seth snorted. "What, demons are listening to Reed now?" His mouth dropped open. He looked at me with wide brown eyes as he said it again, only this time as a statement. "Demons are listening to Reed now."

"Right. And he was aware of the demon in the first place. None of his, 'Oh, I can't see you but leave Luna alone' shtick. He stormed out of there and told it to stand down."

Seth was solemn. "So what does this mean?"

My stomach lurched. I opened the door, spit onto the ground, and wiped my mouth with my sleeve. "This means the game has changed."

Seth started the car and squealed the tires as he pulled out. Not toward home, but toward Reed Taylor's place. Suddenly I loved my brother so much I could have hugged him, if I was prone to such things.

I wasn't.

"It's more than drugs," Seth said. He was going way above the speed limit, my hero in chinos. "He let that cat out of the bag by coming outside. There's something in his house he's hiding."

"Demonic overlords? African diamonds?"

I sucked in a breath just as Seth stomped on the gas even harder. Lydia.

"You think?" I whispered. He didn't even need to ask what I meant.

"I hope."

Tires on gravel. Reed Taylor's house loomed in front of us.

I was out of the car before Seth even turned it off. I stared at the neat little house that had suddenly become the place of my nightmares.

Seth put his hand on my shoulder.

"Are you ready to do this?"

I wasn't. I was terrified at what I'd find inside. My heart hurt at the possibilities.

"I still love him, you know."

"I know."

"What if…he's been the bad guy all along?"

"Then we storm in there and get my daughter back. You'll be all right, Luna. You're strong."

"Nobody's that strong."

"Maybe not alone. But you have me, right?"

"Do I?"

"You do."

The Mark blistered between my shoulder blades. My mouth screwed together.

"Your wound hurts?"

"Like a demon."

"Funny. What exactly does that mean?

It means I wished I was dead. "There's activity in here. A lot of it. It hurt before, but I assumed it was just from the demon attacking me. Obviously there's a lot more going on."

Seth tried the door. Locked, of course.

"How can I best help?" he asked.

"Okay. So I assume this will be like Hell House. Only, according to Reed Taylor, it's not going to look like much to you. But for me…"

"Yeah. I can only imagine."

I shrugged, feigning nonchalance. "Ain't no thing. Except for when I see little girls on fire, or starfish running across the room, or demons under the floorboard and stuff."

His face twisted into something ugly and mean.

"And Lydia."

I coughed to hide my quick intake of breath. I was trying to avoid that particular image. "And Lydia."

He flicked his hot eyes to me, and then back to the road. "So basically you want me to calm you down if you start to go nuts. Be your touchstone to reality. And let you know there are no dead girls unless I see dead girls."

That didn't sound stable at all. "Right."

He looked at me fully this time. His eyes were serious. "I've got your back, Luna. I really do."

"Thanks," I said. Years were covered in that single word.

Using his elbow, he broke the window. The shattered glass sounded strangely triumphant.

"Let's go," he said, and crawled inside.

Chapter Forty-Six

I don't see him," Seth whispered. "I thought maybe he'd come to investigate the window." He started searching behind the chairs, underneath the couch.

"Lydia," he whispered. "Lydia, it's Daddy."

I climbed in and was immediately assaulted by the stench of rotting meat. Flies buzzed around the room in a swarm, blackening the broken window.

"Ugh," I said, and covered my nose with my hand.

"What? What is it?" Seth peered around me anxiously. "What do you see?"

Something that looked suspiciously like entrails hung from the walls. Spider webs made out of skin covered the ceilings. I noticed my feet soaking in the familiar, bloody carpet.

"I see a slaughterhouse. How about you?"

He touched the walls gingerly. "This wallpaper is atrocious, but that's the worst of it. That's it. It's not real, Luna. Let's go."

I nodded, and removed my hand from my nose. If it isn't real, it isn't real.

A small boy swam through the air. He kicked his feet and splashed in nothingness. His dark eyes ran over Seth curiously.

"Soul surfer?" I asked, and pointed.

Seth shook his head. "Nothing."

"Figured. Just checking."

I stepped forward. Seth put his hand on my shoulder.

"Want me to go first?"

"Nah. I've got it. But thanks."

He nodded. "Anytime."

His concern gave me wings. I strode through the room, splashing blood out of my way like it wasn't even there. Which apparently, to the normal eye, it wasn't.

I put my hand on the second doorknob, took a deep breath, and opened it.

Nothing. A blank space. No walls, no floor, no ceiling. I stared at my hand and watched in horror as it seemed to disappear.

"Seth?" I called, and whirled around. He wasn't there. "Seth!"

Nothingness. Absolute nothingness.

"Answer me!"

It's exactly what I was always afraid of. I was abandoned.

"Are you here?"

This is what happens to souls when they die. They disappear. They fade away. They're forgotten.

Was I...calling out for someone?

Suddenly I knew it was true. My conversations at the cemetery with Mom and Dad had been a child's dream. They didn't exist anywhere.

"Luna? Can you hear me?"

There was no life after death. There was only empty space. Empty space meant there were no angels. Or demons.

"I'm right here," a voice said.

No demons. They didn't exist.

"I have your hand. Can you feel that I have your hand?"

They didn't exist.

"Luna, answer me."

I had been seeing them. Talking to them. Being afraid.

Of nothing.

I was crazy.

"Sit down," the voice commanded. It was soft and strong at the same time. "Close your eyes. I'm going to help you to the ground." Someone pushed me gently, and I resisted at first. He was trying to push me backwards into the sky.

"Trust me," the voice said quietly, but I shook my head. I didn't recognize it. I struggled, but was pushed back. I was floating somewhere strange.

"Now breathe. Slowly. You know how. In and out. In and out. You can do it, Luna."

The voice knew my name. I squeezed my eyes shut and concentrated on the feel of his hands.

"You know what I see, Luna? It's a small room. Smaller than the first room. No windows, so it's fairly dark. The floor is firm. I can reach out and touch one of the walls if I want to. There, do you hear that?"

A knocking sound.

"A wall?" I hated how small my voice sounded.

"That was the wall. The nice, firm wall. Are you ready to go? Keep your eyes closed, and I'll lead you."

The hands belonged to the voice. He drew me up, which didn't feel like up at all. It felt like he was pushing me though quicksand. I was afraid I'd choke on it.

He pulled me gently forward, knocking on the wall every few seconds.

"Hear that? The wall. We'll be there in about two more knocks. All right, let me grab the door for you. Did you hear it open? Step through. All right, closed. Take a second."

I knew that voice. I stood there, breathing, still not opening my eyes. "Seth?"

"Yes."

The floor was underneath my feet. I could feel it. Seth's hand was warm. I squeezed it and he squeezed back.

"I was all alone."

"You were never alone. I had you the whole time. Now open your eyes. Better?"

I opened my eyes and gasped. My hands flew to my mouth and I tried to hold back the tears.

My father hung by his neck, just like he had when I'd seen him last. His face was bloated; his eyes and tongue bulged. The familiar letter pinned to his chest. "Seth. Luna. I'm sorry."

"What do you see, Seth?" My voice cracked. Seth didn't answer me. I spun around to face him, suddenly angry. "Tell me what you see."

His eyes were angry but his voice was calm. "There's a TV. An old chair. Reed isn't in here. Neither is Lydia."

I pointed toward our father. My hand shook.

"And here?"

"Nothing. I don't see anything." A beat. "Do you see something?"

My voice sounded ugly. "I see Dad."

The note, written in my father's neat handwriting, somehow angered me more than the rest of it. I ripped it from his shirt and balled it up in my hand.

"Hey, you," I said, pushing my finger against its chest none too lightly. My father's body shook on the end of the rope. This only pissed me off more. "You're skating on thin ice, mister. Better explain why you're wearing my father, and fast."

"Luna." A voice, weak with pain. I stared at Daddy's body, but it didn't come from there. Seth was slowly straightening up, oblivious to any noise. His eyes were searching the air for the corpse of our father.

"Luna. You need to…leave."

I peered behind my father's body and saw a dark shape in the corner. I narrowed my eyes, trying to make it out in the murky gloom. A shine of eyes from inside a hood. Robes that misted at the ends, miserably. Definitely not happy and content.

"Mouth!" Pushing past my father's body, I made my way to the demon. I growled when I saw him. He was hanging high up on the wall, nailed upside down with tapered spikes. His hands, his legs, his shoulders. The black robes were tattered and torn, his skin solidified and flayed open. I saw his ribs. I saw his heart beat inside the well of his chest. I reached up to touch his face. He spasmed.

"Oh, Mouth. What have they done to you? I have to get you down."

He shook his head. The movement was barely perceptible. "Leave, Luna. Take Seth and go. You shouldn't be here."

I studied the spikes. I could pull them out of the wall, or if worse came to worse, actually work Mouth off them. The pain from that would be indescribable, though, and I didn't want to make things any worse.

"I'm not sure how to pull you down without killing you. How did they do this, anyway? Can't you become filmy and slide off? Seth," I yelled over my shoulder. "A little help here."

Seth looked around and shrugged helplessly. Of course. What use would he be?

"No worries, Mouth." I grinned, even though I didn't feel it. "I'm good at figuring things out on my own."

"Luna, listen to me." He was getting angry now. Good, anger was a distraction. I pulled on a spike but it refused to budge. He shrieked.

"I'm sorry! I'm listening. What's up?"

I tried again. The pain made sweat bead on Mouth's forehead. I bit my lip and yanked as hard as I could. He screamed again.

"You don't have time for this. You have to leave, immediately."

"Not without you," I said. "This place sucks. Think I'm just going to leave you here to rot?"

I tugged again. His screams made me wince.

"I'm so sorry," I said. I leaned my forehead against his. "I don't know what to do."

"Why," he bellowed, glaring at me with flaming eyes, "don't you ever listen to anything I say?"

"Why," I yelled back, "are you always screaming at me?"

"One of these days, I'm going to kill you," he threatened.

"Not unless I inadvertently kill you first," I answered. For some reason it struck me as immensely funny, and I started to giggle.

"Luna?" Seth called. "Is everything all right?"

I was losing it. I laughed harder until I felt tears running from the corners of my eyes. I covered my mouth before my giggles turned to screams.

"Luna."

"Seth, Mouth here is nailed to the wall. Dad's hanging over there from a rope. Where will I find Lydia, do you think? I already saw her torn apart once. It would be just my luck to find her in pieces."

Seth slapped me, hard. My eyes narrowed and I bared my teeth at him.

"Don't ever touch me again, or I'll kill you, too."

Seth took a step back. Mouth cursed.

"You see? You have to get out of here. Remember how this place messes with your mind?"

"But that was at the old house. This is Reed Taylor's home. Shouldn't that make a difference?"

The demon snarled. "A nexus is a nexus. Stop wasting time and get out of here."

"Not until I find Lydia."

"I don't know if she's here. I haven't seen her."

"Then what about you?" I eyed the spikes. "I'll figure something out."

He shook his head and his voice softened. "You say that so often, but that isn't how it works. Not this time. I'm sorry, Luna. Thank you for coming after me, but I can't go. Even if you got me down, I'm trapped here, remember? Leaving isn't possible."

I thought. Then I made a decision.

"If you were bonded with a human, then you could go, couldn't you?"

"What are you saying?"

I lifted my chin. "If I opened myself to you, as a demon. Let you put your fingers in the Mark, gave you access to my soul—"

"Don't you ever say that!" His voice was harsh, grating. His eyes glowed so intensely that I had to look away. "Never, never say that. You don't want to invite anything in."

"I want to invite you, Mouth. I know I don't always act like it, but I care about you. I do. We'll get you out of here and find Lydia. I know you can help me. And this Mark literally puts a target on my back. One day it's going to happen. A demon will work its way in, and I won't be able to stop it. I'd rather it be you than anybody else. You'd make sure it wasn't all bad, right?"

He wouldn't catch my eye. I turned away, my cheeks burning.

"Luna," Mouth said softly. He kissed my forehead and it felt very much like goodbye. "I love you, you know," he said, "in my own way. As much as I know how."

Seth grabbed me by my wrists.

"Luna, come here," Seth yelled. "I think we need an ambulance."

"Not yet," I screamed, and reached for Mouth, but Seth pulled me away.

"Go," Mouth told me. "Go now. Get out of this house. Please."

"Luna," Seth begged, and I stopped fighting. I turned and ran after my brother.

Chapter Forty-Seven

Seth was crouched over somebody on the floor. My heart sunk. It's Reed. It's Reed. It's Reed.

"It's Sparkles," Seth said, squatting beside her. She looked like she was barely conscious. Her demon twined around her arms and legs. "I heard her moaning in the back room. She doesn't look so hot."

Understatement.

I narrowed my eyes at the sight of her and spit on the ground. "What's she doing here?" My eyes widened. "Wait, if she's here, where's Lydia? Is she here, too?"

Seth shook his head. "I didn't see her.

I knelt by Sparkles, tried to make her eyes focus. "Sparkles! Where is Lydia? Lydia?" Her eyes rolled. I slapped her in the face, but she didn't even react. Even her demon was moving slower than usual. Groggy. Snapping at me blearily, almost blindly.

What was going on here? Suddenly I had a thought. I yanked up the sleeve of her shirt. Fresh track marks. She was using. Disgusted, I let her arm fall to the ground with a thud.

"You're useless," I spat. "You're a waste of a person and a mother. You deserve everything you get."

"That's enough," Seth said. He sounded tired.

I turned my anger on him. "How can you be so calm?"

"I have to be calm or I'm going to lose my mind."

I turned my back on him and Sparkles. I was out of here. I marched back to Mouth. He was the answer to all this.

"My offer still stands," I said. "I need to find Lydia, and you're going to help me. Ride around in my soul and blow this joint."

A strange giggling in the background unnerved me. It was the demon masquerading as my father, swinging gently back and forth from his rope.

"He's here," Mouth said. I had never heard him sound frightened before.

"Who's here?"

The grotesque body in the middle of the room laughed louder, more manically.

"He's come for you, Luna," the demon in my father sputtered. "He's waited so long." His mirth caused the rope to spin in a slow, jerking circle.

My shoulders tensed.

"Mouth, tell me who's here?"

The Mark scorched anew, forcing a sound of pain between my lips. The laughing demon suddenly started screaming, shrieking, wailing. His skin, my father's faux skin, started blistering and bubbling. I couldn't stand it. I staggered away from both of the demons, toward the door. The knob turned easily under my hand, and the squealing abruptly cut off. I tasted bile.

"No!" Mouth called. He struggled to yank himself free from the spikes. "I warned you. It's too late."

Reed Taylor stood there, looking tired and pale. I took an automatic step toward him, but something stopped me. His body language was off. The way he stood was unnatural, like he was being pulled upward by strings.

"Something's wrong with him," I breathed.

Mouth nodded grimly, and I bit my lip, hard.

"But that's him, though, isn't it? I mean, he's real, even if he is all jacked up."

"That's him." Mouth's voice was very soft, and full of something strangely like pity. I looked at him.

"What aren't you telling me?"

"Look closer."

I didn't want to. It took everything that I had to force myself to clench my fists and study what I saw in front of me. Reed Taylor's handsome face was white and slack. Dark spikes ran from his red hair, spearing upwards. I realized what I was seeing, who I was seeing, and I hissed.

"So you understand," Mouth said quietly.

"I understand."

The darkness flowed from Reed Taylor's scalp up into a long, thin arm. Too thin. Bone-shatteringly thin. The very stuff of nightmares, or at least my nightmares. The arm connected to a shadow so large that its head projected onto the ceiling. The shadow turned toward me and I thought my heart would stop. I tried to breathe normally. I bit my tongue to keep myself from shrieking. I knew if I started then I would never, never, never stop.

The shadow giggled.

"Ah, Luna! It has been, mmm, such a long time!"

The voice was higher than I remembered, squeaky and broken in all the wrong places. As it spoke, its head rotated to the side so far that I braced myself for the sound of snapping bones.

Everything in me screamed to run and hide. The shadow pranced its way closer. It tiptoed on impossibly small feet.

"And how is the brother, mmm? Still a coward? Learned from his bargain, girl?" It sniffed the air. "Oh! I can smell him. He smells like such lovely things. Despair. Shame. Oh, yes, guilt and misery."

It turned his eyeless face back to me. "And you. I missed you, mmm, yes. Little girls and fears are so delicious. But yours, oh, yours were always the sweetest. So delightful to lead down waterways and into the dark places. There was magic there, Luna. Tell me, do you still see magic in the water? Look closer, Luna, and see what you find! Put your face right down into the water and—"

"Shut up," I said. My fists were clenched at my side. "I'm sick of your voice. I'm not six years old anymore. You're gonna have to do better than that."

"Watch it," Mouth breathed warningly.

I pointed at Reed Taylor. "I want him. Give him back to me."

The Tiptoe Shadow cackled in delight. "You want the puppet? My new friend? Oh, but I think not, mmm. I was lonely without you, Luna. No one to whisper to. No one to run my fingers across in the night. I needed, mmm, someone to play with, and someone came. He's a lovely one, don't you think? And he knows things. A great many things. He knows where the New You is."

The New You?

Lydia. Reed Taylor knew where Lydia was.

The shadow moved its great arm, and I realized with horror that his fingers were boring through the top of Reed Taylor's skull. This was how it was controlling him. It danced Reed Taylor closer to me. His left leg turned in awkwardly and his heavy boots dragged on the ground.

"Stop it, you're hurting him," I yelled and rushed forward.

Mouth's cold voice stopped me. "Tread carefully," he said. His eyes never left the shadow man's face. "He's counting on you to get emotional. It isn't Reed he wants."

I took a deep breath, nodded. Reed Taylor's gorgeous greens were vacant, the corners filled with swirling black. I reached forward and ran my hand down his face gently. Cold to the touch, but so beautiful.

I felt the heat of the Tiptoe Shadow's gaze. "Why, you care for this one?" He shook his hand, and Reed Taylor's body danced like a broken doll. "This one, mmm, when he has caused you so much trouble? Oh yes," he said, and his squeaky voice turned deeper, more sinister, "I know this one. I know his consorts: those who think they fly, mmm, higher than us. I know." He suddenly bent over backwards, his head twisting toward Reed Taylor's face. He ran his tongue down Reed Taylor's cheek. "He, mmm, tastes like you. Is that why you want him back? 'Come on, Luna, give me a kiss.'" He opened Reed Taylor's mouth and shadowy black fingers waggled where his tongue should be. The shadow giggled wildly.

I broke.

"How dare you call my brother a coward? You're the coward. How dare you pick on little girls, and men that can't see you, and small boys who are afraid of the dark? If you're going to fight somebody, fight somebody who can fight back."

Mouth made a warning sound, but I was too worked up to care. "Leave Reed Taylor alone, and come after—"

"Luna!" Mouth roared, and I stopped short. My body began to tremble. I suddenly had the sense that I had almost gone too far, said something that couldn't be taken back, and Mouth had saved me.

Moving almost faster than I could register, the Tiptoe Shadow snaked forward until he was face-to-face with Mouth.

"You," he said, and I realized that, until now, he hadn't even known he was there.

Mouth dipped his head.

"Why do you stop her? Why do you, mmm, betray?"

Mouth bowed his head respectfully. "I…I don't betray, master. I forgot myself. She offered to help me and I was…moved."

The demon's giggle went higher, more wild. The hair on my arms stood.

"She? Help you? Then she doesn't know. Oh, mmm, tell me she doesn't know."

Mouth, head still bowed, murmured, "She doesn't know."

The Tiptoe Shadow screamed with laughter. He wrapped his long, thin arms around himself, and Reed Taylor's body flopped and shook with the demon's mirth.

"You're breaking him," I yelled, tears in my eyes. I whirled on Mouth. "What don't I know?"

He looked away from me. "Do you ever wish," he said quietly, "that you could take something back? That you could change who you are?" He met my eyes again. "I never wanted to hurt you."

"Luna." I whirled at my brother's voice.

"Seth, don't come in here."

He looked horrified. "What's happening to Reed?" I realized he only saw me and a broken Reed Taylor levitating through the air. It must be too horrible to comprehend.

"It's the Tiptoe Shadow."

Seth's face changed into an expression of horror more grotesque than anything I had ever seen. I was afraid his heart would stop.

I was sick of this.

"Enough games." I stormed up to the Tiptoe Shadow. "Where's my niece?" Fear didn't have a hold of me anymore. Nothing but rage.

"The little one?" he squeaked. He wriggled, his happiness an obscenity. My mouth tasted sour. "The pigtails, and starfish hands, and laugh like, mmm, bubbles? It had been so long since I had one so small around to play my games, someone to hide under her blankets and pray I don't exist. But I do, you see. I sing songs, all night, comforting, about things that, mmm, crawl in the dirt and things that will eat her eyes, and when she cries for Mama Luna, no one comes. 'We're all alone,' I tell her. 'They've all abandoned you,' and I open my mouth and catch her tears and they are so sweet, so sweet, so sweet…"

The sound that came out of me was unlike anything I had ever heard. It was something I expected from the wolf demons, or something that dreamed of sucking marrow from bones at night, but not from me. It was wild and frightening. From the corner of my eye I saw Seth shrink away, but I didn't care. I rushed at the demon.

"No, no," he said slyly. He lifted Reed Taylor into the air as though he weighed nothing. "I will break my toy. Just you see. Do you like toys, Luna? Do you like when they twist and spin and, mmm, snap?"

He twisted Reed Taylor's arm painfully in its socket. Reed Taylor's expression didn't change, but his face went even paler, and sweat stood out on his forehead.

"No, stop," I cried. "Please don't. I'll do anything."

"Anything?" The demon looked shrewd. I'd been down this road before.

"Luna, think of what you're saying," Mouth whispered. His head was still bowed. "You think he doesn't know what he's doing? He's playing you."

"Whose side are you on?" I hissed and Mouth winced. I turned my attention back to the Tiptoe Shadow, who was nibbling down Reed Taylor's ribs like a hungry dog. I saw blood.

"What will it take for you to leave him alone?" I asked. "For you to put him away and give Lydia back to my brother?"

"You ask hard things," the shadow said. He pointed at Mouth. "Doesn't she ask hard things?"

"Yes, she does," he said respectfully. He cut his gaze to me, but I deliberately avoided his eye.

"The child says yes," the Shadow told me, nodding. "I like my pretty toy. But sometimes…they break."

He snapped Reed Taylor's arm, and I screamed. Seth took a step forward, but the shadow shook his head. "Uh uh, naughty boy. There are more, mmm, wonderful things to snap and spin on my new toy."

"Don't go closer," I warned Seth. I glared at the demon. "Enough. If you break him, then I won't have a reason to do what you ask. It's me you want anyway, isn't it? Not this toy. Not the girl. Me." The demon looked wary but didn't move. "Put the puppet down, and play with me. I'll be your doll. Remember the sound of my terrified breathing as a child? Remember the magic in the water? I can fear you again. Let me. Let him go, and play with me." I took a small step forward.

"Luna."

I heard my brother call me frantically, but I tuned him out. This was for Seth. This was for Lydia. This was for Reed Taylor. What's one life compared to many? Who would really miss me, anyway?

"Games?" The Tiptoe Shadow asked hopefully. "Twistings and playing and ties?"

"Whatever you want," I said. I was closer now. I lifted my arms to show that my hands were empty, that they needed to be filled with nightmares and the dead and whatever horrors he could come up with. "Whatever games you desire. Just put him down, please."

The demon looked from Reed Taylor to me. "Such pretty dollies. So many games that we could play, mmm."

This wasn't going as planned. "But you don't really want Reed Taylor. What kind of horrors could you bring him? You don't know him like you know me. Take me. I'll be more satisfying. I'll scream every night. Take me."

My brother shouted my name again, and the Tiptoe Shadow gyrated angrily from head to toe.

"Enough of brother. No more, mmm, brother. You," he thundered, pointing at Mouth, "silence brother! Kill, burn, twist, break brother." The spikes yanked out of Mouth's body, clattering to the floor. Mouth sank to his knees.

"No," I shrieked. I backed away from the demon, standing between Mouth and Seth. "If you hurt him, I won't stay. I'll leave you with your broken toy, and I'll walk away forever, I swear I will."

"No games?" the shadow asked tearfully. "No stories or songs?"

"No stories or songs or screams. Nothing. Just a toy who can't see you. No Luna doll. No me."

The demon paused. Reed Taylor still hung from the air, his arm lolling grotesquely.

The shadow sighed.

"All right. Go, brother. Goodbye, brother. Come here, plaything."

I turned to Seth. "You have to leave now. Just leave this house before he changes his mind."

He bared his teeth. "I'm not leaving you here with that...that thing. Luna, I remember. How could I do this to you a second time?"

The Tiptoe Shadow made an impatient sound, fiddling with Reed Taylor's legs.

"Go, now. Find Lydia. She needs you." I hugged him fiercely. "I love you." I stepped back before he even had a chance to put his arms around me.

"I'm ready," I said, and walked up to the Tiptoe Shadow. I heard the door close behind me as Seth left, but I didn't take my eyes from the demon's missing face.

"Dolly," he said and ran his trembling hands over my cheek.

Chapter Forty-Eight

Mouth wasn't happy. I could tell it by his wispiness. I could tell it by the way his lips were set into a firm line.

I didn't care.

"Dolly, dolly," sang the Tiptoe Shadow, and he ran his long fingers down my hair, twisted them around my neck. They went around several times.

"Can…can you let Reed Taylor go now, please?"

I wanted to sound strong, but the feel of those dark fingers on my skin made my mouth go dry.

"Reed Taylor, where is Lydia?"

"There's magic in the water."

Reed Taylor's voice, but not his words. I reached for him, but the demon pulled us further away.

"No, dollies. Bad dollies." He shook us, and I choked, grasping at my neck. Mouth clenched his fists, but did nothing.

"Hey, knock it off," I growled as soon as I had my voice back.

The Tiptoe Shadow giggled. "You want to talk to the puppet? Hear what the puppet has to say? Okay. Okay, okay. Oh, it will make you cry. Big, soft, sad tears, and I will lap them from your face, and I will be happy."

He pulled his hand away from Reed Taylor's head slightly. The inky furls cleared from the corners of his eyes. They were filled with pain instead.

"My arm," he gasped.

"He broke it," I said, jerking my head at the monster. "I'm sorry. He's kind of a jerk."

Sweat dampened his hair. "You weren't supposed to see me again. That was the end of it. I was going to live life without you."

I frowned. He didn't have to sound so miserable that I was here. The Tiptoe Shadow giggled and his fingers tightened around my throat.

Reed Taylor's eyes cleared and he looked at me, took in the demon's ghostly fingers.

"No," he said.

"It's okay," I whispered, and tried my best to grin. "It saved Seth. It's worth it. I'd hoped it would get you out of here, too, but now I'm not so sure. The Tiptoe Shadow here seems pretty fond of its pretty little puppets."

He looked at the shadow. "You're breaking the deal. You weren't going to hurt her."

"You…made a deal?"

Reed Taylor winced. When he opened his eyes again, the cloudy whorls were back. "He's laughing. He lies. We're forgetting his true nature." His body seized, jerked, and he reached for me with his good arm. I pulled away automatically.

The Tiptoe Shadow hadn't moved. He just stood there, grinning eerily at us.

"He's not saying anything," I pointed out to Reed Taylor. Maybe the pain was getting to him more than I thought.

He shook his head. "He's thinking it. He's in there with my thoughts. There isn't room in my head for both of us, so sometimes it's mostly him, and sometimes it's mostly me. He's pulling back right now because he wants me to tell you some stuff." He spit on the ground. "He wants you to cry. He hates you, you know. He thinks it's love."

The demon's thumb caressed my neck. I closed my eyes against the oily feel.

"His thoughts make me sick," Reed Taylor told me. His beautiful greens were full of sorrow. "I don't have to tell you what he's thinking. I'm pretty sure you know."

"I always knew."

The shadow half purred, half growled. "He doesn't want to tell you to your, mmm, face. He wanted to fade away and disappear, become something other than what he is. Oh no, he is ashamed, that's what he is."

"Shut up!" Reed Taylor yelled at the Tiptoe Shadow, who began chortling wildly.

"I can't wait, I can't wait, I can't wait," he started to chant, rocking himself in glee. Both Reed Taylor and I swayed with his movements.

"She doesn't have to know," Reed Taylor told the shadow flatly. "It'll only hurt her."

Mouth surged forward. "It's too late. There you go. You went and screwed up, just like I knew you would, and now here you are. Here you both are. Luna, you should have listened to me. You should have stayed away."

The shadow eyed him shrewdly. "She should have what, hmm? Listened to a, mmm, betrayer? A demon who only befriended her so he could bring her to me? Yes," he said to me, twisting down to meet my eyes. It looked like his body had to break in half to do it. "That's why this one approached you. And you, Luna doll. You were so eager to hate, and so eager to say mean, hurtful things that wounded his little soul, and then you felt sorry, but you were, mmm, right. He has a way with words, my little one, but in the end," his voice hardened, "he serves. Don't you, child?"

Mouth dropped his head again. "Of course."

I could hear the anger and hatred in that voice. So could the Tiptoe Shadow, who screamed with laughter.

"Oh, you are so upset. Oh, how you wish to yell and rend and banish me to the dark places. But you can't. You can't even tell her, can you? Because then what will happen?"

I turned to Mouth the best I could. "What will happen? If you try to go against him?"

I could hardly hear him. "I die. Forever. You can't turn against the ones who...you can't even say anything against..."

"I created him," squealed the Tiptoe Shadow, and he clicked his tongue with an insect-like glee. "The one he prays to and the one who tucks him in at night, when I'm not watching you. Dreaming of you. Running my tongue against your window and wishing you would let me in. Why won't you let me in? Why let my little one in? Not me? I was so, mmm, disappointed." His laughter sounded like choking. His head turned slowly on his neck. "That isn't nice. That isn't nice at all."

"You...came because he asked you to?" I didn't know whether I wanted to hit Mouth or cover my face and scream.

Mouth flowed over, put his hands on my cheeks. I could barely feel them. "At first. It was like that at first, but you have to believe me when I say—"

"I don't have to believe anything you say," I spat.

He backed away, eyes averted.

"You're a demon, and demons lie. I knew it from the beginning. I...I made a mistake when it came to you." My eyes burned, but I wasn't going to cry over a demon.

"But you trusted him?" Mouth yelled, and his voice echoed in the room. Even the shadow had gone silent, listening. "You trusted Reed, and what did he do? He can't even tell you."

"I'm warning you," Reed Taylor said.

Mouth roared and screamed a word I didn't understand. It wasn't of this world.

"You're warning me? You're warning me?" He surged forward, grabbed Reed Taylor's good arm and yanked up his sleeves. "Do you see this, Luna? Do you know what's pumping through his veins right now? Do you have any idea how much?" He pointed at the Tiptoe Shadow, sharing Reed Taylor's body. "Enough to affect this guy, right here. And do you see Sparkles over there? Where's Lydia, huh? Where is she, when the person who is supposed to be taking care of her is passed out on the floor?"

"I did this for Lydia," Reed Taylor yelled back. His eyes were burning with a fury I hadn't seen before. His body writhed against the hold of the Tiptoe Shadow. "I did this for Lydia, and I did it for you." He looked like a wild man. I tried to move away.

"Oh, tell her," the Tiptoe Shadow cawed. "Tell her how you and the mother lay together at night and talk about her. And you laughed, and laughed, and laughed. And in the other room, the New Luna cries in loneliness and fear. But who comes to her? I do. I don't leave her alone, no. There are, mmm, songs, and stories and things to tell her. About the dark places, and the fun we shall have, and why nobody loves her but me, the one who crawls under the covers with her when she hides and—"

"Stop it, you monster!" I screamed and tore at the hands around my neck. "You're disgusting and vile, and I don't want anything to do with you! Uninvited! Uninvited!"

"You are all alone," howled the shadow. The pits where his eyes should be burned brightly. "This one, he betrays you for another woman. That one, he betrays you for me. Who is here with you? I am, I am, I am. Who has always been by your side? Me, me, me!"

"I was there, too," Mouth said, and it was so quiet that I barely heard him. The shadow sucked in a breath. "I was always there. Your father let me. Me and one other, the demon you met in the House of Horrors. We watched you grow up. We were careful. We were respectful and kept our distance. I wanted a friend. The other demon wanted to see what life was like for the living. We—"

"They watched when I killed your father," the shadow wheedled. His voice had thinned and wormed its way into my ears. "They watched and didn't say a word, didn't help him. The way he kicked, and his eyes bulged, and his fear was so delicious. And that second when he thought, 'I've made a terrible mistake'…Oh, oh! I could feast on that moment for eternity."

Tears were running down my face.

"Is it true?" I asked Mouth. "Were you there when my father died?"

"I was." His voice was so quiet that I had to hold my breath to hear it. "I was there. I didn't want him to go alone. I wanted him to know I'd take care of you."

That squeaky voice again. "He wasn't alone. He was never alone. We were together, he and I, and when he struggled and his tongue swelled and fell from his mouth, I held his hands. I wrapped myself around his body good and tight so he could, mmm, feel me, and know how together we were…"

"Stop it," I screamed. I covered my ears with my hands. "I don't want to hear anymore."

Mouth flowed up to me again, and his voice was very kind. "Your father loved you and Seth very much. It didn't work out like he had hoped, but he took his life in order to save you. Just like…just like Reed is planning to do."

"What are you talking about?" I looked at Reed Taylor. "What's he saying?"

Reed Taylor's eyes were still full of green fury.

"I joined up with this demon because I wanted to help you. I thought, if it's a part of me, I'll be able to sense the rest of them, right? Only I can hear what it's thinking. And I overhear it think that if you kill yourself while connected to it, it dies too."

My father.

"Your father. I know his death wounded you inside, made you fracture in a way that can't be healed. It's never going to fully heal, Luna," he said when I tried to interrupt. "But now you know why. He was hoping to kill the Tiptoe Shadow, take it with him. Only it didn't work."

The Tiptoe Shadow giggled madly. "He tried and tried."

I felt my face go pale. "You were planning on killing yourself?"

Reed Taylor shrugged his good shoulder.

I didn't know what to say. I felt like crying.

"After everything I said? You were willing to do this for... Are you frickin' crazy? How am I supposed to live without you?"

"You'll do just fine, babe. You always land on your feet."

He grinned, broken and battered and torn almost beyond recognition. My eyes traveled from him to Mouth, who looked stricken, his body slowly healing itself.

I made a decision.

Chapter Forty-Nine

It hurt me to see the ones I loved damaged like this. Seth chased away, Reed Taylor broken, Mouth angry and helpless. All of these people, brought together involuntarily because they cared about me in one way or another. Each, in their own way, only wanted to help.

"Luna," Mouth said, and he sounded worried. "Why are you looking at me like that? What are you thinking?"

I reached for his hand, smiled. I ran my fingers down his cheek. "Thank you for everything. I hope you know how special you are to me."

"Luna," he said warningly, but I had already turned away. "Reed Taylor, I…"

There wasn't anything more I could say. His gorgeous greens that had gone frightened and worried and were now narrowed with resolve. He was perfect. He was my everything. How can you explain that to someone?

"I love you," I said simply, and then turned to the Tiptoe Shadow. "Demon," I screamed, and spread my arms wide. "Taste the Mark. I invite you in."

"Luna, no," Reed Taylor shouted, but the swirling, crashing noise of wind and thunder drowned everything out. It ripped at my clothes, tore at my hair. I squeezed my eyes closed.

"The Mark," shrieked the Tiptoe Shadow. His voice was horrifyingly close to my ear, and I gasped. "She's mine." I felt the long fingers disengage themselves from my neck.

I couldn't take it any longer. I was dangerously close to losing my nerve. "Do it. Do it now," I screamed, and glared at the shadow. His long tongue lolled out of his face, licked his chops. It was long enough to wrap all the way around his head.

"With pleasure," he rasped, and his fingers spread, plunging firmly into the Mark.

I shrieked, launched up onto the balls of my feet by the pressure and the pain. My eyes were wide, wild, and I couldn't control my arms, my legs, my heart. I couldn't close my mouth or stop the sounds coming out of my throat.

"Mmm," moaned the shadow and drove his hand in deeper. I felt him push into my brain, into my lungs. His darkness flowed through my veins, forcing my blood to cling to the walls of my arteries in horror and self-preservation.

Reed and Mouth both shouted, waving their arms and trying to get my attention. I saw Reed Taylor try to wrench himself free of the shadow's hand, but I couldn't focus. I couldn't move. All that existed was agony and the hatred that coursed through me. Reed Taylor had been right: it was hatred the Tiptoe Shadow thought of as love.

The wind hissed and roared, filling my ears as the demon's thoughts filled my head. I saw myself as a little girl, tasted my own fear. It tasted just right, tasted so good...

I fought to keep myself at the surface. I couldn't go through all of this and have the demon divert me from my purpose. Demons lie, don't they? Twist things and make things seem different from what they really are. Panting, I battled with my trembling hand, struggled to slip it inside my pocket and pull out my folding knife. I flicked it open with my thumb, realizing dully that the crazy voice in the wind I kept hearing was my own.

Your father had tried to kill himself, oh yes, but, mmm, it didn't work, you see. He didn't know. Didn't know the secret. Didn't know there must be love and want and that desire, but more than that, there must be blood.

Blood.

Blood, the invisible presence had repeatedly told me that day at work. I'd drawn that extra vial of blood, slid it into my pocket…but what was I supposed to do with it? I remembered the look on Mouth's face when he realized what I held. His anger when he exploded the vial. So angry. Far too angry. How could that small vial possibly affect him?

I'll show you, Luna You. Mmm, I'll show you why.

I didn't want to see, but I did. The images poured into my brain and twisted my stomach. Oh no.

Oh yes. So close. And now, mmm, it is too late.

The knife stopped inches from the side of my neck. So even if I do this, even if I kill myself right here, right now…

I won't, mmm, go with you. I'll move on to New You, and other puppets. Oh, they will be so sad. Putting you in the dirt where things will grow on your skin. I'll creep behind them and run my fingers down their spines. Forever.

Despair. Anguish and hopelessness flooded me. If I had managed to take you with me, I thought, using the blood…

You would have destroyed everybody in the line under me, yes, Luna You. And he loves you.

I dragged my eyes to meet Mouth's. His gaze was serenity in the chaos, his robes whipping around his wispy frame. The sorrow in his eyes surpassed anything I had ever seen. He saw my realization and the corner of his mouth quirked slightly.

The knife shook in my hand. I heard Reed Taylor scream my name over the wind and rage, but I couldn't tear my gaze from Mouth's.

The Tiptoe Shadow tsked inside of my brain. So fickle, girl. Never saw him when you were young. Never saw him when you were older. Never saw him when he stood before you, telling you what he was and how he felt. And now, mmm?

The demon scraped his long nails over my soul. The layers peeled, split, were torn and shoved aside like pieces of sliced flesh. I saw my fingernails blacken as he ran underneath them.

The demon's high giggle made my back arch in disgust. I saw my father thrashing, kicking at the end of his rope. The demon splayed his final thoughts before me. Realization that the demon would merely leave him and float away, that it wouldn't be taken down like he had hoped, merely slowed down for a while. It would end here, his children orphans, his daughter to be tormented by the being who now grasped him by the hair. His death was for nothing. All of the torture, the second-guessing. Seth's anger, my loneliness. He had died thinking he was saving us, but he didn't know about the blood. I had nearly left Lydia the same destitute legacy my father left me.

The knife was pulled from my hand. I hardly felt it leave my fingers.

I...I've made a terrible mistake, I thought.

The demon laughed. Your father said the very same thing. But you belong to me now.

He forced his way into my soul utterly, and it was more than I could take. The bombardment of pain, the ugly memories and thoughts and whims that flooded my being. The Tracing, it burned, it scorched, it ached and hungered for the filthy soul screaming to feed it. By now I was screaming again, too. Then the darkness became too heavy for me. It covered my eyes and my nose and filled my mouth. It became everything.

Chapter Fifty

I opened my eyes and gasped. The stabbing between my shoulder blades was too much to take. Every nerve was raw, a silver blade raked down each centimeter of skin. It felt right somehow, like hitting somebody on the head and killing them felt right, like running your car into a retaining wall felt right.

"Let me die, let me die, let me die," I screamed. I writhed on the floor, trying to cover my head and curl my body into a protective ball.

"I have you," Reed Taylor shouted to me over the noise. Wind roared and howled. No, not wind. The Tiptoe Shadow. The shadow and somebody else.

Mouth.

My eyes rolled up in my head. Reed Taylor gently shook me.

"Luna, stick with me. Mouth managed to pull most of Tiptoe out of you, but it won't last long. I have to tell you something, okay? Okay?"

My lips pulled back from my teeth and my body convulsed from the agony, but I struggled to meet his gaze, blinked.

He tried to smile, but it didn't reach his eyes. "Baby, I'm sorry. About everything. All of it. But I have to tell you something very important. Can you remember?"

I was trembling so hard that my body kept cracking against the floor.

Reed Taylor gathered me as closely as he could.

"Lydia's safe with a friend of mine. I left a message on your phone telling you where to find her. Cecilia and I," he said, nodding his head toward her body in back of the house, "we got high together. The needles are in the other room. Tell the police I called you, and when they come, you need to show them everything. Understand?"

I was blacking out again. He shook me, took my face in his hands and kissed my mouth desperately.

"Listen. Show them the needles. Show them our marks. They'll give Lydia back. Cecilia's unfit. I'm sorry I got her back into it, but I did it for you. You and Seth and Lydia."

My eyes cleared. I could almost focus them on his beautiful face.

"I didn't know how else to help. It was the only thing I could think of to do."

He hugged me, rubbed his scruffy chin in my hair. "I love you," he said. He kissed my face again and again. "I do. I see what you see, and you're braver than I ever could have been. But maybe I can stop it."

He set me down gently, looked at me with the same eyes that made me fall in love with him.

"Goodbye, Luna."

His face hardened, and he stood up. I was still jerking on the floor, my jaws clenched together so I didn't scream the house down, didn't bite my tongue in two, didn't start shrieking out the vile visions the demon flooded my memory with.

Reed Taylor put his hand on Mouth's shoulder. The demon turned and they exchanged a look. It was a look that terrified me. I tried to reach out to them, but my body wouldn't respond.

Reed Taylor pulled a hypodermic needle from his pocket. It was full to the brim. Mouth nodded his head once and flicked his eyes in my direction. He raised his arms to the sky, tipped his head back, and screamed something into the wind. The pressure on the Tracing immediately deepened.

The Tiptoe Shadow growled and snapped at Mouth with razor teeth. Mouth didn't budge, but stood his ground, still chanting his indiscernible words. Reed Taylor bowed his head and injected himself with the needle.

There was a tearing, ripping sensation on my back. I shrieked, flailing my arms as I tried desperately to flip onto my side, keeping my shredded back and the demon's protruding hand from touching the floor. And then suddenly the pain was gone.

The pain. The itching feeling. The open, broken part of my soul that had been the demonic Tracing. It was closed for the first time in months. I covered my face and breathed a sigh of relief. The Mark was gone.

"Wrong," squealed the Tiptoe Shadow. It skittered on broken little legs. "Wrong puppet. Wrong puppet!"

Another voice, deep, yelling in a way that made my stomach twist. Reed Taylor, driven to his knees. The shadow's long arm twisted out of his back. It emerged from the Mark that, until just now, I had been wearing. Mouth had somehow used his power to transfer my burden to Reed Taylor.

"No!" I scrambled to Reed Taylor, ran my fingers though his hair, examined the bloody holes in his back. The Tiptoe Shadow's pointed fingers fit perfectly. I glared at Mouth. "No, no. How could you do this?"

"Step back," he said, and wrapped his dark hand around my wrist. He couldn't get a grip. I pulled Reed Taylor into my lap and rocked him back and forth. His eyes were already pinpricks, his breathing shallow.

"Luna!" Mouth said loudly, and I looked up at him though my tears. His eyes were agonized. "You have to let him do this."

"Do what?"

My brain wasn't working right. I saw Reed Taylor's agony, saw him being overwhelmed by not only the demon but the Mark. Darkness flowed out of the many holes in his arms. The Tiptoe Shadow thrashed, unable to pull itself away from the temptation of the Tracing, feeding on pain and sorrow in a frenzy even as it felt Reed Taylor's body dying around it.

"Luna!" Mouth's voice had an edge of desperation that pulled me out of my cloudiness. "He's doing it for you! You have to let him make this sacrifice."

I didn't have words. I simply wailed.

"Stupid puppet! Stupid, broken puppet!" The Tiptoe Shadow spun on the ground like a top. His eyes found me. "Back to my Luna doll," he trilled, and Mouth grabbed my hand.

"Come with me. Now," he commanded and tried to pull me from Reed Taylor's dying body. I shook my head, but the demon bent down until we were nose to nose.

"Blood, Luna. Blood."

"Blood? But…"

"We don't have time. You need to trust me."

I looked into his eyes. Wiped my face with my sleeve, staggered to my feet, and ran after him. We ran past Cecilia, through the room with my father's corpse and into a back room. Several used needles were strewn on the floor. The room was dirty and grungy, and the headless demons who were trying unsuccessfully to grasp the needles only made it worse.

"Take one," Mouth said. His voice was loud in the relative silence of the room. "You need to collect Reed's blood while he's still joined with the demon."

"I can't."

"You have to."

My knee-jerk defiance took hold. "I don't have to do anything! I just watched somebody I love kill himself, and now you want me to stick needles into his corpse and—"

"You can't take his blood as a corpse. He has to be alive. It's very specific. We have to contain the shadow, and the only way to do that is to take a piece of him, brimming with life, and inject it back into the host body after its death."

"You mean siphon his blood while he's still living, with the shadow inside, and then sit around waiting for Reed Taylor to die?"

"Yes."

"And then inject the shadow back into him?"

"Yes."

"I can't do it. It's too horrible."

"Reed did this to save you from that thing, and you're just going to go all helpless when it counts? You can kill the shadow, Luna. Otherwise he'll just come for you, and what was it all for?"

Mouth, radiant in his fury. Robes flowing around him like torrential rains, like licks of flame. His eyes blazed fire. I heard the Tiptoe Shadow squalling in the other room, spitting and cursing and feasting on the soul of a beautiful, lonely, green-eyed man who traded himself for me.

I bent down, picked up a needle.

"The Tiptoe shadow showed me, Mouth. What will happen to you if I do this."

Mouth sighed, looked away. "I had hopes," he said finally. He reached out for my hand, and this time is was rock solid. "Stay with me while I fade?"

I took his hand, gripped it hard. "Absolutely."

We ran back to Reed Taylor. He was nearly still. I bent beside him, searched for his vein. Thick scar tissue, marks to work around.

"Reminds me of when we first met," I whispered to him and withdrew the blood. It wasn't coming out as fast as I'd hoped.

The Tiptoe Shadow eyed me. "What, what? What is that, dolly? What do you have there?"

I hid the needle behind my back like a child. "Nothing." I peered past him at Reed Taylor, who had stopped moving completely. I bit my tongue to keep myself from sobbing.

"Not yet," whispered Mouth. He wrapped his arms around me, and I could actually feel them. "I'm sorry. I'm so sorry, Luna."

Me too. It killed me to see Reed Taylor there, dying all alone. It killed me that he was doing this because he loved me. And it killed me to think that soon I'd lose Mouth, too.

"I don't think I can do this," I said, turning to the demon. "I can't lose both of you. Would it really be so bad if the Tiptoe Shadow stayed?"

Mouth wiped the tears from my face. "You're stronger than this. You'd hate yourself for it in the future. And you'd hate me."

I shook my head. "I'd never—"

Suddenly Mouth flung me away. I landed hard on my back, the needle bouncing out of my grip and spinning on the floor. My skull hit the floor with a loud crack.

I shook my head, trying to clear it, and stared up at Mouth. The Tiptoe Shadow had disengaged from Reed Taylor's back and was pacing back and forth like a tiger where I had just been standing. I hadn't even heard him move.

"You can't, mmm, defy me. You can't deny me. Girl. Girl! Toys are meant to be broken."

Quick as a snake and just as sinuous, he flowed in my direction. I grabbed the needle and darted away.

"Uninvited," I yelled at the top of my lungs.

The demon laughed. "Abra Cadabra. Open Sesame. Just words."

He lunged again, and Mouth stepped in front of him, spitting out phrases I didn't understand.

The Tiptoe Shadow snarled. "You can't deny me. I made you! I, mmm, own you. You are mine."

His long arms snapped out, wrapped around Mouth and pulled him close.

"Break," the shadow said, and squeezed. I heard Mouth choking, struggling for breath.

"Leave him alone," I yelled, but the demon didn't even look my way.

"Oh, so good. So tasty, this fear. To, mmm, kill one's own, it…" He chirped happily.

There was nothing I could do. I knew it. I wanted to stand and scream until I couldn't scream anymore. I wanted to pound my fists into the dark blot where the shadow's face should be. I wanted to break every bone in its formless body for tearing my family apart, for terrorizing Seth and my father and me, for causing Reed Taylor's death and, I could see, the eternal destruction of Mouth.

I would kill the shadow.

Mouth was kicking his feet. I closed my eyes briefly and zipped past them, over to Reed Taylor's white, white body. His eyes were open and empty. I felt for his pulse, put my cheek to his mouth and felt for breathing. Nothing. He was dead. I dashed at my eyes and searched for his vein.

"I'm so sorry, baby," I whispered. I slid the needle into his vein carefully, carefully, even though he would never feel the pinprick. His blood was thick and red and so painfully, heartbreakingly beautiful. It was full of life and heroine and the very black essence of the Tiptoe Shadow swirling inside. Hope through death. Escape for some of us, but not all.

I injected the small vial of cold blood back into his body, then sat cross-legged and cradled his head in my lap.

The Tiptoe Shadow made a strangled sound and whirled around, dropping Mouth. "You! What did you do? What did you do?"

I didn't answer him. He gasped and railed and roiled, tried running toward me, but fell and landed on his toothpick knees. There was a sound like splintering wood, and he screamed.

"Dolly," he squealed, grabbing for me with both long hands. "Puppet." He scrabbled on the floor, mewing pitifully. I touched my forehead to Reed Taylor's and cried.

Mouth sat beside me, barely substantial. He looked exhausted. I slid my hand into his. It went right through.

"So this is goodbye," I said. The wailing, groaning sounds of the shattering Shadow Man sounded behind me. He wasn't worth turning around for.

"So it is." Mouth looked at Reed Taylor's body, sorrow in his eyes. "He was a good guy, Luna. I'm sorry I gave him such a hard time. I was just—"

"I know."

We sat there, side by side, listening to the death throes of the shadow. I stroked Reed Taylor's bloodied hair with one hand.

"I wish things could have been different," I told the demon. He was completely translucent now, a mere breath of fog.

"Different how?"

A scuffle behind us. A gurgle.

"I don't know. Just different. Anything but this."

Silence, and then he said, "You're brave, you know."

I snorted. "Me, brave? Do you even see me right now? Did you see me bolting away from everything in this house of horrors?"

His voice was fading, becoming softer. "I saw you do what you needed to do. I saw you stand up to something terrifying. I saw you ready to kill yourself because you thought it would save us."

Tears came to my eyes again. "And instead you and Reed Taylor—"

He shrugged. I caught a faint shine like crystal out of the corner of my eye, but that was it. He was nearly gone.

"I'd do it again in a heartbeat, Luna. I'd do anything for you."

I reached for his face. I couldn't feel a thing.

"I know. Thank you so much, Mouth."

There was silence behind us. No sounds, no struggles.

The demon grinned, his teeth flashing. "My name used to be Dorian, you know. I haven't thought of it in ages."

"Dorian," I repeated. A tear ran down my face, and I smiled back. "I won't forget it."

He leaned forward and kissed me on my cheek. I closed my eyes and felt nothing but a brief moment of sweetness. When I opened my eyes again, he was gone.

I doubled over and sobbed into Reed Taylor's shirt. I was still crying when the police arrived. They gently pried me away from that spot of death, wrapped a blanket around me, and led me away.

Epilogue

I wish I could say I had imagined everything. For once I wished that I was crazy, but that isn't how life ends up. I'll tell you how it ends up: it finishes out in its own fine way.

After Seth bailed out of the House of Horrors, he headed straight for the police department. Half of what he said didn't make sense, but they managed to piece together something about the mother of his child being totally strung out and unresponsive, and his daughter was missing, and demons were frickin' everywhere.

"Demons everywhere" is usually code for "Holy crap, everybody has gone nuts in that crack house" so they loaded up their gear and came. They made Seth wait outside while they entered and found me sobbing over Cecilia's boyfriend, who had overdosed on heroine. Poor little me, I was absolutely traumatized by seeing death so up close and personal, they thought. They carted Reed Taylor off and took Sparkles away in an ambulance. Then they turned their attention to Seth and me. Good, hardworking siblings. Going to counseling, trying everything in our power to get Lydia back. We were stable. The courts would still keep an eye on us, but Lydia was brought home, where she belonged.

Seth and I couldn't get enough of her. We fought over who she got to sleep with until we finally calmed down enough to let her out of our sight.

She, of course, ate the attention up with a spoon. Every morning I woke up to "Mama Luna!" and hugs, kisses, and giggles. Even after everything, she's happy. She's safe. She has her daddy who adores her more than life and her Mama Luna who will kick any foe in the face.

But the boys…their loss destroyed me. I'd hold Lydia and cry, thinking about how much I missed their constant bickering and one-upmanship. I missed having Reed Taylor's heart and Mouth's sarcastic but fierce support. Knowing they had died because of me…well, that was more than I could take.

The demons had backed off considerably, giving me extra space since I had proven I could take down one of the baddies and his entire line. I see them peeking at me from behind shrubbery or from the sewer grates, but they hardly ever cross my path anymore. They never call me by name. I'm surprised to find out how lonely that makes me.

I went to Reed Taylor's funeral. I went to Sparkle's court date. Lydia and I go to Mommy and Me ballet. I don't have to tell you what a disaster that is, but she loves it, and she loves to see her Mama Luna twirl. "Arabesque" has become a dirty word to me.

One evening I dropped a flower on my mother's grave, another on my father's, and slid the third behind my ear.

"Hi, Mom. Hi, Dad. Just wanted to let you know things are going well with us. I know how you worry. Seth says hi, and Lydia drew you a picture. It looks like, I don't know, a tornado or a cow or something. I can't really tell."

"Maybe she should stick to dancing."

I froze. That voice.

"Ah, Luna. Still ignoring me, I see. Some things never change."

I whirled around. Mouth—Dorian—stood there, hands in his pockets. Pockets. Actual pants, and a shirt, and no flowing robes at all. He wasn't dark. He was created out of light instead.

My hand flew to my mouth.

His smile was crooked. "Hi."

He held out his arms and I dazedly walked into them. They were solid. Solid as the earth. I ran my hands over his shoulders. His face. His hair. He was real.

"How can this be?" I asked. "I don't understand."

He looked uncomfortable. "I'm not alive, exactly. I mean, uh…"He looked at me shyly. "I'm demon patrol."

Silence. Then I couldn't take it anymore. "You're an angel?"

He cringed. "Don't put it like that. That's not exactly right. I mean, it is, but…ugh. I'm still not used to playing for the other team, okay?"

I gawked. "But how?"

He sighed. "It's 'cuz I gave up immortality for you. Not only that, but it was in order to pull a major demon off of the Earth. Kinda got extra bonus points for that, if you know what I mean."

"But I can see you."

"Oh, that." Mouth-Dorian waved his hand casually. "That has something to do with you and I being connected to the same demon right before we died, and then taking him out. They explained it, but I kinda got bored and didn't listen much." He leaned forward conspiratorially. "They make you go to angel school. It's really mind-numbing."

I hugged him. "I've missed you so much."

He hugged me back.

"I'm glad. I know it's been hard without Reed. "

I sighed. "It's been awful, but it isn't any more than I deserve. Besides, some people were born to be alone, you know?"

He gave me a strange look. It made me nervous.

"What?"

"Maybe, but you're not one of them. Now listen, Luna. Something big is going down, and it's been going down for a long time. Remember when Demon Patrol disappeared?"

"You know why?"

"Yeah. Tiptoe Shadow was the tip of the iceberg. He was almost a non-entity compared to what we're dealing with now."

"There's something more?"

He looked grave. "So much more. And I'm kinda in a jam about it, you see. As you know, I was a demon of some authority. Now I'm going after members of my old kind."

I nodded. "I get the predicament."

He looked at me slyly, and his eyes glittered. It was the old Mouth again. "So I say to myself, hey, I need some backup, right? I need somebody who I can hash things out with, who not only understands me, but is familiar with the demonic. And I say to myself…"

"Why not hit up the ol' Demon Girl, my Luna?"

I felt the grin spread across my face. It felt delightfully wicked and free. Finally, something I understood. Carnage. Justice maybe tipped with a little revenge. Something to fill my mind so I'm not dreaming of haunting gorgeous greens at night.

He shrugged. "Two outcasts should stick together, is all I'm saying. You up for it?"

"You know it."

"Good." He took the flower from my hair and held it up to the moon, like he had so long ago. It was a splash of bright color in a dark world. "So tell me how Lydia talked you into ballet. You're terrible. I have to turn away about half the time."

I flicked his ear, hard. "Hey, watch it. I killed you once and I'm not afraid to do it again."

He laughed, and I started talking, telling him about Seth's law school and how I found a super sweet deal for parts on my motorcycle. I told him I start every day by burying my nose in Lydia's sweet-smelling hair. Her pigtails, they still wave like banners.

HELLO, MY DARLINGS!

I'm so pleased and honored that you took the time to read my very first full-length novel! I love Luna, Seth, Mouth, and Reed Taylor so much, and it was a pleasure to introduce you to their world, as crazy and diabolical as it is.

Luna's tough, but even the strongest of us break under the weight of our experiences. Now that she's on Team Demon Patrol, what else is going to happen to her? Will she find acceptance? Will she stitch together her broken heart? Or will she find solace in the darkness?

I've received quite a few opinions as to what should happen in the next two books, and I'm curious to know what you think. As an author, I love to hear ideas and suggestions. It jumpstarts my brain and gets the literary machine going. Writing is an interactive process for me, so if you have any feedback (good, bad, or downright demonic), I'd love to hear it! You can contact me at BoneAngelTrilogy@gmail.com and visit me on my blog at abrokenlaptop.com.

If you don't mind, I'd so love it if you would post a review of my book at sites like Amazon and Goodreads. Letting the author—and other readers—know whether or not you enjoy their book is one of the most important things you, as a reader, can do. Reviews are vital. They help new books get written. Your opinion counts!

If you enjoyed *Nameless: The Darkness Comes*, please have a look at my other work, and thank you so much for taking this journey with me. Let's see what happens to our Bone Trilogy friends in the future, yes?

All my love,
Mercedes

ABOUT THE AUTHOR

MERCEDES M. YARDLEY wears red lipstick and poisonous flowers in her hair. *Nameless: The Darkness Comes*, book one of The Bone Angel Trilogy, is her second work for Ragnarok Publications, the first being the 2013 Stabby Award-winning, *Apocalyptic Montessa and Nuclear Lulu: A Tale of Atomic Love.*

Mercedes has been published in several diverse anthologies and magazines, ranging from John Skipp's horror anthologies, the *I Will Survive* book with Gloria Gaynor, and *Neverland's Library* by Neverland Books.

She has also worked as a contributing editor for *Shock Totem Magazine* and currently lives in Sin City. Her short story collection, *Beautiful Sorrows*, came out in 2012.

Made in the USA
San Bernardino, CA
19 September 2014